NB WINNER OF THE INAUGURAL
NORTHBOUND BOOK AWARD

'From start to finish, I was spellbound by the characters ... the narrative voice, and the vivid imagery. Mensah intricately weaves complex characters, vivid descriptions, universal topics of love, loss, identity, religion, with themes like the search for a place to belong, into a well spun tapestry, a mind-spinning tale, a heart-pounding novel – and I'm hooked. I absolutely love this book.' *Yvonne Battle-Felton*, author of the Women's Prize-longlisted novel *Remembered*

'[I was] gripped by *Castles from Cobwebs* from the first page – with its arresting opening, lyricism, and unconventional narration. There are moments of real beauty and clarity in the prose, especially around race, a subject handled skilfully and thoughtfully by the author. There is something real, powerful, and unique in this debut.' *Chitra Ramaswamy*, journalist and Saltire Award-winning author of *Expecting*

'A compelling exploration of memory, race, mothers and the fractured self, Mensah questions the frameworks through which we understand the world and interrogates how to put disparate parts of our identities together to become the most true version of ourselves.' *Jessica Andrews*, author of the Portico Prize-winning novel *Saltwater*

Castles
from Cobwebs

J.A. MENSAH

Saraband

Published by Saraband,
Digital World Centre,
1 Lowry Plaza,
The Quays, Salford, M50 3UB

ISBN: 9781912235766
ebook: 9781912235773

Printed and bound in Great Britain by Clays Ltd, Elcograf S.p.A.

10 9 8 7 6 5 4 3 2 1

*The author would like to acknowledge the financial support of the
NorthBound Book Award, run by Saraband and New Writing
North, supported by Arts Council England as part of the Northern
Writers' Awards.*

For Mum and Dad

CONTENTS

The sand looked so beautiful then, so many little individual grains in the light of the night, giving the watcher the childhood feeling of infinite things finally understood, the humiliating feeling of the watcher's nothingness.

Ayi Kwei Armah, *The Beautyful Ones are Not Yet Born*

But we who live at various places along the coastline of the British Sea know that where the tide begins to run in one place it will start to ebb at another at the same time. Hence it appears to some that the wave, while retreating from one place, is coming back somewhere else; then leaving behind the territory where it was, it swiftly seeks again the region where it first began.

The Venerable Bede, *The Reckoning of Time*

Prologue:
In the Beginning

A baby lies naked in the snow. Doughy brown arms and legs jostle with an unseen playmate. It is dawn on a day of brilliant light, and besides our foundling no one stirs. No one, that is, except Reverend Mother Michaela Maria, who stands in the vestibule of St Teresa's Convent on Holymead Island, tying a triple knot in her walking boots.

Whenever possible, she begins her week with a brisk walk before the rest of the world is awake. She likes to wander along the edge of the island, trying to circle as much of it as time allows. If the tide is low and the flats are dry enough, she may venture onto the sands that connect the tidal island to the mainland, but this morning, the tide is high. The sea fills the causeway and the waters are undecided – choppy one moment, calm the next. Reverend Mother steps out; the air is cold but still. She walks the narrow roads and tangled lanes of the village. The buildings offer some shelter, so it's a while before she notices the wind, pushing at her back, increasing her speed. She wonders whether to return home.

No, follow me, the North Wind whispers, *follow me and I will make you fishers of men.*

She wraps her coat tighter and continues on. That's the morning assembly sorted, she smiles to herself. This is precisely why she likes to walk at dawn – the fog in her mind clears and answers come on the breeze. At the end of the village, she leaves the shelter of the buildings and heads out to the old castle on the hill. In truth, it was built primarily as a fort, not a castle, but people rarely use language or stories from the past accurately.

As she approaches, she decides to circle the base of Beblowe Hill and then head home. As she wends her way around the hill, she notices an odd shape jerking on the incline. It's a wounded gull, she thinks. The weather grows angrier as she climbs. The sea battles the shore, and a slurry of wind, snow and hail beat her face and clothing. When she finally reaches the thing, she has to bend in close, blinking against the elements, to see what it is. As if controlled by a secret hand, the weather calms, the wind settles, the sea slows, and the snow dwindles to a dusting and then stops completely.

The baby lies bright-eyed and serene, looking up at her. Soaking her joints in snow and mud, Reverend Mother kneels beside the child. Hands shaking with cold and fear, she picks the baby up and wraps it inside her sheepskin coat, spreading her long white hair over her shoulder to curtain the bulge. She treads carefully down the hill and onto the lane.

Reverend Mother crosses my path with her stolen cargo. I smile, with some melancholy, at her back as she disappears. I am happy and sad for what these two have yet to come. I've already seen it: the child is me and this is my story.

Book One:

Sunsum

Sunsum
Noun

1. Spirit
    • some things are Sunsum – God; while others have Sunsum – people;
    • an element of God within the human being;
    • unified touch with the Divine.

2. The mystical force of destiny.

3. One's character, spark and morality.

4. That which connects the body (*honam*) to the soul (*okra*).

Arrival

Sparrows chirrup and settle on the cold slate shingles of the old shop roof. The shop used to be called Eady's Saintly Sherbets. It had a wooden sign hand-carved by Edward Grimauld with a little symbol that looked a bit like a soldier's helmet but was meant to be the rice-paper fizzy sweets that gave the shop its name. Mr Grimauld's sign has been replaced by a white plaque with EP written in a large blue font and *Eadberht's Place* scrawled beneath it like an absent-minded doodle. I stand in front of it, examining the shop's transformation. A layer of snow powders the shop roof and lightly covers every surface, from the trees, to the parked cars, to the cobblestone paths. No one is around and the frosting is unblemished, but the sun has started to break through the clouds and the suggestion of warmth has begun to melt the sprinkle. I'm back. It's winter again and time has folded in on itself to confuse me. It offers reflections as keepsakes then snatches them away before I can catch them. I see ghosts everywhere: in the gloom of the trees, the nooks and crannies of the lanes, in shop windows, and out in the waves.

A shadow crosses my path; my nineteen-year-old-self steps out of the shop with a paper bag in her hand and a rucksack on her back. Her focus is on the contents of the paper bag; peering inside, she inspects the sweets. She bundles the bag into the side pocket of her coat and looks up – straight at me. Squinting, she shields the glare of the sun with her hand, as though trying to see me more clearly. She pauses for a moment, then turns and walks away.

My twelve-year-old self nudges past me and drops a book in the brief collision. I bend to look at the fallen thing, but she's snatched it up before I can read the title. I find myself running along to keep up with her and realise too late where she's heading. The large iron gates are confrontational and the redwood trees beyond it cast huge shadows. 12 walks into the grounds and strides along the path to the main building. Cradling her books in one arm, she searches inside her satchel and retrieves a key; unlocks the door, pushes it open and is gone. I'm left alone. Outside. The old building looks frail and infirm in the winter sun. Light is so unforgiving; I've always preferred the warmth of darkness, where you can hide until you're ready to be seen. I open the gate tentatively and walk towards the first redwood tree that lines the path. I hesitate, then touch it; press my cheek against its spongy bark and wrap my arms as far around its trunk as they will go.

Voices from the distance pull me out of the embrace. A group of tourists has stopped and they peer through the gate. I let go of the tree and walk towards the building, escaping their gaze.

In front of the convent, I wait before knocking. I pick up the brass knocker and bang on the door as a guest might. The sound is deep and full. After a few moments, the oak door creaks and staggers open. Sister Alma smiles up at me. We stare at each other from opposite sides of the threshold: me, the gangly, dark Amazon; her, the squat, yellowing cherub, her skin almost transparent now.

'We've missed you.' Her words are whispered, her eyes are wet.

'I've missed you, too,' I say.

She wipes a tear from the side of her eye. I bend to hug her. My dreadlocks brush her face. I'm sure they horrify her, but she doesn't say anything – she's so unlike Mother.

'She'll be glad you came,' Sister Alma hurries to say, as though she's heard the mention of Reverend Mother in my thoughts. 'We didn't know if you would.'

'Of course, I ... how could I not?' I feel ashamed and break our gaze.

She smiles apologetically, 'You're early.'

I try to explain and we end up talking over each other in a flurry of words and misjudged pauses.

'I arrived in Newcastle late last night–' / 'I need to go to the mainland to pick up a few things–'

'I thought I'd come for a walk…' / 'Odds and ends really–'

'Come early, I mean, to just walk around the island.' / 'I shouldn't be long–'

'I didn't mean to come here so early, though.' / 'No, no, it's not a problem…'

'I just … sort of … found myself here.' / 'That's fine, dear, it's fine, really.'

She reaches for my hand and strokes it. 'It's fine,' she says, stroking me again. 'You always had such beautiful skin.'

I pull my hand away defensively, and repeat that I didn't mean to come so early.

'Really, you don't need to apologise,' she says gently, looking a bit bruised by the way I snatched my hand from her. 'This is your home.' She asks if I'd like to go to the mainland with her, but I'd rather not. 'Of course, of course,' her voice is almost shrill. 'You'll want to look at the old place again. That's not a problem at all.' She steps aside and ushers me in, 'Come here, come in, don't stand on ceremony. This is your home. This is your home.'

Leading me through to the library, she fusses constantly, repeating the unnecessary over again. She brings in a china teapot with chrysanthemum tea and fluffs the cushions on the chair beside the window. Mr Bojangles pokes his head around the door. I put my hand on the floor and beckon him towards me. He sneers and turns, walking out with his tail hanging low.

'It'll take Mr Bo a while to get used to you being back,' Sister Alma says, in defence of her cat.

'He's probably forgotten me.'

'Never,' she snaps. 'He knows this is your favourite spot. No one's really sat there since you left.'

I wonder if this is true or an indirect slight: if there's one thing I was taught here, it was the poetics of guilt.

'Reverend Mother will come soon and, Imani, promise me something? Don't blame her. You mustn't blame her, ok?'

A smile tugs at the corners of my lips; I wonder how I can use this opportunity for guilt creatively, though the look on her face defeats the impulse. 'If you don't blame her, how can I?' I say, trying to reassure her. 'But are you ok?'

'I'm fine,' she says. 'You can see that with your own eyes.'

After more to-ing and fro-ing she finally leaves. It feels like there is more oxygen in the room. I sip the tea, and try to relax. I'm glad Sister Alma seemed ok; the email had been cryptic and I wasn't sure what state I'd find her in. Looking up from the teacup, I notice it for the first time, the tapestry of the Assumption of Mary, hanging on the wall. Mary rises to heaven surrounded by clouds and cherubs. It caused quite a stir when it was given to the convent as a gift: not because it wasn't an accurate copy of Rubens' original painting, or because the embroidery framing the main image made the piece look too busy, as Sister Magdalene had complained. The main issue, although no one said it, was that Mary, Mother of God, was depicted as a black woman, rising to heaven, in clouds and cherubs. I smile at the image and fiddle with my dreadlocks, trying to break one strand from another. They've started to grow into each other, webbing and tangling without permission.

I wander down the halls and stop when I reach the kitchen. The old Aga stands in place, the matriarch still. A microwave and a blender sit to the right of it, next to the alabaster pestle and mortar. They are new and bright, but she offers them only a little of the spotlight. My twelve-year-old self walks in. Mother is cooking at the Aga; she turns as 12 enters.

Two of the classes from the day school are being taken on a trip to the mainland to visit the Grace Darling Museum. I wanted to go, but Reverend Mother refused. She turns her back on 12 and dismisses her with a wave. I can't hear their conversation, but I remember the moment. 12 is crying as she moves to leave. Before she reaches the door, a cupboard opens, then slams shut. 12 stops, cheeks wet with tears. She turns to look at Mother. The cupboard opens again: a plate lifts from the shelf, hangs in mid-air then falls, shattering on the ground between them. I hear it.

'Stop that at once, Imani!' Mother says, her voice suddenly audible.

'It's not me,' 12 whimpers.

'Now! Stop it right now!'

A patch on the floor beneath 12 grows progressively wetter. A mug flies from the cupboard and hits the wall.

Mother raises her voice, 'Imani! I'm not telling you again.'

I can't see her, but I know - it's Amarie.

12 hangs her head, staring at the puddle that's formed between her feet.

'Go! And don't come out until you've thought about the things you've done,' Mother says.

12 runs out. Hunched over the Aga, Mother has her back to me. The kitchen smells of burnt milk and urine.

I'd been sent to sit in the confessional, the penitent's booth. No priest would enter the adjoining compartment. The curtain wouldn't be drawn from the grille because I hadn't been sent to confess. Mother would send me there to think about my actions and pray for forgiveness. After a time, she'd send one of the sisters to get me out. The door was always left unlocked, so I could go to the toilet if I needed to. I suppose I could just have left if I'd wanted to, but the thought never occurred to me.

After I'd been sitting on the wooden stool for a few moments, I heard Mother's footsteps. Her approach was distinctive; she was the only nun who wore a slight heel. I heard the key and its turning screw, and I understood that this time I wouldn't be able to get out, even if I'd wanted to. At this stage in our lives together it had been years since I'd mentioned Amarie. I'd learnt not to talk about her. I think Mother hoped she'd gone, and this reappearance confirmed that I wasn't becoming the person Mother hoped I would be.

Six

My six-year-old self passes me in the corridor wearing a gummy smile. Both of my front teeth had fallen out and, if I didn't concentrate as I spoke, it gave me a lisp. 6 is wearing an oversized brown tunic, one of the sister's hand-me-down habits cut to fit me. The only clothing I received as 'new' were the cloth belts Sister Alma would sew for me each birthday. They were made from offcuts of the sisters' habits, but as well as the brown and cream of their clothes, the belts were made from bits of tablecloth and curtains – any fabric she could get her hands on – and they were always colourful. Each year she would sew my age into the belts in a style that turned the number into a pattern. Those belts were mine in a way that not many other things were.

I sneeze and sneeze and sneeze and it seems like the sneezing will never stop. Mother sits on the bed next to me and rubs my back. It doesn't stop the sneezing, but it feels like the times I hold the fabric of my birthday belt to my face because Sister Magdalene's telling me off. The fabric pressed up against my cheek doesn't stop the telling off, but it makes it feel not so bad. Mother rubbing my back is like that. I've mostly stopped putting the cloth belt on my face now when Sister Magdalene gives me a talking to, because she told me off for doing it. She said I'm not a baby and I'm not to act like one. While I'm thinking of Sister Magdalene, the sneezing stops. Harold told me that if you think of something scary when you're sneezing or hiccupping it can sometimes scare it out of you. I hadn't meant to think of Sister Magdalene, but it seems to have worked.

'Ok?' Mother asks.

I nod and smile. When I breathe in, the cold air runs along the gap in my teeth and it makes my gums tingle. It tickles. I can't decide if I like the feeling, so I switch to breathing through my nose. Mother pulls the bed covers over me and opens the book: *Tales from Africa and Other Exotic Lands*. It is a heavy, dark red, leather book with a lot of little wrinkles on the cover. It's my favourite. The other sisters read biblical tales like *Jonah and the Whale* or *Noah and the Ark* to me; Sister Alma and Sister Maria sometimes read fairy stories like *Alice in Wonderland* and *Sleeping Beauty*. Mother is the only one who reads to me from this book.

When Mother finishes the story about Anansi the spider man, I beg her to read another. I hug her waist and listen to her voice. I'm scared and happy; part of me wants the moment to come now, but something about it also makes me shy. Tonight, I'm telling Mother about Amarie. The sisters have always said I was a gift from God. Reverend Mother said I had a Divine purpose and it would one day be revealed. Amarie is the proof of that – she is a Holy Being sent by God to guide me. When Mother finishes the story, she kisses the top of my head and is about to stand.

'There's something I need to tell you,' I say.

'No more stories,' Mother says, getting up. 'It's late.'

'I've been sent a Holy Spirit.'

Mother looks confused.

'God sent me a Holy Spirit,' I say again, smiling up at her.

'What do you mean?'

'Her name's Amarie. We play together and we talk about all sorts of things. You'll like her, I know you will.' The words fall out at once like a handful of marbles dropped on the floor. 'There she is!' I point at the door where the shadow of a girl stands. She's holding her hands together and crossing one leg behind the other.

Mother turns to the door and sees Amarie. Her mouth opens and she pulls me out of bed, never taking her eyes off Amarie.

'You're hurting my arm,' I say, trying to tug it loose.

Her fingers dig into my arm even more. She crosses herself before reaching for the door. She opens it and pushes me out of the room, then comes out and slams the door behind her. Reverend Mother whispers something over and over; I think I hear it, she's saying, 'Satan be gone, you cannot have this child.'

My chest hurts and a lump grows in my throat. I want to say something, to defend my friend, but the words won't come. Mother leaves me in a spare dormitory, the cell where postulants stay before taking their vows. She comes and goes, putting candles everywhere and sprinkling oil all over. I blink when the wetness hits me. She puts rosary beads in my hand and closes my fingers around them in a fist. She makes the mark of the cross on my forehead with her thumb, which is still wet with oil. She locks us both in the room. Mother tells me to take the bed by the wall and she takes the bed by the window. The candles glow and it makes shadows in the places the light doesn't touch. I try to look for Amarie without Mother noticing, but she's not anywhere.

Seven

This year for my birthday belt, Sister Alma's stitched 7s in rainbow colours. I preferred the six belt; she did all the 6s in different shades of blue and they looked like a row of cresting waves. The 7s all together look like diagonal bars, and it makes me think of a brightly coloured, wonky jail. Above my tunic and the cloth belt, I'm wearing a fleece, a jumper, a cardigan, long thick socks with my boots, a fluffy scarf that hugs my neck and my winter coat. I don't have gloves on. The only things that aren't covered are my face and my hands. I'm standing outside the door to the main house. Everywhere is becoming white, like God's dusting the grounds with icing sugar. There's a mix of snow, hailstones and rain – slush-weather, Sister Alma calls it. The hail hits the back of my hands like a million little pinpricks. My hands are turning a grey colour. Sister Magdalene said to stand here and that she'd be back in a short while to get me. She told me to think about what I'd done and why I was being made to stand outside. I call to Amarie under my breath, but she won't come. So I stand and think about what I've done.

I'd been cleaning the chapel during the morning work meditation. My job is to clean the floors and the pews, never anything higher. Sister Maria usually comes in to wipe the altar and the statues, but she'd not been feeling well, so Amarie and I decided to do her cleaning for her. Amarie was polishing the small statue of the Virgin and Child in the alcove and I did the altar. Then there was a crash and, when I turned around, Sister Magdalene was already in the room. Her eyes went towards the alcove where the statue should have been. I looked there, too. The Holy Mother and Child statue was in pieces on the floor and Amarie was beside it.

Standing in the cold thinking about what I've done, I decide that my hands are being punished for Amarie's accident. But more than that, before Sister Magdalene had a chance to speak, I started shouting that it was Amarie's fault. So my hands are also being punished for betraying my friend. I rub my palms together to try to warm them up, but they feel fake. I try not to think about how much it hurts, or that I can't feel my little finger any more. Instead, I think about the wounded hands of Christ. I think about his death, as Mother says we should whenever we feel pain. I think about forgiveness. I think of the poem that Sister Alma taught us in assembly, St Teresa's poem: 'Christ has no body now but yours. No hands, no feet on earth but yours... Yours are the hands, yours are the feet...' / *Years later, scholars will argue that St Teresa had not written this poem because they could not find it among her other writings. But that doesn't matter at this moment; it's what you've been taught, and you think of it over and over.*

Mother comes out. She walks towards me and takes my hand, leading me back into the building. The warmth of her touch around my numb fingers makes them feel real. She takes me into the common room where the fire has been lit. Dr Trewhitt is called. He advises the sisters that they should wrap my hands in towels and blankets, and I should be given a lukewarm bath and avoid hot water for a day or two. He says I've got mild frostbite and I'll be fine once my hands have thawed. He promises to call in again to see me and says the sisters should let him know if I have any pain or numbness once my fingers have warmed up. He tells me off softly. He says I shouldn't spend too much time playing in the cold and I should take better care next time. He says, at nearly eight, I'm a big girl and I should know better. / *Years later, you will still feel a strange tingling sensation in your right hand when the weather grows too cold or sometimes when you become emotional. You will presume the nerves in that hand never completely healed.*

❖

It's dark. Half-asleep, I walk down the hallway, tracing my way back to bed after using the toilet. The cold of the concrete floor on my bare feet wakes me a little with every step. There's a light on at the end of the hall. It's coming from Mother's office, spilling out from the gap at the bottom of the door.

'What would you have me do?' Mother says.

There's no answer.

'Send her away?' She pauses. 'How's she going to make sense of that?'

There's still no answer. I wonder if she's on the phone; the only phone in the convent is in Mother's office.

A second voice speaks then, 'What's the penance for what we've done?' It's Sister Magdalene. 'Where can we find redemption?'

'We, all of us, made the decision.'

'Had the sisters and I been given proper spiritual counsel, we would not have kept her.'

'You feel I didn't give you proper spiritual counsel? I was not the only person–'

'With all due respect, Reverend Mother, by the time the Bishop arrived, the decisions had all been made.'

'What is it you're accusing me of?' There is a long pause. 'Three sisters left us at the time, you chose to stay.'

'I isolate myself.'

'And now that's not enough? Are you sure it is Imani that's the problem, Sister?' The sound of my name is like a pinch in the leg. The shock of it wakes me up completely.

'Or does her presence aggravate another wound that you're tending?' Reverend Mother says.

There is a long pause.

'The sisters have concerns,' Sister Magdalene replies, 'that it is not my past but yours that has created this situation.'

They're both quiet. I hold my breath and listen.

'My past sins are between me and God, Magdalene. As are yours.'

'That was until you brought them into our home,' Sister Magdalene shouts.

Feet shuffle. Someone clears their throat. I'm worried that one of them will walk out and find me there listening.

'Now it's about collective responsibility,' Sister Magdalene says. 'Today should have been a holy day, her presence in the chapel – what she did in there…'

'She didn't mean to, Magdalene.'

'It doesn't matter! She still did it – she can't help it, there's darkness inside her. We have to let her go.'

'She is not some creature we can release back into the wild! She is a seven-year-old child.'

There's a bang as someone hits the table or a bookshelf and something falls.

'God blessed us with a child.'

'She is not like us, Reverend Mother.'

They go quiet. I wonder if I should move, get out of the way before I come face to face with one of them.

'She was given to us,' Mother says softly.

'It's a sin, it's a sin, it's a sin! And that shadow of hers, this demon – whatever it is – is proof of that.'

'She has an imaginary friend; it's quite common in children of her age.'

'There is nothing common about that child. When she calls the name of that *thing*, she makes everything unclean. She could have destroyed the sanctity of our holy space with what she did today. I'm not unsympathetic, I am not saying she is completely to blame – it is where she's from, *what* she's from: those people, *her* people, they worship … darkness … do ritual sacrifices … kill people …

cut off their limbs ... they keep severed body parts ... keep them to give to their unclean gods!'

Mother takes a deep breath and sighs loudly. 'Hysteria will get us nowhere. You asked me earlier; you asked, what penance will we have to do to absolve ourselves of the sin you think we've committed – let's raise her to the light. Her life lived and fulfilled in God's will – that will be our redemption.'

❖

I move away with Sister Magdalene's words echoing inside me: '...it is where she's from, *what* she's from...' My room is mostly dark, but the light from the moon spills onto the bed and makes her easy to see: Amarie sits on my bed. I feel uncertain when I look at her. Amarie's head is bent down. She's looking at something cupped in her hands. She doesn't look up when I walk in; she keeps staring at the thing in her hands.

'What is it?'

She doesn't say straight away. I ask again.

'It's a human finger,' she says.

I look down at my own hands. They're still rubbery from the cold, but all of my fingers are there.

'I have a human finger,' she says.

Sister Magdalene's words are still moving in me: 'Those people / *her* people / they worship ... darkness ... ritual sacrifices ... kill people ... cut off their limbs ... severed body parts to their unclean gods.'

I scream and keep screaming. By the time Reverend Mother runs into the room, Amarie has gone. Mother tries to comfort me and keeps asking what's wrong. I cry and cry but can't get the words out. I'm scared. Scared that I'll always feel this afraid and that no one will be able to protect me. I hadn't noticed her at first but then I spot her, Sister Magdalene, standing by the door, watching.

Twelve

I roll the sack-cloth fabric, wrap and tie the yellow, green and brown twelve-belt around it. Then I shove the bundle into the tall dune grass, hidden from view. Racing towards the sea in my vest and leggings, I don't stop until the water reaches my belly button. That first touch of it shocks and my skin tightens around me. I wait for a bit, but there's only one way to get used to it: I dive in. Swallowed by cold and dark, I blow all of my breath out and it bubbles in front of me. I pull wide on a breast-stroke, come up for new air, then swim freestyle in the direction of Outer Farne.

I notice it then: she's not with me. I stop and tread water, look-ing out for her. The sea spreads wide, salty and deep, its waves gently rolling and tossing. The movement feels playful, as it rocks me in position. But I've seen its strength, depth and darkness and I know never to forget what the sea can do. I can't see Amarie any-where, but before panic sets in she appears, hovering just beneath the surface like the black ink of a cuttlefish. I swim on, stronger with her beside me.

Outer Farne is the only Farne Island that is completely swal-lowed by the sea at high tide which keeps other people away. We arrive at low tide and crawl onto the bank. The ground is covered in blotches of guano that make me think of Dalmatian spots. We settle on a clean grassy area to catch our breaths. The sun dries my skin and leaves a trail of salt crystals, little white specks shimmer-ing along the skinny brown of my arms and legs.

'What are you going to do about the trip?' Amarie asks.

I shrug. 'I guess I could talk to her.'

Amarie sits cross-legged looking at me, 'How?'

'Stop pressurising me. I'll think of something.' I pause. 'Maybe, maybe I'll say something like … about, how it's the end of the term and the end of the school year … and how everyone's really excited about the class trip to the Grace Darling Museum. I might say, how they're all talking about it, so I was looking forward to it too – but that Sister Maria told me I might not be allowed to go. I could maybe ask Mother about it, like it's a question, like I'm not sure of the answer.'

'She didn't even have the decency to tell you herself.'

'She'll be trying to protect me.'

'From a museum?'

'She'll be thinking that it's for my own good. And maybe the Grace Darling Museum won't be that special – we don't know… It would be nice to leave the island – the proper way for a change – and to see the mainland, to actually walk on the mainland.'

Amarie doesn't say anything. I get up and wander away from her, feeling judged. It is barely the end of June, but it has been so warm that the tips of the grass have started to turn yellow. I brush my toes through strands of blonde grass as I walk, pulling a few out that are practically straw. I stop beside a rock pool, dip my feet in its waters and then settle myself on its incline. I grab at flotsam and seaweed that's trapped there and kick the water up a bit. We should never have started talking about the trip to the museum; it's completely changed the mood of the day.

A dazed-looking mackerel circles the edge of the water, trying to avoid my feet. I lean in to touch it, and it slips along my palm and swims towards the farthest wall, putting as much space between us as it can. Its scales are smooth to the touch, like undersea velvet. Having nowhere else to go, it turns around, trapped. We look at each other. It feels like a challenge. I'm on my feet in the water, but crouching as though I'm about to catch a ball in rounders. It moves, slowly, away from the wall. I lunge. It tries to escape, but my hands are around it. I tighten my grip. Gotcha! I squeal and jump, nearly lose my balance but manage not to fall. I hold it up to show Amarie. It thrashes between my fingers. Amarie gives me a thumbs-up, then turns away. Deflated by her response, I nearly lose my hold on it. I steady myself, then throw it and send it flying up and out – it glides through the air, then splashes as it falls into the open water, to freedom.

The sky is bright blue with no clouds at all. The air is warm and the breeze feels like when you drink juice after running really fast on a cold day: your throat burns and is a bit sore from the run, and when you breathe through your mouth the air is icy cold and it stings the back of your throat, but then you drink juice and it's the right amount of cold and it just soothes and quenches at the same time. The only thing that interrupts that just right, soothing, quenching feeling is the squall of seagulls fighting in the distance. I can't see them, but their racket puts my nerves on edge. Amarie feels my frustration.

'This is their home and we've decided to come here,' she says, telling me off.

'But do they have to be so loud?'

She doesn't say anything. She's still in a mood. I lie back on the grass and turn away from her. There's no use her being in a mood with me; it's not my fault. I'll hate it just as much as she will when the day school girls come back after their day at the Grace Darling Museum with all these stories and I wasn't there and I have nothing to share and nothing to say and it becomes another reason why no one really wants to sit next to me or talk to me or work with me.

'Do you remember that day we went to Brownsman?' Amarie asks, breaking me out of my thoughts.

'Yes.' I don't turn to look at her; she can't just switch in and out of moods and expect me to be ok with it.

'Go on, tell the story,' she says.

'I don't want to.'

'Go on!'

'You were there, you know the story,' I snap.

'Tell it,' she insists. 'And tell it in the past tense.'

I don't want to look stupid, so I ask without missing a beat, 'Do you want it in past simple, past continuous or past perfect?' I've never paid much attention in Sister Alma's grammar lessons, but if they'll help me avoid looking like a complete idiot when Amarie plays the smart arse, I'll start to concentrate a bit more.

'Currently, you're trapped in the present,' Amarie says, as though she's explaining a simple maths equation to a small child. 'So, tell it in the past tense – in whatever way you want.' She sits up and looks at me. 'Telling stories of the past, *in the past tense*, builds up your appetite for history.'

'I don't like it when you start being weird.'

'Just tell the story,' she says.

I'd wanted to try somewhere different, to go a bit further out. You didn't fancy it. You were worried about the distance and the deep – and in case there was a caretaker on the island. But I convinced you it was worth a try, and we did it. It was exhausting, but it felt great once we got there. We had to scramble up the rocks to get to the flat part of the island and to keep low until we'd checked everywhere – the cottage, the old lighthouse, the lot. It was all clear. I felt vindicated and was doing a little victory dance, then you said, 'Don't celebrate just yet.'

Off in the distance, a Billy Shiel's tourist boat was making its way towards us. It was going to dock on Staple Island, but it would ferry around us on Brownsman Island to give people more chances to take pictures of the puffins and terns that were flying above us and nesting on the island. All we needed to do was stay out of sight until it passed. We hid behind the lighthouse ruins and waited.

There was a little boy on the boat. He must have been about three or four, shaggy brown hair and big, bright eyes. He wore a burgundy jumper with a tiger on it. He stood on the bench at the side of the boat looking overboard. A woman, who I guessed was his mother, held onto his waist and he was waving and laughing at everything he saw – the birds in the sky, the seal sunbathing by the water's edge, and me peeking beyond the edge of the lighthouse ruins. He jumped and shouted and started to point at me. I crouched low behind the crumbling walls, but it was too late. I wasn't sure if the woman had seen me. A few moments later, she started to scream. I risked it and peeked over the side again. She wasn't looking in my direction at all. She was leaning over the edge of the boat, staring into the water, which was rippling around a centre point, and the boy had vanished. Before I could properly think about what I was doing, I ran to the edge of the island and dived into the sea. I tried to open my eyes, but it was impossible to see – the water was dark and full of silt. I felt the push of the current against me as I swam deep in a direction that I hoped was right. *This way*, you said, and I followed your lead.

Here, you said. And I grabbed at the place I thought you meant, but I was only ever grabbing at water. You told me to calm down, not to waste my breath by panicking. You led my arms through the dark until my fingertips touched something that felt like fabric. I grabbed it and pulled him towards me. His body felt small and limp next to mine. I might have felt afraid but there was no time to feel anything really – it all happened so quickly. I swam in the trail of your voice and followed you to the surface. I didn't hear your words with my ears, your voice was in my chest.

We came up at the edge of Staple Island. You told me where to leave him and where to hide so I wouldn't be seen. You went quiet then, and I could hear shouting and crying coming from the boat. Above that came a man's voice; he was shouting, 'Look, look over there!'

From where I was, I couldn't see the boat. But I could see you standing on the causeway between Staple and Brownsman, waving in the open air. You were creating a diversion; it gave me enough time to creep out of hiding. I ran to the edge of the island, jumped back into the water and swam away.

Within seconds, you were already back on Staple Island, standing beside the boy and gesturing at the boat again. The people on it started cheering when they saw you with him, and the boat made its way towards you. When they were near enough but had not quite docked, you stepped out into the glare of the sun and disappeared in front of their eyes.

That evening in the common room during quiet time, Sister Alma was reading the paper. She gasped. Sister Maria asked her what it was, and Sister Alma said, 'There was an accident on the Farne Islands and a little boy nearly drowned!'

The other sisters stopped what they were doing and huddled around her asking questions. She read silently for a moment, then told them, 'It was one of Billy Shiel's boats to Staple Island. They were circling Brownsman and a four-year-old boy fell overboard.'

My neck grew hot and you tensed beside me. Reading directly from the paper, Sister Alma said, 'A shocked bystander said, "He fell out near Brownsman Island and then appeared ten minutes later on Staple Island. It was a miracle." Many of the passengers on the boat reported that there was a shadowy figure standing beside the young boy when he was later recovered from Staple Island. Some believe it was the ghost of Grace Darling who saved the drowning child. The mother of the child said this morning, "I don't know if it was the ghost of Grace Darling, but whoever or whatever it was, I'm grateful my son is safe." The story of the lighthouse keeper's daughter who helped her father save survivors from the Forfarshire, the famous steamship that sank off the Farne Islands, is well known around these parts–'

'We should simply thank God that the boy is fine and stop this nonsense about dark shadows,' Reverend Mother interrupted. She hadn't moved from the cross-stitch she'd been working on. 'If you speak too often of darkness, you never know what it might bring you.'

My face burned but no one seemed to notice. I was grateful my skin was more loyal than Sister Alma's. Mother didn't look at me the whole time she was talking, but I sensed the tension in her body the way I felt yours. And I heard her accusation in my chest.

❖

Amarie was right: telling the story did make me feel better. It made me realise that we have our own Grace Darling story. We spend the rest of the day foraging, looking for an oddity to add to my shoebox collection of uncommon things. Neither of us mentions the school trip again.

Dusk creeps in and the temperature drops. Goose pimples form on my arms. 'Do you get goose pimples, Amarie?' I ask, watching my skin clot.

'Can you see goose pimples on me?'

'No.'

'There you go.'

'What are you?' I ask, examining a rock, trying to determine if the pink mottling across the grey makes it worthy of joining my collection.

'If you don't know what I am, nothing I say will make sense.'

'You could try,' I say, discarding the stone, deciding it's too similar to something I already have. 'I know, we could play the "I am" game. I can go first,' I offer. 'I am twelve. I am strong breaststroke in the North Sea – or a front crawl, if we're going far out. I am pulling myself forward, body soaring through the deep. Cresting, head breaching to take a new breath and inhale the light. I am my first period. Something about original sin and Eve. I am dandelion and burdock hard-boiled sweets. I am stones, shells and sea glass collected on the muddy banks of Holymead and the rocky shores of the Farne Islands. I am running and climbing and rolling down hills. Starlings, gulls, terns and puffins and seals. I am salt crystals on my skin after I emerge from a swim and dry off. I am my own Grace Darling story.' I take a breath, happy with myself. 'Ok, your turn.'

'I am questions forming, about to be known,' Amarie says, and she doesn't say any more.

There are some things Amarie and I never talk about, things we've agreed to forget without ever really knowing them. But a fearsome memory stalks me and won't let go – a finger points at me; it's an accusation of something, but I don't know what. I dream about it, but when I wake up, the image is foggy. I don't know who the finger belongs to or if it was pointing at me at all.

'Do you ever think about good and evil?' I ask.

'In what way?'

I think of how to respond and can't quite form an answer, when Amarie says, 'Look!' She points up and into the distance. A flock of starlings, hundreds, maybe thousands of them, are on the horizon. I sit up with her to watch. The sunset in the distance melts from orange to red to purple, and the birds dance in patterns against the sky. In unison, they twist, rotate, break apart and then come together again. Dancing with one spirit, they pivot and soar across the sky: dispersing, connecting, then disappearing in unison.

I wash my hands in a rock pool. 'Whatever it is, it'll come off as you swim!' Amarie says, irritated by how long I'm taking. The tide has started to come in and she wants to leave quickly. I ignore her and continue to rub my palms together under the water. A teeny, tiny pollack bumps into my feet, struggling to find a way out of its surroundings. I reach for it, miss and reach again.

'Leave it alone,' Amarie says. 'The tide will be in soon and then it'll be back in the sea. We have to go.'

'Who knows what could happen between now and then. I'm doing a *good* thing.' I grab at it, gently this time, and it slips into my hands.

'We need to go,' Amarie insists.

I step out of the wet rocks and throw the fish out to sea, to freedom. The little fish sails through the air and a low-flying tern swoops down and grabs it just before it hits the water.

I keep seeing it happen, over and over. I desperately want to admit it during weekly confession, but I can't. If the sisters found out I'd been swimming that far out, they'd never let me leave the grounds again. Days go by until, finally, I come up with a plan. Amarie and I are in my room and I want to know what she thinks. I have to find the right way to tell her; she can be stubborn, and if I say it in a way she doesn't like, she'll just refuse. I lie on my bed flicking through Spanish magazines that Sister Maria has given me. Amarie is at the window. The daylight erases the top half of her, so I can make out only her legs on the wall under the windowsill.

'What are you looking at?' I ask.

'The walls around the convent.'

I move to stand beside her.

'It's like a prison,' she says.

'It's like a castle,' I correct. 'We could be royalty.'

'Or captives.'

'It's a castle...'

'...for slaves.'

'Castles are not for slaves! You're in a mood.' Now is not a suitable time to tell her. 'Maybe it's more like the castle that St Teresa speaks of, the holy one that we all have inside us, that we need to explore and understand. The grounds and the walls are like a moat. They keep people out unless we say they can come in.'

'We're like the island within the island,' she says.

I take this as a victory, 'Exactly! And the gate is like the causeway. Perhaps we should get the sisters to publish the tide times for safe crossing, like with the proper causeway,' I giggle a bit.

'Why are you so happy?' she asks, suspiciously. 'You've been unhappy for days.'

'Because of what I did to the fish.'

'And now you're fine?'

'I realised something I could do ... that might help.'

'And what's that?'

She's talked me into a corner; I can see I'll have to tell her, but I'm not sure it's the right time.

'Go on,' she says.

'I have to confess.'

'If you confess, we'll be trapped here forever. It's our one escape!'

'Don't be melodramatic.' I pause for a second. 'I've thought about it, and as long as the person I confess to swears not to tell the sisters, it'll be fine.'

'Do you trust anyone enough?' she asks, and before I can respond, she says, 'And if you do, you're stupid!'

This is going to work; she feels very strongly about our access to the Farnes. 'I trust you. I want you to be my confessor.'

She moves from the window to the wall. I can see all of her now: a silhouette, her outline identical to mine. We are tall for our age, a bit bony, with bumps and curves starting to grow.

'If you say the Lord's Prayer and Psalm 23 and ask him to make you his right arm and his servant, I think then it will be ok for you to be my confessor. We were all made in his image and we are all connected to him, so I don't see why you can't be my confessor.'

I'm speaking quickly, my mouth is dry and I can feel my pulse in my throat.

'I'm not Christian, Imani,' she says.

'What are you, then?'

She doesn't respond.

I wait, fighting the urge to cry.

'Don't you know me?' she asks, gently.

'No,' I splutter, throat hot, eyes starting to leak.

She moves beside me and puts a hand on my shoulder. I see it, though I can't feel its weight.

'I don't mean to upset you. I can try to help – in my own way.'

'Which is?'

'I can ask the ancestors to speak with Nyame.'

'Who?'

'The One Who Knows and Sees All.'

'God?'

Her voice sounds more grown-up than usual, 'You can confess to me, I will pass your message to them and they will pass the message to … God.'

'How will I know if I'm forgiven?'

'The forgiveness will travel along the same routes as the message, in reverse.'

'Will you say the Lord's Prayer and Psalm 23 before you do it?' I ask. This is a matter of principle, a matter of faith. I feel there is something wrong in speaking to God through so many inter-mediaries. I'm sure that Mother would disapprove. She would be convinced that several people along the chain of communication were demons. I'm scared and insist that Amarie says the prayers that I've asked for. She is quiet for a while, pacing along the back wall, then she agrees and recites the prayers. She takes her position standing by the wall close to my bed. I sit with my back to her and begin: 'Forgive me, Sister, for I have sinned…'

Ten

Harold and I have spent the morning foraging in the grounds of St Teresa's. Sitting in the rose garden, we catch our breaths. Harold's cheeks are red and his button nose, which is usually red anyway, has turned a beetroot shade of purple. When he turns those colours, we have to lie down for a good while for him to cool down.

'What've we got?' I ask, settling on the grass.

'Dandelions for sandwiches, weed for the salad, and I can get pond juice to drink after we've rested.'

Mother said Harold needs to lose weight, but I think he's fine as he is – people need to just leave Harold alone, I think.

'Perfect picnic,' I say, closing my eyes and enjoying the sun on my face.

Harold breathes heavily next to me. I have a vision: Harold sitting in an armchair watching something on TV. His floppy blonde hair is so overgrown that it creeps into his eyes. He's still as big as he's ever been, maybe bigger. His nose is red – the normal red, not beetroot – and his cheeks are their normal kind of beigey colour like the rest of his face. I'm in the kitchen, which is beside the living room, and there's an open arch that connects the two rooms. I'm chopping onions on a cutting board and I use the back of my hands to wipe away my crying from the onions.

'Do you think we'll get married?' I ask Harold in the here and now.

He sits up and looks at me; his cheeks, which had started to calm down, begin to go red again and his nose goes mauve.

'Do you want to marry me?' he says, looking concerned.

'I don't know. I just wondered.'

'Would we have to do it now? I don't want to leave my mam and dad.'

'No,' I reassure him. 'We're only ten, we're not allowed to do it now anyway. But if you don't want to, we don't ever have to – we could keep on as friends. Some people never do it – the sisters and Mother, they never did. They married God instead. Actually, I don't know if I'm even allowed to do it. I'm special. You know I'm special, don't you?'

'Yeah,' he smiles. 'I'm special, too.'

'No,' I correct him. 'We're special in different ways. We know how you're special. But I'm special and we don't know how yet. We don't know what it'll mean for me.' I look at him, trying to work out if he understands. 'Maybe when it's revealed, it will also be revealed that I'm not allowed to get married.'

Harold stands and walks away. I wonder if I've offended him. He goes to the other side of the grounds and stuffs his pockets with flowers. He comes back and empties them on the ground – tons and tons of daisies.

'They're for us,' he says. 'We can make a daisy chandelier for when we get married and have our own house.'

'What's a chandelier?'

'A huge lampshade that hangs from the ceiling. I'll get a picture of one and I'll bring it to you for next week.'

'If we were to get married, what do you think our lives would be like?' I ask.

'I don't want to think about it.'

I feel offended. 'Why?'

'Because it would mean my mam and dad aren't here any more.'

'What?'

'People get married when they don't have mams and dads or when their mams and dads are about to go.'

'Go where?' I don't let him respond. 'That's not true!' I shake my head, feeling a bit irritated with him. 'What about Sally Hetherington? She got married and her mam lives in the village, just two doors down from her.'

He sits beside me and looks up at the sky.

'People don't just get married because their parents have … gone away.'

He doesn't say anything; he leans backwards until he's lying flat.

'We can stop talking about this now if you want.'

He's silent for a while longer and then says, 'Ok, let's do that.'

'I'm sorry if I worried you, I didn't mean to.'

He doesn't respond. We lie on the grass looking at the sky; wisps of cloud and not-quite-cloud float over us.

'That one's a tractor,' I say, pointing at a thick angular form that's drifting over us.

'And now it's turning into a dragonfly,' Harold says, as fragments break off and the cloud distorts and transforms.

'And that one's a cow,' he points to a roundish one.

'But it's turning into an eagle.'

'Look, the dragonfly's become a fish.'

'What is it becoming now? Wait…' I put my hand over his mouth, not wanting him to jump in too quickly. He pushes my hand off and we both shout, '…a bow tie!' and laugh.

I always try to have grown-up conversations with Harold. I'd heard Sister Magdalene telling Mother that I shouldn't spend too much time with him. Mother said it was good for me to be with my peers and Sister Magdalene had said, 'He's not her peer.' She's probably right, but I'd be really sad if they stopped me from seeing Harold. I know I'm special and that I need to develop more quickly than I am doing; that's why I try to have grown-up discussions with Harold, to help me progress. I'm sure it'll make him develop quicker, too, and help with his Down's.

'Do you think it's possible for a tractor to become a dragonfly, or a cow to become an eagle?' Harold asks. It's a childish question, but I've abandoned any hope of grown-up things, so I choose to enjoy the day and the time with my friend. I sit up and I'm silent for a long time – really taking his question seriously.

'In reality, it probably isn't, but in faith everything is possible.' I'm pleased with my answer.

Then Harold asks me, 'What's the difference between faith and reality?'

'That's a good question, Harold! That's a really good question. I'm going to ask Mother and I'll tell you what she says. We can swap when we see each other next week – you can give me the picture of the chandelier and I'll give you the difference between faith and reality.'

He smiles and nods. I decide that trying to have grown-up conversations with Harold isn't a bad idea after all; as awkward as the conversations feel sometimes, they are obviously having medicinal benefits to Harold's brain and general development, so I should definitely continue.

That evening after dinner and evening prayers, I shower quickly and hurry into my room to get changed for the relaxation period before lights out. That will be my chance to ask Reverend Mother my grown-up question and I want to get there as early as possible.

'Why are you rushing?' Amarie asks as I'm threading my arms through the sleeves of my pyjamas.

'I have something to ask Mother.'

'About Harold's question?'

'You heard that?' I ask. I hadn't noticed her with us.

'Of course. I've always thought that faith and reality are words that people often use for different kinds of knowledge.'

I rub cream into my face and pull my dressing gown on. 'That's interesting. Let's see what Mother says about it, eh?' I slip my feet into my slippers and run for the door. 'Come on!' I call to her.

We gather in the common room and I'm bursting with my grown-up question. I have to wait, though, because the TV is being brought out. It's kept in a locked cabinet, which is opened only a few times a year. We watch things that Mother calls Edifying. This means wildlife documentaries or programmes about history. Whenever there are people in the programmes, I search the screen to see if I can see anyone that looks like me. I never do. I wasn't expecting to watch TV tonight, so I should be excited, but I'm full of my grown-up question and I can't wait to ask it. We settle into our places and hot drinks are given out: a warm malt drink for me, Earl Grey for Mother, Sister Maria has camomile, everyone has their drink in their cup. Sister Alma stands in front of the TV, ready to announce the programme. Before she starts, I put my hand up.

'Yes, Imani?'

'I have a question.'

'About the programme?'

'About life.'

They chuckle.

'What is the difference between faith and reality?'

Sister Alma flushes and looks at Mother. 'Imani, can we talk about that later?' Mother says.

Deflated, I nod and Mother signals that Sister Alma should go ahead.

'The BBC has made a programme about our very own St Teresa. It's a two-part drama called *The St Teresa of Avila Saga*. We'll be watching the second half next week.' A gasp goes through the room; TV, twice in two weeks and about the founding mother of our order. I should be excited, but I'm too busy feeling lousy and I don't really want to watch the programme now.

Whenever we watch wildlife programmes and the animals start to mate or fight, one of the sisters, or Reverend Mother, will tell me it's time for bed. When I ask why, Mother says the content is Inappropriate. During *The St Teresa of Avila Saga*, I keep expecting someone to send me to bed. I close my eyes tight to block out the things she does to herself. I cover my ears, but I can still hear her crying. Then the pictures I'm trying to block out start appearing behind my closed eyes: the nail pressing into, then piercing, her hand, the blood filling her palm. I squeeze my eyes tighter but I can't stop seeing it.

'I'm going to sleep now,' I announce, standing up, because clearly no one else is going to send me to bed.

'Are you sure?' Mother asks, her eyes never leaving the screen.

'I'm tired.'

'You'd prefer to go to bed and miss watching the history of our Mother?' Sister Alma asks.

'I'm tired,' I repeat.

'Don't you think she grew tired, of suffering, of people doubting her?' Sister Magdalene says.

'You right,' Sister Maria adds. 'Watching this make me remember how far we come from her original vision, of poverty, of humble, of suffering. How easy and lazy we make it for ourselves. Sit down niña, this is education.' She strokes my arm and pulls me down at the same time. Sister Maria gets lost in the drama, more so than anyone else. She comes from a place in Spain that's very close to Avila, and I wonder if she's entranced by the film because it's about our founding mother, or if watching people who look like her on the TV fills something inside of her. When the film is finished, I go to bed without speaking to anyone. Later, Mother comes into my room and I pretend to be asleep.

I skip school all week and go to see Dr Trewhitt at his house instead. He's been stuck at home recovering from a knee injury and needs company. I don't tell him what's happened and he doesn't ask. Today he makes me a lemon cordial and we sit down to do a crossword.

'A six-letter word for a pelagic bird that sheds its colourful bill after breeding.'

I count the letters off on my fingers, 'Puffin.'

'You're a bright spark,' he says. 'You'll do great things.'

'What if I don't?'

'Pardon me?'

'What if I don't "do great things"?' I ask.

He puts the back of his pen in his mouth and looks at me. 'It depends what you consider to be great, I suppose. Many people achieve greatness and the world never hears about them. They're great friends, mothers, fathers, daughters – you'll be whatever greatness is to you.'

I like his response. I wonder whether doctors are a bit like dads, and then I ask, 'Dr Trewhitt, what's the difference between faith and reality?'

He chews on the pen, really thinking about it. I knew it was a grown-up question.

'Well, I guess reality is the way that things are, and faith is a hope in what may be or, perhaps it's better to say a belief, yes, a belief in what you can't see.'

I stare into space as I listen to his words. I can't wait to tell Harold. I daydream about telling him and putting on the same thoughtful grown-upness in my voice that Dr Trewhitt has now. I know exactly the example I will give to Harold, too: in reality, he is my best friend; he is here, I can touch him, he is solid. I know he cares about me and will never let me down. In faith, Amarie is my best friend; she's my shadow, she's of the spirit world; when I touch her, I am always touching the thing she is beside. It's a bit like how we don't see the wind, we just see the thing it moves; but even though I can't touch her, I know she's there and that she also will never leave me or let me down, just like Harold.

❖

Mother knocks on my bedroom door. She comes in, although I haven't said come in. I sit with the pile of books on my lap; sandwiched between them are two sheets of paper with daisies in the middle.

'Are you ok?' Mother says sitting beside me.

I push down harder on the books.

'What are you pressing this time?'

I point at the pile of leftover daises on the windowsill.

'You're developing a habit for knick-knacks and ephemera, aren't you?'

I don't know what ephemera means and I don't want to talk. I keep pressing; my legs start to hurt, but I keep pushing.

'We've missed you in school this week,' she says.

I'm not sure if I'm in trouble. I push the pile on my lap until my legs feel a bit numb.

'You needed time to absorb the things you'd seen,' she says. 'The people on television are actors. They're performing a script that someone from the BBC has written. Those things may or may not have happened to St Teresa in the way they were shown. She experienced many spiritual trials … and put herself through vigorous religious exercises.'

I'm relieved – I'm not being told off, but I really wish she'd stop talking and leave. She explains that the trials St Teresa endured were all in exploration of a deeper connection with God: 'We don't adopt her practice explicitly here because our culture wouldn't permit it.'

I lift the first book and the top sheet to see how the daisies look. I feel Mother's eyes on me.

'I don't know if we need to adopt it explicitly,' she says.

The daisies have set better than I expected. The stems and petals have spread out and are connecting and overlapping, making criss-cross patterns along the page.

'I do feel that we need to adopt ... the spirit of it, though,' Mother says, 'and as far as possible, I think everyone at St Teresa's tries to do that.'

I touch the criss-cross pattern softly with the tips of my fingers.

'We are all human, we forget or grow complacent, we make mistakes. But we try to remind one another, and an opportunity like this, to watch an adaptation of her life, it's just another chance to remind ourselves of the origin of our order.

'We're not going to start asking anyone to ... hurt themselves. In fact, I won't tolerate it. But reminding ourselves about poverty, the importance of meditation, thoughtful conversation with one another and with God, the learning that can be gained from the experiences of suffering that life opens us to – those are our foundations and if we dilute that any further, we won't be connected to what we came from.'

I look at her for the first time.

'You don't have to watch the second part if you don't want to,' she says.

'Will I have to do that?'

'What?'

'Will I have to hurt myself ... so that I can learn from suffering ... and find my Divine purpose?'

'Your first purpose was to bless fifteen cranky old women with motherhood. Not many young girls are so blessed or burdened,' she says. She gets up to leave.

'Can I have warm milk with cinnamon?'

'In the common room or the dining room?' she asks, putting a hand gently on my head.

'In the common room,' I say. 'I'll come watch.'

The second part of St Teresa's BBC adaptation isn't as frightening as the first. It begins with St Teresa sick in bed. Two women fret over her and when she's alone she sees visions. Her bedroom grows foggy and this man walks out of the mist. He's short and gold and I think he's ugly, but St Teresa narrates and she tells us he is a great beauty. He walks over to her bed and his skin releases a golden mist that mixes with the fog. In his hand is a spear. St Teresa's voice tells us, '*He appeared to be one of the highest types of angel who seem to be all afire.*' Choral music starts, he moves in slow motion towards her and she looks very calm. I feel the sisters shift beside me.

'Imani...' Sister Alma begins.

'Let her watch,' Mother says. I wonder if something Inappropriate is about to happen and I'm happy that I get to see it.

The golden man reaches St Teresa's bed. I think he's going to climb on it, but he rises into the air above her. The end of his spear lights with a flame and drips liquid fire onto her sheets, but they don't burn. The angel draws his spear back and plunges its fiery head into her chest. St Teresa convulses; her head is thrown backwards as she lets out this soft groan. Her voiceover tells us: '*He seemed to pierce my heart several times so that it penetrated to my entrails. When he drew it out, I thought he was drawing them out with it and he left me completely afire with a great love for God. The pain was so sharp that it made me utter several moans; and so excessive was the sweetness caused by this intense pain that one can never wish to lose it, nor will one's soul be content with anything less than God.*'

At the end of the programme, the BBC narrator talks about the convents St Teresa established in Spain. Two hundred years after her death, he says, a convent was established on Holymead Island in her name. The image of our convent fills the screen, a sprawling building, all on one floor except for its spires. I wonder if the sisters knew that this would be coming. Everyone holds their breath as the BBC narrator talks about us: she says the convent was built on the site of the Cunningham family mansion. The prominent tobacco baron and his family made their fortune through the Triangle Trade. I make a mental note to ask Harold to use the Yahoo search engine to find out about the Triangle Trade. Yahoo is like a living encyclopaedia that Harold has access to at school, and with it he can find out about the world beyond the island. It's called Yahoo because that's the sound real surfers make when they're riding the waves; Harold's teacher told him so.

'In its heyday the convent housed over a hundred sisters,' the presenter says. 'There are now fewer than twenty in residence and what was once a closed community has become more out-ward-looking. It is the only Carmelite convent to house sisters who are cloistered and semi-cloistered. The convent manages a day school for girls, and jointly manages the Holymead Archives with Durham Cathedral.' The picture of our home fades to white, and black words creep up the screen.

Dream:
Wounded Hand

I'm running along the causeway, trying to reach the mainland. A figure is walking behind me, at a steady pace that I can't outrun. I'm holding something; it's small and moist and my right hand is balled into a fist around it. Liquid drips from between my fingers. I open my hand into a hooked claw: there, in the middle of my palm is a finger. *I have a human finger*. Butchered, bloody and still warm.

The footsteps behind me grow louder. I shut my fingers tight and run as quickly as I can. It's getting dark and the sands of the causeway are becoming boggy. The mainland flickers in the distance, threatening to disappear. The person walking behind me calls out or screams. The sound makes no sense – it's all fury and incoherence. I turn to look; the figure following me is a woman. She appears to be several metres away. She shakes a wounded hand in the air at me. My feet pound the softening earth, working hard to avoid getting stuck. My heart beats wildly and I sprint with all my might.

'Demon!' she screams clearly. The word is unmistakeable. 'Demon!' she cries again.

I feel her breath on my neck, though she is still far off in the distance. My thighs burn with the effort, and the more I run, the more the mainland creeps away. Her breath is loud beside me now, although her steps have faded. At the side of my vision, a bloody hand reaches for my shoulder. Where its index finger should be is a gaping black hole that drips.

❖

BOOK ONE: SUNSUM

I wake up in a sweat and nearly fall out of the armchair. The Black Madonna tapestry looks down at me, knowingly. There's a sharp pain in my lower back and my right hand tingles. I adjust myself in the chair, sit up to catch my breath, massage my hand a little. The cup of tea Sister Alma made me is on the side getting cold. I try to steady myself. It isn't the first time I've had that dream: it was a recurring nightmare when I was growing up. But in the mornings I would remember only part of it – the running, or almost being caught, or the finger. Sometimes, I'd simply know there had been a finger in the dream and I'd feel it marking me out as something wicked.

Rhythm and Roses

I drain the teacup of the last dregs of chrysanthemum tea. The final sip is cold and leaves a strange aftertaste – not quite bitter, not quite sweet. It's been a while since Sister Alma left. Reverend Mother hasn't arrived but the Black Virgin Mary is still with me. I'm torn between thinking I should never have come, and I should have come much sooner. In the distance, Mr Bo scratches at an object, shredding it with his claws, if the noises are to be believed. I get up and go to find him, using the sound to track him. The dull thud of my rubber-soled shoes against the concrete floors almost echoes – perhaps I am the ghost in this place and the spirits I see have more substance than I do. Mr Bo stops scratching. I'm in the middle of the hallway, no nearer to finding him. The corridor at the end leads to my old bedroom.

At the door, I pause. It whines as it opens. 11 is sitting on the bed thumbing through a glossy magazine. It will be one of the ones Sister Maria bought on her last trip to Spain. She was the youngest sister by a good thirty years, and I don't know if it was her age or the fact that she was also an outsider, but she was always warm towards me.

There's a faint tap on the bedroom window. 11 ignores it; she's focused on the thick, shiny pages. I approach her tentatively and sit on the bed beside her. I reach for her shoulder – she seeps through my hand, like ink absorbed in a clean sheet of paper. She turns to see who is there but looks right through me. The rapping at the window starts again.

'Perhaps it's hail,' she says, and I look to see who she's talking to. There's no one there. I wonder if Amarie is in the room; eleven-year-old Amarie. But I can't see her. The noise outside grows louder. It's inconsistent and messy.

'It can't be hail,' 11 says, to herself, or to Amarie, or to me. 'It's got no rhythm.'

I smile, remembering the theory: at eleven, one of the things I loved about Mother Nature was what I saw as her natural rhythm and artistry. The year we held a ceilidh to raise money for the repair of the roof of the parish church, Mrs O'Shea, one of the mothers of the day school girls, said I was a good dancer: 'She's got rhythm,' I heard her tell Sister Alma, 'all black people have. They have a sort of creative exuberance just in them.' By then I knew I was black and not brown, as I'd previously thought. And I'd realised I wasn't the only black person in the world. But apart from that, I knew very little about black people, and I took Mrs O'Shea's comment as a statement of fact. Even with my limited knowledge, I was sure Mother Nature was black: she had rhythm, symmetry and style. Throughout Northumberland and the holy islands, there were extravagant displays of Mother Nature's 'creative exuberance', from the giant redwood trees that lined the grounds of St Teresa's, to the flame-billed puffins on the Farne Islands, to the way the old monks' priory had aged, somehow blooming in its own disintegration.

'It's a person. It's not Mother Nature,' 11 says. 'Listen to how random it is.'

I turn around, looking for her, certain now that a young Amarie must be in the room somewhere. 11 stands and moves to the window. I follow her; we look out but there's no one in the grounds. Beyond the periphery walls, a small figure catches my eye – jumping up and down outside the convent is Harold.

'Come on, Amarie, let's see what he wants.' For a moment it feels like she's addressing me. She pulls a coat from the small closet, puts it on and walks out.

'Hola, niña,' Sister Maria calls.

11 jumps and turns around, 'I'm just going for a walk around the grounds,' she says, answering a question that hasn't been asked.

'In this weather?'

'I need some daylight.'

'It's very cold.'

'I like the snow.'

'You arrive in the snow,' Sister Maria says, stroking 11's short afro hair. 'On a day of brilliant light and the place was covered, unblemished in white,' she says in words that are not her own.

11 smiles and nods.

'Don't leave the ground and don't stay long, you'll be sick.'

11 walks out. Once outside she waits until Sister Maria's footsteps fade, then runs to the wall, pressing herself against it, trying to remain hidden. I follow her, struggling to keep up.

'Harold? Are you there?'

'Yes. Walk to the gate so I can see you,' he says.

'Someone might see. This is better.'

With access to TV and the Yahoo search engine, Harold was my eyes and ears to the outside world. Harold was my gateway to information about black people. By surfing the World Wide Web he was able to verify Mrs O'Shea's claim that black people had rhythm. He put it into Yahoo and wave after wave of information came crashing out, with images and words which proved that all black people did indeed have rhythm. From these, Harold compiled a list of eleven of the most rhythmically blessed black people and he presented me with it as a Christmas present. The crumpled piece of paper with the names of people I'd never seen was kept with my favourite Spanish magazine in a shoebox under the bed. It also housed single feathers (wigeon, merlin, bluetail, pheasant and goose), shells, stones, sea glass, two of my milk teeth, one of Harold's, the rosary beads I'd fashioned from pebbles with holes in them, some orange yarn, and my best attempts at flower pressing. The names on the list Harold gave me were: Michael Jackson, Eric B & Rakim, Curtis Mayfield, Carey Mariah, Sammy Davis Jr, Earth, Wind & Fire, Etta James, James Brown, Stevie Wonder, Sam Cooke and Samantha Mumba. I used to read each name out loud every night before I went to sleep. Eventually, I memorised them and didn't need the paper any more. I'd repeat them to myself before sleeping: Michael Jackson, Eric B & Rakim, Curtis Mayfield, Carey Mariah, Sammy Davis Jr, Earth, Wind & Fire, Etta James, James Brown, Stevie Wonder, Sam Cooke and Samantha Mumba. It became a bedtime litany, reciting the names of others of my kind that I didn't know. The magazine I kept the list in was my favourite because it had a picture of a woman so dark that she was only a bit lighter than me. When I first saw her, I carried the magazine everywhere. I'd sneak out of classes to sit in empty rooms and stare at her.

'What's up?' 11 asks.

'Up? Nothing. I just wanted to see you.' Harold pauses, 'This isn't what I thought it'd be like. Let me *see* you. Please?'

'No, I've told you, if we get caught, I'll get in trouble. I'm reading magazines today; I can do without being sent to the penitent's booth.' I'm growing impatient, 'It's freezing out here; what is it, Harold?'

'I love you.'

'What! Harold! Did you come out here in the middle of the freezing cold to tell me that? Couldn't it wait?'

'No.' He pauses. 'I have a present for you.'

'Today's not my birthday. Harold, why are you being so strange? I wouldn't have come out here if I knew you were going to be strange with me. I only came because I thought you might have found out something new and interesting or that something might be wrong.'

'Something was wrong: you didn't know that I loved you, so I came to tell you.'

I remember this conversation well. I watch them live it for the first time.

'Oh, Harold.'

'Don't say, *"Oh, Harold"* like that. I don't like your voice when you use it like that.'

'Couldn't this have waited until it wasn't snowing?' That was a very sensible question.

'The snow might not melt until tomorrow and today is the day you tell people you love them.'

'St Valentine's Day, I forgot! We rarely do a service on his behalf–'

'Let me see you. I want to give you a present.'

'Harold, I've told you– '

'Please…?'

11's voice softens, 'Let's make it a game; why don't you find a way of giving me the present without handing it to me through the gate. Go on, I dare you to think of a clever way of giving it to me.'

Harold doesn't respond.

'Harold? Harold?' 11 calls.

Clumps of softness fall on my head and nose and glide off; red covers white as the rose petals land. In the breeze, tufts of scarlet hover above the snow. Another cluster of petals comes from beyond the wall and then another. I look up and let them caress my face.

'Did one touch you?' Harold asks, his voice jumping up and down as he continues to throw the petals over the wall.

'Yes, Yes! Lots have!' 11 says.

11 and I dance in falling snowflakes and petals.

'Every one that … touches you … is a kiss from me,' Harold says between jumps.

'You are silly!' 11 giggles, this time not in the grown-up voice.

'That's it,' Harold sighs when the last handful floats down. 'I'm going now, Imani, bye.'

'Don't you want to stay and talk a bit? I can tell you the real history of St Valentine.'

'No, thank you,' Harold says. 'Bye then, I will come to see you next week.'

'Ok, bye, Harold – I love you.'

11 bends down and picks up a handful of petals. She'll dry them and press them and put them in the shoebox with her magazine, the one with the dark-skinned Spanish woman in it and the list of black people with rhythm.

Eleven

I overslept and missed morning prayers at 5 am, morning work meditation at 5.45 am, and breakfast after that. We've got an early start to school because the tide is low earlier than usual, so I'm late for everything by the time I arrive at the schoolhouse for assembly at 8.12 am. Reverend Mother is at the front of the assembly hall and the girls are sitting looking afraid, guilty and confused. I sneak in at the back and hope no one notices.

'Someone somewhere in this school has committed a grave sin,' Reverend Mother says.

My stomach lurches.

'We received a Divine Sign from our Mother Mary this morning. As you all know, these are rare and sacred and must be treated with the utmost respect.'

Our sister convents in Spain and Ireland have had Divine visitations, messages and signs, but we've never had anything. Well, the convent received me, but I wasn't a sign. I was a gift. Reverend Mother said we would receive a sign that would tell us how my promise should be realised, and my stomach does another little flip as I listen to her now. From the tone of Mother's voice, I really hope this sign has nothing to do with me.

'It was a message of transgression,' Mother says, confirming my fears. 'It is unclear exactly what the transgression is, but the implication is crystal clear. Therefore we, the sisters and I, would ask the girl who knows what has passed to come to us immediately and tell us so that we can deal with the matter.'

I try to catch the eye of one of the sisters. They're all concentrating on Mother. I look at Sister Maria, trying to get her attention. It was Sister Maria who'd suggested to Mother that they give up their attempts at wrestling with my afro and just cut it short like hers. Before that, I went through nights of torture when the sisters would sit me on the floor in front of the hearth in the common room and try to comb and plait my little curls. These nights always ended in tears. Often one sister would give up halfway through in a sweat, and another would do as much as she could until all of the senior nuns had had a turn or until my whole head was done, whichever happened first. Trying to sleep after it was impossible; my head would throb all night. Then Sister Maria stepped in and said that although they could portion out their ordeal and each take part of my head, I had no one to share the pain with and suffered their efforts alone. I think they all felt bad when she said that because they'd never thought about it that way before.

Once, a few people from the village saw Sister Maria out gardening without her habit covering her head and they said she looked like a butch lesbian. The girls were whispering about it in school all week. Harold discovered the meaning of the word 'lesbian' for me – his mother told him it's when a girl kisses another girl, and since then I decided the villagers were incredibly stupid; didn't mothers kiss their daughters? Don't friends share a peck on the cheek? Wasn't every girl a lesbian then? It was only when Harold was caught going onto Yahoo to investigate further and his teacher caught him, banned him from surfing the net for two months, and sent a letter home to his mum, only then did we guess that there might have been more to it than we'd been led to believe. Afraid of getting Harold into more trouble, I didn't bring it up again.

Mother continues detailing the gravity of the Divine Sign, but she still hasn't said what it was. 'In the early hours of the morning,' she says in a hushed voice, 'Sister Alma came across the sign from our Divine Mother. The blood of Mary lay staining the snow that had settled yesterday evening.'

We breathe in as one, shocked.

Mother continues, 'We believe this symbol was left to tell us that one, or some, of our girls has been immodest, indecent, immoral, sinful.' She throws adjectives on top of each other with relish – we'd get marked down if we did that in an essay.

'The blood of the Virgin signifies a union that has not been ordained by God.'

There's a long silence. Mother scans the room, glancing over each of us slowly.

'We will hold confessions all day for anyone who knows what happened or what this symbol signifies, so they can come to us and *confess*.' The last syllable is a hiss.

A hand in the middle of the hall goes up, it's Shannon.

'Yes Shannon,' Mother says, thumbing the rosary beads that hang from her pocket.

'How do we know it was the blood of our Holy Mother?' Shannon says. 'How do we know it wasn't the blood of someone or something else?'

The silence in the hall is as thick as fog. I tense up, wondering if this is going to be another very public conflict between Shannon and Reverend Mother. Once, Shannon arrived at school with her hair bleached from its naturally mousy colour to platinum blonde. Mother called her parents to come and take her home and when they refused, the sisters held Shannon in a chair as Mother shaved her head with Sister Maria's trimmers. Mrs Turnbull screamed when she came to pick her up at the end of the day.

'You left her in my charge,' Mother said calmly. 'I asked both you and your husband to come and pick her up and deal with the matter in your own way, but you refused.'

Shannon's mother was grey and weary-looking; she was proba-bly much younger than Mother, but this didn't give her any visible advantage.

'This is not the last you'll hear of this – I'm furious!'

'As am I, Mrs Turnbull. I had to delay one of my classes while I was forced to attend to this matter – a GCSE class no less! Those girls will be sitting their exams soon and instead of guiding them through this challenging time, I was forced to deal with your errant little girl, so gluttonous for attention that she forces the teaching faculty to dedicate one-on-one tutelage to her.'

'Tutelage, you call what you did to her tutelage?'

'A fine lesson was learnt today, was it not, Mrs Turnbull?'

'This is not the last you've heard of this, Reverend Mother – we may even take this to court. Who knows what emotional trauma Shannon will suffer now.'

'Nonsense, Edna, I've known you since, well, back at Carmel College. You must have been what, twelve, were you, when you joined us? You drive nearly sixty miles a day to bring your daughter here, even though the tide timetable must be a nightmare for you, and why do you do this? Because you know the type of *tutelage* she'll receive. The same sort you received from me all those years ago. If anyone should be taking anyone to court, it should be the parents of those wee girls, who'll be sitting exams this month. Now, get in that extravagant car of yours and head back home. All this racket because a silly girl wanted some attention. Well, she achieved her aim and what have you achieved, Edna, other than pushing your blood pressure up a few more notches?' Mother steered Mrs Turnbull towards the door as she spoke, 'Go now and drive safely. God bless.' Before Mrs Turnbull could respond, Reverend Mother had closed the door.

Mother takes a moment before answering Shannon's question, enjoying the wait. 'Purposeful question, young Shannon. I hope you'll be as insightful later while we try to uncover the meaning of this sign. It was not merely blood that we found lying on the snow, no – not blood at all, in fact. Had it been blood, we may not have recognised it as a Divine Sign and would be putting our questions to adult powers like the police. No, it was a symbol of blood and a message of impropriety. Red rose petals were found floating just above the surface of the snow. As I am certain you remember from your spiritual symbolism classes, the rose is most commonly associated with the Holy Mother; she is, after all, "the rose without thorns". And what does the rose *with* thorns symbolise, Shannon?'

Shannon flushes and mutters something.

'Louder, please?'

'Original sin,' Shannon says.

'Exactly. Therefore, red roses dismembered in this way – completely torn apart – this is a symbol of impropriety and a puzzle left for us to solve. The Holy Mother compels us to ask, which of our *girrils*' – Reverend Mother's usually light Glaswegian accent becomes heavier when she gets excited in this way – 'has been improper and in what way? What can we do to help them?

'We will hold confession all day today in room C16, to try to get to the bottom of this. Let me reassure you that no one will be in trouble; we mean to help you, to protect the sacred castles and chambers of your souls. The founding mother of our order...'

My heart beats in my throat and I struggle to breathe around it. My face is hot; a paler complexion would struggle to hide the blood that's rushing to my cheeks. I don't go to the confessional, but there's a long queue at the door of C16 all day. Every girl in the school joins the queue at some stage, and some of them queue twice or more. I wonder about their improprieties and, if everyone else has something to confess, shouldn't I, the real perpetrator, be joining the line? And it's not only the day girls who queue – everyone who works, studies or lives at the convent joins the queue at some point. A second classroom is opened to accommodate all of the confessors. The sisters take turns in confessing and bearing witness to confessions. Even Sister Magdalene, who is fully cloistered, sends a message across to the schoolhouse requesting one of the sisters come to the main house and hear her confession. I wonder what improprieties *she* has to confess.

In the evening, I sit cross-legged on the common-room floor, playing Scrabble with Sister Maria. Mother sits in the burgundy armchair with Earl Grey cupped in her hands and a cross-stitch in front of her. Sister Alma is marking homework books with Mr Bojangles sleeping on her lap. Sister Magdalene is doing a puzzle of the Sistine Chapel, and some of the other sisters are sitting at the back reading.

'Imani, I noticed that you didn't confess today,' Mother says.

'No.'

Sister Maria has just spelled the word 'bra' and I wonder whether Mother would find it improper. In the rules of Scrabble, it is definitely improper because it's an abbreviation. I don't say anything. I take my Z and E and make zebra.

'Bueno,' Sister Maria says.

'What?' Mother asks.

'I speak about the game,' Sister Maria rushes to explain.

'Well, Imani, why didn't you go to confession today?'

I pause, 'I thought it wasn't meant to be compulsory.'

'You are getting far too bumptious, young lady!' Mother puts her Earl Grey down. 'Yes, it was not our weekly confession, but a ritualised confession planned by man should not take priority over a God-ordained order to confess!'

'Did you find out the meaning of the sign?' I ask.

'Yes, without your contribution.' She takes a big gulp of tea before continuing, 'When Sister Alma showed me the sign this morning, I thought it was a warning about an indiscretion. But as I shared the sign with our community and extended family here, we saw their response, all opening up and coming to speak of the things that were heavy in their hearts. I realised the sign was calling for all of us to cleanse ourselves of ... everything. It was a call back to the womb of our Holy Mother, for us to become innocents once more. This building and all of the people who dwell in it are renewed and clean now. You are the only *stain* that remains.'

Blood rushes to my face for a second time that day. But this time it's different; Amarie runs towards Mother and I fight with all my strength to hold her back. Mr Bo stands up on Sister Alma's lap and she drops the book she's marking. He hisses at me, then turns to the wall to hiss at Amarie. Sister Alma strokes him to try to calm him down, but it doesn't work. If I let Amarie reach Mother, I don't know what she'll do. Mr Bo seethes at her, his back arched and his tail reaching up behind him. Within me, I pull at Amarie, trying to slow her down. The effort pushes me back and I tumble, sending the Scrabble pieces flying. Mr Bo jumps off Sister Alma's lap and runs out of the room.

'You never threw tantrums as a child, so don't for a moment think we'll accept that type of display in your adolescence,' Mother says.

I wriggle on the floor holding my stomach.

'She is having a fit?' Sister Maria asks, coming near me.

'Leave her,' Mother says.

I can see Amarie by the wall, her movements slowed by my struggle, but getting closer to Mother.

No! I call to her, *please don't!*

We squirm and fight and, finally, she gives in.

Tell the sanctimonious old witch the truth.

Ok.

She stops struggling and I try to catch my breath. My eyes water and my nose begins to bleed. All of the sisters are standing now, looking down at me, frightened. Mother is the only one who remains seated, giving deliberate attention to her cross-stitch.

'The rose petals weren't Divine,' I say. 'They were from Harold.

He brought them yesterday, for me. He threw them over the wall of the grounds because I wouldn't go to the gate.'

'Sometimes it is those who are not completely of this world who commune best with the higher powers. Harold's *condition* may give him insight and access to spiritual chambers we are yet to penetrate – and as such he was acting as a vessel for our Holy Mother.'

'No!' I shout.

Sister Alma kneels beside me and dabs a tissue against my bloody nose.

'He brought them to me as a St Valentine's Day present– ' I say, then quickly add, '–he threw the petals over the wall, I didn't even look him in the eyes ... nothing improper happened.'

'Whatever your memory of the event may be, and whether or not the boy knew the reason he was doing the things he did, we are all instruments of the Divine. Nothing in this world is without significance. Because of the pure and generous gift of love he shared with you, today we were all able to shed our loads and receive blessings from the Virgin. This changes nothing.'

'But–'

'Enough! Go to your room.'

Fourteen

It's exam season and the sisters are preparing the final-year girls for their big tests; they're running after-school lessons all term. This means the usual boat that takes the mainland girls off the island won't be enough, so Sister Alma's arranged for two boat trips instead. Mother's asked me to bring the younger girls to the harbour for the first boat, and Sister Maria will bring the final-year girls later, in time for the second. It used to be that the school times, like everything on the island, depended on the tide. When the mudflats were safe to cross, parents from the mainland would drive in and drop their girls off. High tide usually lasts four to six hours, so the length of the school day depended on what the tide was doing, and parents would pick their girls up when the tide was out again. That was until Mrs Turnbull started a petition. Another one of her many battles with Reverend Mother. The petition called for school times to be standardised. She complained that with the amount they pay in fees, it was unacceptable for the school to be so irregular. The parents of the other mainland girls all signed the petition, but none of the families from the village did. Reverend Mother just ignored it, then Mrs Turnbull wrote to the Bishop and he told Mother she had to standardise.

'I don't see why Mother made you come with us,' Shannon Turnbull says.

'You'll have to ask her about that,' I respond.

'I could have made sure everyone got on the boat. You've never even left the island before. I mean, if something happened to one of us, what would you do?'

Shannon's goading me for her own reasons; what she doesn't realise is that I know why she's doing it.

'Why are you ignoring me?' she asks. 'Don't you speak English? No understandy Englishy, eh, eh?' she continues.

We reach the boat and I turn to the group and count the top of their heads. Twelve; I left with twelve from the school and twelve have reached the boat.

'Don't pretend you can't hear me. The silent treatment isn't exactly clever or mature. You're not clever.'

'There are twelve,' I say to the boatman when he asks how many. 'Their parents will be waiting at the port. Please will you make sure that they're all picked up before you leave them?'

'Oh, aren't you important!' Shannon continues behind me.

'Of course, dear,' the boatman responds, and he starts to usher the girls on. 'We can drop this one overboard on our way if it would be any use?' he nods in Shannon's direction.

'Are you talking about me?' she snaps, glaring at him.

He ignores her and counts the other girls onto the boat.

'That won't be necessary,' I tell him, trying to hide my smile. 'Here's our number at the convent – if any of their parents aren't there, please give us a call. We want to make sure all of the girls get home safely.'

'All of the girls get home safely!' Shannon says, in a singsong voice. 'Listen to her, like she's not a girl, too. She's in all of my classes, I'm three months older than she is – she's fourteen and I'll turn fifteen before her. Listen to her, with her airs and graces, like she's older or as if she's a sister or above us or something,' Shannon says to the boatman. 'She's not above us, she's far below … she's a, what do you call it – stray, no … feral … no … what do you call it when people find cats that someone's tried to drown and they decide to take them home and raise them? That's what she is.'

Heat rushes to my face and I blink to stop the tears.

'On the boat and enough of your chat,' the boatman says to her.

'Really, that's what she is – someone else's unwanted thing that the sisters decided to take in.'

The boat sets off and as it begins to pull away, the boatman calls over the engine, 'A convent school, eh? Good to see that the best values are being given to the young 'uns. I'll be sure to rec-ommend to me son that he sends the grandbairn there. Charm school itself by the look of this one...' he nods in Shannon's direction.

He waves and I wave back, trying to smile through the cloud.

Just before the boat is out of earshot, I shout, 'Don't worry, Shannon, if I see Duncan Ogilvie, I'll tell him you're sorry you couldn't meet him after school as planned. Shame about that!'

Shannon's mouth flies open. She recovers herself and yells, 'He'll punch your lights out, you dirty little...' The wind carries away the rest of her words and I turn away.

From what I've seen of Shannon and Duncan's relationship, I completely understand why the sisters chose celibacy. Duncan lurks around the schoolhouse gates at break times and when he manages to sneak into the grounds, all that seems to happen is they huddle in a corner whispering; he rubs the top of her jumper as though he's polishing a cabinet, then he licks her lips and sticks his tongue in her mouth. That goes on until she pushes him off and tells him to go.

'Why are you wasting your energy thinking about her?' Amarie asks. 'You should have let me smack her for what she said.'

'It doesn't matter. Anyway, I wiped the smirk off her face in the end, didn't I?'

'I know she's not the brightest, but Duncan's a horrible, horri-ble boy. I don't know why she'd spend time with him.'

'If she'd told me about their plan for today – or just not been so horrible, I might have been able to help ... because I've never told anyone what I've seen between them. I might have...'

'And got into trouble yourself if the sisters found out? What are you talking about?'

'If she'd just trusted me...'

'Why do you want her to share anything with you?'

'Anyway, she didn't tell me, so ... there we go.'

'Is that Harold?' Amarie asks.

'Where?'

In the distance, at the bottom of the bank, two figures stand under the arches of the lime kilns.

'It's probably not.'

Amarie runs towards them anyway. I follow, lagging behind. Duncan Ogilvie has Harold pinned against the inside wall of an arch. Harold's face is bright pink and his nose is turning purple. He has a mark on his cheek as though he's been slapped.

'Come on, Spastic, tell me! Where did they go?'

'I was g-g-getting buttermilk,' Harold stutters.

'Where did the girls go?'

'Leave him alone!' the words come out as a shout.

'If it isn't the love child of Quasimodo and King Kong. Why don't you piss off back to whichever jungle you came from?'

'Leave him alone,' I repeat.

'Where's Shannon?'

'On the boat going home.'

'You idiot! She'll be sat at the port for ages, she's not being picked up till six.' He pushes Harold harder into the wall.

'Crying, Spaz? Don't be a girl as well as a–'

'I said, leave him alone,' I repeat.

'Or you'll do what, Paki?' Duncan says, slapping Harold's face. 'Are you soft on the spaz, Paki? Are you?' he laughs, looking between Harold and me.

Duncan hits Harold again and this time Harold cries. I ball my hands into fists, ready to launch at him.

'Stop crying, idiot, you're embarrassing yourself in front of your little Paki girlfriend,' Duncan says.

Before I have a chance to step into the arch and threaten him, Amarie launches herself; she runs down and grabs Duncan by the throat and pulls him off Harold. She pushes him to the ground and kicks his face into the dirt. He rolls away, panic in his eyes, not understanding what's happening. She follows him, bending to punch him.

'What the fuck!' Duncan shouts as his nose explodes with red.

Amarie pulls him up by the collar and headbutts him, before pushing him back down. She steps on his side and he curls into himself for protection. The flow from his nose stains the grass with crimson and snot.

'Imani,' Harold says.

I run towards him and we hug.

'Are you ok?' I ask.

We're both shaking, looking away from the scene. He nods, wiping his eyes with the back of his hand.

'Make her stop,' he whispers. 'Make it stop.'

I turn to look at them. Duncan lies unconscious on the ground, but Amarie's still kicking him. He's not moving, but she won't stop. Or can't stop. She steps on his arm and then his hand; his fingers poke out grey and motionless from under her feet. She lifts her foot high to stamp on his face.

'Stop!' I scream. 'Stop it, Amarie!'

She freezes with her foot in mid-air and turns to look at us as though waking up from a dream. Her hands are covered with blood and she has a smudge of red on her forehead from head-butting him.

'What did you do?' I ask her.

Old fears gather and almost form into memory. *What did you do? Get out! Go! Go away!* Do I already know what Amarie is capable of? Sister Magdalene's voice from another time, warns or accuses me of something: 'There is darkness in her!' / '*her* people worship … darkness.' / '…give severed body parts to their unclean gods.' / A severed hand points a finger at me.

'Take Harold home,' Amarie says, breaking through my thoughts.

Harold's cheeks are more than ruddy and his eyes are swollen from crying. His mother is hysterical when she sees us. She repeatedly asks what happened, never leaving space for me to answer. Then, before I've finished saying Duncan's full name, she says she is going to press charges. 'That bloody Ogilvie boy! I'm going to have him arrested!' I leave with her still shouting questions and threats about Duncan. I run back to the lime kilns, but when I get there, there's no sign of Duncan or Amarie.

Back at St Teresa's, the after-school club has finished, Sister Maria is preparing to take a group of girls for the last boat to the mainland and the village girls are getting ready to walk home. Sister Maria tells me that the boatman called about Shannon; her parents weren't at the port waiting for her like the others.

Shannon! I'd completely forgotten about Shannon. I start apologising and confessing that it's all my fault.

'What?' Sister Maria asks. 'I call her parents and they come immediately. No problem. They were confuse about after-school club.' She smiles at me, 'You, too sensitive. You must no feel responsible for all the things in life.' The rhythm of her words is comforting; she touches my chin and squeezes it. 'Rest, you look tired.'

'Here you are!' Sister Maria says. 'I am looking everywhere.'

Disorientated, I rub my eyes as the light floods in. 'I thought you were taking the girls to the boat?' I say.

'I go and come already.'

'I was meditating,' I say, stating the obvious. Standing up from the cushion on the floor and rubbing my knees, which have started to hurt.

She's exasperated and her English is affected when she's emotional. 'The police is here. They want see you.'

My stomach clenches. I take her hand and we leave the meditation cell together and walk downstairs. Inside the common room, the fire is lit and two police officers sit talking to Sister Alma and drinking tea. When we enter, they fall silent. They ask me questions. I'm careful not to answer questions I haven't been asked, as I'd done earlier when Sister Maria told me about Shannon.

'Did you see where Duncan ran off to?'

'I last saw him down by the lime kilns...'

'Near the castle?'

'Yes. I was walking back after dropping the girls off at the boat...'

Their radio goes off and interrupts me. The policewoman excuses herself and steps out. I look at the policeman, expecting him to pick up where she left off. He's draining his teacup and finishing off a flapjack. Sister Maria is looking at him disapprovingly, but Sister Alma is smiling at his appreciation of her baked goods. Outside the room, the policewoman shouts into her radio. My heart races in my chest.

'We've located the Ogilvie boy,' the policewoman says as she steps back in. 'He's at the community hospital in Alnwick.'

I cough back surprise and try to look calm. 'Apparently Harold wasn't the only one Duncan picked a fight with today. My colleagues have been with him for the past hour. They've been trying to radio into me but the signal out here's horrendous... It seems after Duncan finished with Harold, he took his father's mini jet boat and went off to meet up with his girlfriend. He didn't know she'd already been picked up. He docked a bit off the port at Seahouses, but as he was getting off, he got into a fight with a group of local lads. Right now, he's not in a good way, and the jet boat's a write-off. He says the lads took it for a joyride and he saw them crash it just south of the port. He's given a statement and described the whole thing, so we'll look into that separately.' She turns to address me, 'Can you tell me what you saw happen between him and Harold? Harold's quite shaken up, and he's not saying much. His mother wants to press charges.'

'When I got there, he had Harold, but when he saw me, he ran off.'

'You didn't see anything at all?'

I shake my head.

She thanks me and the sisters for our assistance, and then the two police officers leave. My palms are sweaty and my heart won't slow down. I tell the sisters I need some air and walk out before either of them has the chance to call me back. I drift into the evening and keep going. By the time I'm aware of where I am, I'm at the sands of the causeway. The sky is indigo and the tide is coming in; I head up the sand dunes and away from the rising water. Sitting at the top of the bank, I watch the sea swallow the path that leads to the mainland, making us an island again.

'What are you, Amarie?' I asked her. We sat on this bank together, watching the causeway flood. It was one of the only times she actually answered the question – and I didn't feel afraid.

'Your shadow,' she said simply.

When Reverend Mother and the others called Amarie a demon, I didn't have the words then to say what she really was, and Mother seemed so afraid that we both stopped talking about it and pretended Amarie didn't exist at all.

'I'm the sun and the sum,' Amarie said. 'Sunsum.'

'You're talking in riddles again,' I said. She did that sometimes, it felt like I was being tested and I was always failing.

'Take this hand and touch the other one,' she said.

I used the fingers of my left hand to touch the palm of my right.

'What's happening?' she asked.

I felt myself getting irritated; it was another test, but I decided to go along with it – it wasn't exactly challenging.

'My left hand is touching my right.'

'Now rub both of your palms together.'

I did as she said and rubbed.

'What's happening now?'

'I'm rubbing my hands together, like you said.'

'Which hand is being touched and which one is doing the touching?'

I stopped, then did the action again. 'Neither, they're both doing ... both.'

'That's what I am; not object or subject, not body or soul, I'm the space where they meet; both and both.' She pointed at the causeway, which was disappearing under the sea: 'I'm that patch of land ... not mainland or island; both and both; unified touch.'

Sitting on the bank, I watch the remaining sands turn to rust in the sunset then slowly start to disappear as the North Sea swallows them. There's a shape moving in the middle of the disappearing flats – it's her.

'Amarie!' I shout. She doesn't move. I rush down the bank towards her. As I reach the bottom of the dunes, I catch sight of Sister Maria and Sister Alma, who are some distance away and walking towards me. Sister Maria calls out, but if I wait to talk to them it will be too late. I run into the causeway.

Go back, Amarie says, her words vibrating in my chest.

'No!' I shout and continue towards her.

The beach turns to mud and then swamp the closer I get to her. By the time I'm with her, boggy waters are at my thighs. I wrap my arms around her. 'I'm not leaving you.'

'You should,' she says.

'You were protecting us. You were just trying to protect us.'

The reflection of the moon sends silver streaks rippling in the water and the sea rises to our hips. The flow pushes against our legs and it takes effort to remain standing.

'Imani, go back to the sisters.'

'I won't, I won't.'

'There's something in me that you can't control.'

My right hand tingles and I can feel my pulse at the centre of my palm. 'Something evil?' I ask her, tentatively.

'No, but the more you ignore it, the more it will frighten you.'

The current sweeps at our legs and we hold each other and fall, letting the sea take us. My head goes under water. I could try to swim, but I don't. If this is what she wants, so be it.

Imani, don't, she says, *swim, swim.* Her words echo in the hollow of my ribs; part voice, part movement of my internal organs. I'm cold and I've swallowed water, but I start to kick. This bobs my head out of the sea and gives me enough chance to cough out some of the water I've swallowed and snatch at air. The causeway is covered; we hold on to each other as the sea throws us like driftwood. There's the whirr of an engine from somewhere but I can't see a boat. The push and pull of the waves alters, and I know someone is there. I hear them coming, but the deluge stuns my ears. Hands grab me; they pull me up and out. I hold Amarie tight; *don't let her go, don't let her go.* I don't know if the words are theirs or mine or hers.

Thirteen

Brightness and gloom blend. Light takes over. My eyes adjust. I draw myself out of meditation, uncross my legs, stretch, blow out the candle. The dark wins over the light for a moment. Amarie isn't with me. Her voice vibrates softly in my chest, though. I can't make out the words. She's talking to someone. I leave the meditation cell to look for her.

'How old are you?'

'Thirteen. You?'

'Twenty-three.'

'You're younger than Sister Maria.'

'How old is she?'

'Over thirty. I think she's older than you are older than me.'

'That's a complicated thought.'

'I have several. Daily.'

'Is that right? Do you go to the day school here?'

'Yes, but I live here as well.'

'Oh … I didn't know they had boarders.'

'They don't. It's just me.'

'What a fascinating place: cloistered, semi-cloistered, active nuns … and just you.'

'Only Sister Magdalene is cloistered, and no one's active.'

'How long have you been here?'

'All my life.'

'Will you come into the light so I can see you?'

'What if I don't want to?'

'Why would you not want to?'

'That's for me to know.'

'Oh really!'

I hear laughter coming from the library. I creep towards the door. It's the visitor. She's facing the far corner. It looks like she's talking to the curtain and the areca plant but she's addressing the partial shape of a girl, who seems to be hiding. I sneak in, slam the door behind me and duck behind the armchair.

The visitor turns around. 'Is someone there?'

While she addresses the door, I creep behind the sideboard and along the wall, until I'm next to Amarie. I give her a slap. My hand hits the wall. 'Ouch!'

'Serves you right,' Amarie whispers.

'Are you ok?' the visitor asks, spinning back towards us.

I crouch behind the plant and pull the curtain to cover more of myself. 'Yes, fine.' Though my hand doesn't feel fine.

'I think someone might be in here with us.'

'It's an old building,' Amarie says.

'Doors close by themselves here?'

'Sometimes.'

'Will you come out, so I can talk to you properly?'

'I thought you said you hadn't come here to talk?' Amarie says.

'It's too early for a silent retreat. This is just the beginning, I've got a long way to go.' She stares into space. Then, abruptly, she comes back to herself and asks, 'Where are your parents?'

'Where are yours?' Amarie says.

'In America. What do you do here?'

'What are *you* doing here?'

'Hey, I'm answering your questions but you're not answering mine! That's not fair.'

I want to hit Amarie, but every time I try, I end up hurting myself. I tap on the wall where her head rests, hoping the vibration will irritate her enough to make her stop.

'Are you going to be cloistered or semi?' Amarie continues, ignoring me.

'Sister Magdalene is cloistered, you said, tell me about her?'

Amarie launches into the story of the time George Cranston came to fix the central heating in the schoolhouse and saw Sister Magdalene without her face covering or gloves on. As she's telling the story, the library door swings open and Mother's tall, slim form fills the doorframe.

'Melia, what are you doing?' Mother asks.

'It's Mel-e-ya, not Melly-a.'

Mother face is stone. Melia flushes.

'Sorry Reverend Mother, I was err...' she stutters.

I step out from behind the curtain to save her from having to lie.

'Imani, what on earth are you doing back there?' From her tone, I know she doesn't want an answer. 'Sister Alma is looking for you, Mel-e-ya,' Mother says, not waiting for my reply, as I'd suspected she wouldn't. 'She's preparing to give you a tour of the grounds.'

'Of course, Reverend Mother, I'll go right away,' Melia says, rushing past Mother.

❖

Mealtimes are observed in the community dining room; everyone arrives at 5.50 pm and stands. We sit only when Mother arrives at 6 pm. Melia arrives too early and takes a seat when she should be standing, or comes in late and has to scurry to find her seat, apologising as she squeezes past people to take her place. Then the food comes: the broccoli bowl makes its way down the table, zigzagging as everyone serves themselves and passes it on. You receive from the left and opposite, and pass across to the right, and in this way the mealtime routine is ordered. You don't need to think about what you'll do next; all of the decisions have already been made. But Melia forgets to turn the serving spoon to face the person she's passing to, or passes in the wrong direction, or forgets to pass at all. She flushes and apologises loudly with every mistake, forgetting that mealtimes are meant to be silent. One day, as I'm coming out of the community dining room and heading to my room, an arm reaches out of the communal toilets and pulls me in: I'm in the small cubicle facing her. She's shorter than I am, squat and doughy with a storm of black curls around her head that she's tried to tame into a ponytail. She stares intensely at me and locks the door behind us.

'I feel like everyone hates me and I'm doing everything, everything wrong!'

'No one hates you, but you have been doing most things wrong.' Her face falls. 'I need help.'

'I'm not usually supposed to be around the postulants much.'

'I'm not a postulant yet.'

'I have even less to do with non-postulants.'

She looks at me helplessly. 'I just need someone to show me the ropes ... be, like, the human face of this place, you know?'

'Sister Maria–'

'Hates me! Every time she sees me coming, she rushes off in the opposite direction.'

It feels nice to be needed. 'I guess no one has officially told me I'm not allowed to spend time with non-postulants. It's just sort of always assumed. So, until they say, I guess we could spend time together ... but we'd have to be discreet.'

Melia is Greek American. She was born in England but moved to the US as a baby. She's hyped to be back in Britain and gets extremely excited whenever someone suggests we have some tea. She's disappointed to discover that the fluffy scones she'd pictured herself eating with clotted cream and strawberry jam look a bit different here. 'It looks like the roadkill version of the pastry I had in mind,' she says when we sit in Pilgrim's Café eating them after a long walk around the island.

'It's a Singing Hinnie, pet,' Mrs Blenkinsopp tells her. 'What did she expect,' we hear her shout from the kitchen moments later, deliberately speaking loud enough for us to hear. 'This is Northumberland, not Devon!'

Pilgrim's is the only café on the island, so Melia doesn't have many options. We're back in Pilgrim's for Singing Hinnies again the following week.

❖

Melia and I sit at the back of the parish church; she's smoking the last of her cigarettes. She's promised me that if she joins us officially she'll give up smoking. What she doesn't know is that if she isn't able to give up, I won't tell any of the sisters her secret. The ground is wet and cold and we huddle together for warmth.

'Is it always this cold?'

'Mostly.'

She puffs at her cigarette then blows out, staring into the smoke as though it will give her answers. 'You've still never told me how you ended up here,' she says. I tell her the story of the child who arrived in the snow – on a day of brilliant light as the island was covered, unblemished in white.

'Do you really believe that?' she laughs. 'Don't look at me like that, all doe-eyed and sad.'

'Why don't I ask you some questions?'

'Fire!'

'How did you find us?'

'The prioress has an amazing reputation internationally.'

'Reverend Mother does?'

'Yeah, she's a bit of a...' she searches for the word and settles on 'maverick.' She nods, happy with her choice. 'She's basically a badass. So, I came to study under her.'

'Mother is a badass?' I repeat, shocked at the discovery of this new word and its implications.

'You come here and you choose how to be with God. She lets you choose the path that's right for you.'

'When will you decide?'

'Well … I don't know. Sister Alma explained the process to me and … well…'

'Sister Maria told me that when she decided to be a postulant, she came to stay a few times, like you're doing, and when she knew her answer wasn't no, but she still didn't know that it was yes, the sisters suggested she go on retreat.'

'The silent retreat?'

'Sort of, you go into the hermitage for some days.'

'How many?'

I shrug. 'With normal retreats, when you're an actual nun, you can choose how long you stay in there, but when you're deciding if you're going to become a postulant – so not a nun, not even a novice – then it's not in your control. It could be anything, a day or two, a month, but I think it's usually about a week.'

She stares at the cigarette between her fingers, its head glowing in the cold air.

'*A Week in the Hermitage* – it sounds like a horror movie.' She looks out into the distance and sucks at the cigarette. 'Where is *The Hermitage*?'

'Just behind those trees – it's hidden so it feels secluded.'

'And what do you do while you're on retreat?'

'What do we do all the time? Pray, meditate.'

'And you're left by yourself for a whole week to do that?'

'Mostly. Mother comes in a couple of times to talk to you – spiritual counselling. And one of the sisters will bring you food three times a day.'

'Right,' Melia says, looking horrified.

After Melia leaves, I start to wonder about the things she'd said; if Reverend Mother allows everybody who stays to practise their faith in their own way, when will I be allowed to choose? Will Mother put me in *The Hermitage* for an unspecified time and talk me into knowing what it is I have to do with my life?

The second summer Melia visits she brings a rose cutting. It's dark purple. It's a gift for all of us, for the rose garden, she says. Melia hopes to help Sister Magdalene plant it. But with Sister Magdalene being cloistered and Melia being an outsider, they can't go near each other. Mother explains this to Melia, several times.

'But I brought it for the rose garden and Sister Magdalene looks after the roses; it would be so great if she could be the one to show me how to plant it,' Melia insists.

After the third attempt to explain, Mother loses her temper. 'Mel-e-ya, would you prefer it if your little rose cutting died while you stood here insisting on doing something that is against our rules? Sister Magdalene is cloistered – which part of that are you struggling with?' That's when Sister Alma steps in and agrees to help Melia plant the cutting instead.

Within a year the purple rose cutting becomes a sprig. It's not impressive, not in comparison to the other bushes and vines in the garden, and although some of its buds never properly open, it has promise. The year after that, the bloom is bigger and three flowers appear and last longer. The next year the plant is a tuft and five full dark roses bloom. There is one that is so dark that unless it's a very bright day it looks like black velvet. When its petals fall, I take them, press them on a clean sheet of paper and put them inside the Spanish magazine, beside the dark woman and the list of names of black people with rhythm.

Melia visited every summer. For months before she'd arrive, I'd count down the days. I would plan where to take her when she arrived, what new things I'd tell her in my role as her unofficial guide to convent life. I even imagined that one day we might swim out to the Farnes together.

❖

The third year Melia visits, she brings the Black Madonna tapestry. The Holy Virgin is ascending to heaven surrounded by clouds and cherubs – and she is mesmerising. 'I thought you'd like it,' Melia says, when she finishes rolling it out.

'That's distinctive,' Mother says.

'She's beautiful,' I say, and the words come out as a whisper.

Several of the sisters start to speak. I don't hear what they're saying, I'm so captivated by the tapestry. As the days go by, it becomes clear that they don't like her. The Black Virgin Mary is rolled up and squeezed behind the sideboard in the common room. One day, in between periods at school, I go into the main house and pull her out, spread her on the floor and lie on the ground looking at her face. Before I know it, the whole afternoon has gone and I've missed the rest of my classes.

Mother walks in and finds me and I know I'm in trouble. But when she sees what I'm doing, the sternness in her face softens. She clears her throat before she begins. 'You shouldn't have missed your last two classes,' her tone is firm but not angry. 'There's no need to lose a whole school day looking at this thing. We'll hang it up, ok? Then you can look at it whenever you want.'

Lost for words, I just nod.

When Mother suggests we hang it up, the real controversy starts: 'It's gaudy!' / 'Too bright.' / 'It's rather loud, don't you think?' / 'What's all of that embroidery around it? It looks too busy.' / 'It wouldn't really fit in anywhere.' / 'Which wall would you hang it on?' / 'Is it appropriate?' / 'Is it blasphemous?' / 'Of course, *I* don't mind, but the sisters who do, they shouldn't be made to look at it every day.'

I would have hung it in my room, so no one had to look at it except me, but we're not supposed to decorate our cells. Then I'm scared they'll ask Melia to take it back.

'Hang it in the library,' Sister Alma suggests, and that seems like the solution. I am the one who uses the library the most anyway and, for anyone who didn't like the presence of the Black Madonna, there is always the schoolhouse library, which is used more regularly because it's bigger and stocked with a wider range of books. But then Sister Magdalene isn't happy; as the only clois-tered sister in the community, she doesn't take part in the running of the day school, so she would have access to the schoolhouse library only when school is closed. There are a few more days of discontent. In the end, the Black Madonna is allowed to stay. She is hung above the fireplace in the library, directly opposite my favourite seat.

Once the tapestry was hanging, and for the rest of Melia's stay, whenever there was a personal contemplation period, we'd meet in the library and sit across from Her, contemplating – not always in silence.

'My mom says my affliction is the disease of the adopted,' Melia says. 'She figures I'm not really looking for God, I'm looking for my birth mother.'

We look up at the tapestry and not at each other.

'I didn't know you were adopted.'

'Yeah, a bit like you, I guess,' she says.

Like me?

The dinner bell sounds, signalling the end of personal contem-plation. Mother is a *badass* and I am *adopted*. Each year, Melia brings me a word, a concept, a gift that changes the world around me. We walk to the community dining room in silence.

The fourth year that Melia comes, when she leaves she doesn't officially say goodbye. One evening she is there and the next morning at breakfast she isn't. Mother says she had to leave unexpectedly. Later that day, I find one of Melia's bags, a rucksack, in my wardrobe. Other than two items, it's been emptied of its contents. The first thing is a note, which reads: *A little something x*. At the bottom of the bag is a small, gold, jewelled object – it looks like a little pocket pen: it's rounded in shape, and has an intricate filigree pattern with red and blue gemstones dotted throughout. They could be rubies and sapphires. I twist the middle, trying to ease the cover off or draw its nib out, but nothing happens. I put it inside the shoebox under my bed for safe keeping and plan to ask her how to open it when she next visits. But the following year, she doesn't come back. I wait and count down the days, but when the time comes for her to arrive, she doesn't. And she never returns.

Nineteen

When a tree falls in a deserted forest it causes an impact. The wind carries a murmur of this across land and water. Skirting over sea foam, it loses some of its resonance, but the vibration travels on. This trace, when it finally lands, is a shiver down your spine, a tickle between your nose and eyes that makes you sneeze or shed inexplicable tears. When my birth mother fell, I didn't hear it. I felt a shiver down my spine at around 2 pm on a Saturday at the end of October. I was nineteen and hanging clothes out to dry in the courtyard. I dismissed it as a chill in the wind. Then, days later, I received the message. The phone rang in Reverend Mother's office; I let it ring, thinking someone else would pick it up. When no one did, I walked in and answered it as I'd heard Mother and the sisters do so many times before: 'Hello, St Teresa's Convent and Day School, how may I help you?'

'I need to talk with Imani,' a woman said.

My body trembled when she said my name.

'It's me,' I answered.

'Imani, I am your aunty, Grace, from Ghana. Your mother is dead.' No need for pleasantries to cushion the blow, we were family. My aunt Grace from Ghana told me that my mother was pronounced dead on Saturday afternoon, just after 2 pm. She had been unwell for some time.

'The funeral is in two weeks,' Aunt Grace from Ghana told me. My aunt continued to talk, but I'd lost the ability to process information. She told me a number, an address, names and dates; my hand wrote it all down, but my mind didn't quite register any of it. I searched the room for Amarie, frantically looking up and down. Then I saw her, crouched by the door on the opposite side of the room, head between her knees, rocking back and forth. Still holding the phone to my ear, I noticed that my writing hand had stopped. I was nodding in response to something my aunt Grace from Ghana had said. She couldn't hear me nodding and kept repeating the phrase. Finally, she said goodbye and I put the phone in its cradle.

When my mother fell, I didn't hear it, but I felt it. It took a while for the vibrations to be understood, but the shiver down my spine, the peal of the phone, and my aunt Grace from Ghana saying my name, these were the gongs that announced a change in the weather.

Mr Grimauld lets me fill the paper bag with whichever sweets I want and doesn't let me pay for anything. He says he wants me to remember where the best sweets in the world can be found so I'll remember my way home. He says, 'Once you've finished with your travels', repeatedly, as though I'm going on holiday.

I only really had a day to make the decision after the call from Aunt Grace. Sister Alma went to the mainland to sort out a passport and my travel arrangements. Once that was all confirmed, I had a day to pack and that was pretty much it. Mother didn't speak to me. She refused to answer my questions and said if I left, I should understand that I would be doing so without her blessing. I didn't have my own suitcase, so I used the large rucksack Melia had left behind. With my goodbyes said to the sisters, I walked into the village. I stopped off at Pilgrim's Café and Eady's Saintly Sherbets to say some last farewells. That's when Mr Grimauld gave me the sweets and the lecture on finding my way home. Staring into the bag of sweets, it takes all my effort not to cry. I take my head out of the sweet-bag and put the bag into the inside pocket of my coat. The sun is in my eyes and I think I see someone watching me, a woman in the shadows with thick plaits in her hair. I shield my eyes from the sun to see her better, but then she's gone and I'm just looking at the way the light hits the path.

I walk down the bank, rucksack on my back, holding the straps with my hands. Sisters Alma and Maria approach and Dr Trewhitt is beside them. Behind them are five or six other sisters and a crowd of people from the village.

'Let me take that bag of yours,' Dr Trewhitt says.

I move the bag out of his reach and stick my tongue out at him, then walk with the crowd slowly down the bank towards the boat.

'You take good care,' Sister Maria tells me, 'and you forget anything we said about Amarie. If you stuck or threatened and you need her, you let her do what she do, understand?'

'Maria!' Sister Alma chides.

'I don't think we equip her to go into the world, do you?' Sister Maria says.

'Do you think she'll come?' I ask.

'She'll have wanted to come,' Sister Alma says. 'She's busy today, she may not be able to make it.'

'Stubborn old woman,' Sister Maria says.

'Maria!' Sister Alma chides again. They bicker for a while until they both, abruptly, fall silent. We've arrived at the boat.

'How many?' the man asks.

'Just one,' Dr Trewhitt answers.

'Has the Queen been for a visit or summat?' the boat man chuckles. 'What a gathering for *just one*.' He takes the money for the ticket.

Sister Alma hands me a thick envelope: 'It's in case you need to get yourself anything while you're away. Put it somewhere safe.' She leans in and hugs me tight.

I turn to hug Sister Maria. Dr Trewhitt shakes my hand, 'Good luck,' he says. 'How will I finish a crossword while you're away?'

His voice sounds boyish.

Sister Maria pushes him into me, 'Hug her, foolish man!'

'I don't know what's got into you today, Maria!' Sister Alma says.

Dr Trewhitt holds me for a long time. As I come out of the embrace, I notice that his face is wet.

'I'll write,' I promise.

Harold breaks free from the crowd and runs towards me. We hug.

'Did I do something wrong?' he asks.

'No. I just have to go away for a while.'

'Don't!'

'I'll be back soon,' I say. I pull out of the hug to look at him. Crimson ruddies the balls of his cheeks and his nose is light purple and running. I wonder if there's any point trying to explain things to him with so many people watching. One day I'll come back and tell him everything. He puts a crumpled piece of paper in my hand. On it, he has written happyharold@yahoo.com.

'It's a way to talk to people who are far away,' he says. 'We made them at school last week.'

'See, you know all this stuff about the world – you've been my spy for too long. I have to go out and find out about my people for myself.' I put the paper in my bag and promise that I will use it to keep in touch.

'Will you leave Amarie here with me?' he asks.

I attempt what I hope is a reassuring smile, 'I can't, Harold.'

I look into the crowd for the first time and wave goodbye; Mother's not there.

'Popular girl,' the ferryman remarks. 'You'll have to go down to the lower deck, though, no passengers on the top deck while the ferry is moving.'

I go down and stand by the large rear window as the ferry pulls out. Sister Maria and Sister Alma stand waving beside Dr Trewhitt.

The other sisters who'd been walking with the crowd have joined them; my coven of mothers, but the matriarch is missing. I settle down in my seat and tell myself not to look, but soon I'm rushing back to the rear of the deck and waving fiercely at their shrinking image. A tall, slender silhouette appears in the long grass, up on the dunes in the distance. I smile and wave at her; she blows a kiss, then turns and walks away, heading out of the shade of the dune-grass and into the light. As the sun touches her, she disappears. My eyes fill with tears. I hope it was Mother or her shadow, her own Amarie, come to wish me well in spite of herself.

A short, squat man pops his bald head through the door of the lower deck. 'Cuppa? Ordinarily, we wouldn't, but as you're the only one today we can treat you like one of us.'

I open my mouth to say 'Yes', but the word doesn't come out. He notices my surprise and says, 'No worry love, one cuppa coming right up.'

When he's gone, I try to speak again. A choked burst of air comes out but nothing more. I look around for Amarie; the light below deck is sparse and there are shadows everywhere, but no Amarie. I try to remember when I saw her last. We haven't spoken much at all over the past few days. I just thought we both needed to absorb what had happened. I guess I never actually asked her what she thought or if she wanted to leave. But then, she'd *always* wanted to leave. I climb to the top deck, panicked.

'Careful lass,' the squat man says, stepping back without losing balance of the teacup. 'You can't come up here while the ferry's moving, Captain's orders.'

'Captain?' I ask and realise my voice has returned. I search the area to see if Amarie has also reappeared.

'Well, I know it's not much of a boat, but we could still have a captain if we wanted.' He winks at me and guides me back down the stairs.

'I have to go back, I've lost something.'

'Sorry pet,' he says ignoring my concerns. He ushers me into a seat before putting the mug of tea in my hand. 'Frank's finest brew is that. It'll make you forget all your worries and every and any little thing you might have lost.'

The Tale of the Child

I keep coming back to it; that story. I can't say how old I was when I first heard it – no more than six and possibly as young as three. I don't remember a time when I didn't know it. When I think back to my first memory of it, I'm not sure it was the first time it was told to me, but it's as far back as my mind will take me.

I was tucked in bed. The lamplight created a sunset on the walls. With only a single bed and a wardrobe in my room, there weren't many shapes that could form shadows, and the areas the light didn't touch glimmered like dusk and foreboding. I waited for Mother to come in and read me a story. When she finally walked in, her mouth was tight and her shoulders hunched. The Bishop had been to visit. They spoke in raised voices behind her office door. I thought he was sending me away. Mother said they were discussions and not arguments and there was nothing to worry about. The door whined as she entered. She sat on the bed and opened her arms, letting me crawl onto her lap.

'Where's the book?'

'Not today,' she said, sounding tired.

'Why not?'

'I'm going to tell you another story.'

'A made-up one?'

She nodded. 'The baby lay naked on the snow-covered banks of the old fort.'

'What's a fort?'

'It's a strong building that protects people from their enemies,' she said.

I thought we needed a fort to keep the Bishop out, but I didn't share the thought with Mother just then.

'The baby lay naked in the snow, its umbilical cord upright as though attached to an invisible womb.'

'What's an umbilical cord?'

'It's what links you to your creator,' Mother said. 'It was a day of brilliant light and the place was covered, unblemished in white. The winter sun gleamed, reflecting off the snow on Holymead.'

I jumped. 'It's a story about our island! Is the baby cold? Is it ok?'

'The baby is protected by a Divine warmth … because she has a great purpose.'

'It's a girl? Is the fort Holymead Castle?'

'They're wrong to call it a castle. It was built as a fort and it was much later that they attached a residence to it. Did you know it was made from the bricks of the old monks' priory?'

I shook my head.

'It's a special place because it was built from the bricks of a holy house. For the child to be left on the banks of such a place meant she had to be very special indeed.'

I listened, absorbed in the Tale of the Divine Child, as Mother explained how the Reverend Mother found the baby, took her home and raised her to the light. She wove into the story the cake catastrophe of my third birthday, in which Sister Alma baked a cake that exploded when she took it out of the oven: '...the sisters and the Precious Child spend the day cleaning the cake mix from the cracks, corners and crevices of the large old kitchen. They clean with anything and everything they can find – soap, water, sponges, brushes, mops and towels – but most importantly, they cleaned some places with their tongues.' Mother added details I'd forgotten and hearing her retell it made it more real than the memory.

'The sisters love the Divine Child very much. They take care of her to the best of their ability and with God's blessing. One day,

God may call for the Divine Child to leave the convent and take her place in the divinity of life. When that day comes, they must all be brave. The sisters and the child will be sad, but they'll know they are carrying out God's will, so they will also be happy.'

Book Two

Fugue

Fugue

In Twi, pronounced: fu-goo (also spelled *'fugu'*)

Noun

    1. Clothing. A woven cotton shirt or plaid smock traditionally worn in the northern regions of Ghana.

From Mossi *fugu,* 'cloth'.

❖

In English, pronounced: fju-g / fewg

Noun

    1. Music. A polyphonic composition in which a subject is announced in one voice, repeated by other voices, with small variations, and developed by interweaving the parts to a marked climax.

    2. Psychiatry. Dissociation; an altered state of consciousness; sudden, unexpected travel away from one's home with an inability to recall some or all of one's history; a rare disorder characterised by reversible amnesia for personal identity.

From Latin *fuga,* 'flight'.

Brown

Chickens cluck and gossip nearby. A car honks in the distance. Someone, somewhere, shouts a greeting. Wheels screech, several of them, successively. I wait for the crash: it doesn't come. Voices rise in a confused, or angry, chorus. A group of children chant a playground anthem. They clap and stamp in sync. I can't make out the words. The soft lap of a skipping rope beats the ground repeatedly. Something hits the window. A ball? I don't move to see. Soupy air rests on my skin and the sun through the blinds crosses my cheek with a lick of dry heat that is surprisingly refreshing; the crisp light soothes against the cloying humidity. I open my eyes and close them. Open, then close. The ball hits the window again. Close eyes. Open. Close. I do that thing where your eyes are open behind closed lids. I watch the light filter through the skin that shields my gaze; the back of my eyelids glow ochre – Brown. I'm Brown again.

I'd always known that I was Brown. I don't remember it being a discovery: putting my arm against Sister Alma and noticing the difference between us; paddling on the beach with Reverend Mother and realising the contrast in our reflections as they rippled in the stream. There was no one moment when I suddenly knew. Amarie was a blackish-grey and Mother was whiteish-pink. Amarie was spirit and Mother was flesh. I was Brown, somewhere between them, more flesh than Amarie and more spirit than Mother. They were my coordinates and I knew where I was rooted between them. Black was different, though; it came announced. It was the year the parish roof couldn't be repaired any more. There had been so many patch jobs done, it was like an old quilt, all threadbare and no good at blocking water. That autumn we had a ceilidh to raise money for a new roof and Mrs O'Shea from the village, Penelope-Marie's mum, she told Sister Alma that I was a good dancer because all black people have rhythm. And there it was: suddenly I was Black. After that, there was a world outside with others who were Black like me and this hunger formed. Perhaps it had always been there, as a cloud maybe, but it hardened, became granite in the pit of me. Every time Harold found another morsel about Black from Yahoo, I savoured it. But Black also made me dizzy, like when you're little and you spin around, then in the middle of the spinning you realise you can't stop and stand still, and you'll fall over if you try. Black came with expectations, of rhythm and other things that might trip me up.

At Heathrow Airport, there were people of all colours and combinations. I saw a woman, Brown like me, with hair the colour of a postbox. A boy, paler than Sister Alma, with black hair down to his knees, silver chains hanging from his wrists, and blue and purple around his eyes. I watched them – ravenously. I wished Amarie was there to see it all. I prayed she'd stop being so stubborn and appear. At Kotoka Airport, the faces were all kinds of Brown: chestnut, mahogany, oak, chocolate, terracotta, hazel, copper, gold, umber, rosewood, ebony, coffee, onyx, dusk.

'I knew it was you,' Aunt Grace says, pulling me from the multitude flooding out of the airport.

'You have your mother's face exactly.'

Aunt Grace is a small, plump woman. She smells of cocoa and musk and her cheeks shine in the glow of the streetlights that brighten the exit of the airport. I am tall and sharp next to the roundness and softness of her. She takes my arm and strokes the back of my hand, looking up at me. I notice that the skin on my hands has chalky lines again. It was because of these lines that I told the girls at the day school that God had carved me from rocks on the Farne Islands.

'Are the dry, white bits the places God didn't manage to wash all the bird shit off?' Shannon had asked, and the other girls all laughed. I don't know if they actually found it funny or if they laughed because, if you go ahead and laugh loud enough, it means you're not the one being laughed at right now. Standing beside Aunt Grace, I wonder if I'll learn to make my skin shimmer in the light like polished marble the way hers is doing now.

'Yes, you have her face exactly,' Aunt Grace says, then pauses, 'only she was a little bit fairer.'

She notices my rucksack and takes it off my back and hands it to a young man. I wonder if he's a relation and as though she's heard my thoughts, she says, 'This is Boateng, we call him Boat. He's nearly family but not quite.' She touches his arm affection-ately. 'He speaks Twi and Ga fluently, but his English is not the best.' She says this chuckling as though she's made a joke. 'He's been with us since he was a small boy, as a house-boy, and now as our driver.' She leans in, like she's about to share a secret. 'We paid for his lessons and he passed the test, no bribes involved.' She says this with pride.

Boat has old eyes in a young face. He has a sprinkling of hair over his top lip and he's gangly – he moves as though he's been given more body than he's used to and is only just beginning to master all of the parts. I guess he can't be much older than me. I say hello and he smiles and nods but doesn't speak. He grips my oversized rucksack awkwardly, not quite sure which part to hold. Then he steps into the flow of people, confidently parting the stream of bodies to create a path for us to walk through. Away from the crowds and onto the car park, we zigzag through stationary cars. We reach one with a man leaning on it and stop. I wait to be introduced. Boat reaches into his pocket and hands the man a bundle of paper money.

'He was just minding the vehicle,' Aunt Grace explains as the man thanks us and walks away. What he was minding the car for, I have no idea, and it strikes me as odd that no other car has anyone 'minding' it.

We inch through traffic and the speckled lights of Accra at night flicker beyond the window. Beside me in the back seat, Aunt Grace clasps my hand with both of hers. 'This is really very bitter-sweet for us. We've lost our sister and gained a daughter.'

The air conditioning hums and spurts like a smoker with a raspy cough. Aunt Grace continues, 'We don't know how to feel, really. You must give us time and be very patient. At times we may laugh and others we'll cry or argue...' She looks lost for a moment. 'This will be hard for you as well. We have to remember our patience with you, too.' She takes my face in her hands and pulls me into her chest for a hug that I'm not expecting, I'm sur-prised and resist initially, before giving in to it.

'Several people want to meet you. I have been quite strict, though. Not too many, not all at once. First, you relax and see Ghana. You will see Ghana,' she says with emphasis. 'We will go to the village for the funeral, and you will attend. It is why you are here after all. After this, there can be meetings and such. But first you see the place and then you do what you came here to do. My girls will take care of you. They're your sisters, you must think of them like this. I know you say cousin in the UK, but here we say sister. They'll take you to see all of the things, the parks, the cas-tles, beaches, anything you want. Then the funeral and other such things... But first things first.'

A ball smacks against the windowpane. The skipping rope slaps and the chickens cluck. Sunlight filters through the blinds and my closed eyes. Black fades to brown, and my eyelids glow ochre again. I emerge from the haze of half-sleep and memory. Open. Close. Open.

The room is large and busy. There are two wardrobes, each

stacked with multiple suitcases on top. There is a double chest of drawers in dark wood and a towering Victorian dresser with a hefty oval-shaped mirror. As well as the double bed that I'm in, there's another bed on the adjacent wall. Three brightly coloured rattan stools huddle in the corner between the wardrobes. On the wall opposite the window hang individual pictures of members of the family. Each one has its own bright frame: gilt, bronze, silver, metallic red and so on. At the centre of this gallery is a large group photo, framed in wood. Who would I have been if my picture was on this wall? I stare at each face, questioning. I try to see if I can recognise her: my mother. Two faces stand out; each has something that feels familiar.

A rug with a picture of a lion on it stretches across the floor; grassy plains spread out behind him and the sun sets on the horizon. Above the chest of drawers is an embroidery of the Last Supper. The room brims with furniture, fabrics and textures – unlike anything I've known. The sun creeps through the blinds, bouncing off the walls and surfaces, drawing my attention here, then there. Now to the mahogany Thinking Man ornament, next to the ivory lamp stand with the bird engraved on it, then it highlights a corner, some colour, a detail that could easily be missed when trying to take in the whole. My eyes spring and scurry across the room, poring over one item, searching through the rest, letting the sun guide me, then looking at those things that hide from the light – like the jewellery box that sits in the shade at the corner of the dresser. I get up to stroke the stools in the shadow of the wardrobes; look under the beds; behind the dresser, exploring the shade and dark places. Then, I'm blinking back tears, trying to swallow the lump that's forming in my throat. I'm looking for her, that's what I'm doing, in the places the light doesn't touch. I'm searching for Amarie. I crawl back to bed, pull the covers over my head and let the lump in my throat burst into the pillow.

Breakfast at the Fire of Ebenezer

'Is she awake?'

'If she was, her eyes would be open.'

'Not necessarily.'

'Don't do that, Adjoa!'

'It's just so ... not even short, just ... basic. Like she's in SS.'

'Shhh.'

Silence, then fumbling.

'I've got it. Come on, let's go before she wakes up with your hands in her hair.'

'Even SS girls, when we're out of school, we do things with our hair – even if it's not full weave or braids, something simple, like a parting on the side, texturizer, just something! And she's from abrokyire – you'd think...'

'She looks just like her, don't you think?'

'Not the hair.'

'The shape of her face, her nose...'

'But she's not as fair, Aunty Dofi was fair.'

A pause.

'Don't! We're leaving!'

There is a faint tussling; one dragging the other. Their steps fade and the bedroom door thuds. I touch my hair, rubbing away the indent left by her finger. Moments later, a head pops through the door.

'I dropped my...' she begins, still speaking to the one outside.

'Good morning.'

She turns, 'You're awake!'

'She's awake?' A second girl pops her head through the door.

A ball smacks against the window. The girl standing outside comes in, crosses to the window and opens it. She sticks her head out and starts to shout: the sounds bellow but never turn into words that I recognise. The children outside laugh and run away.

'If they break the glass, we will send the bill to their grandparents!' She bangs the window shut. 'This is a house in mourning and they come to play like that.' She makes a sound with her teeth, clenching them together and sucking the saliva through them. It's like the wail of an old hinge and that first long fizz of opening a carbonated drink – it says she is not impressed.

'There it is,' the first girl says, grabbing at something at the side of my bed. She stands up and looks down at me.

'Hello, I'm Afua. That's Adjoa.' She points at the girl by the window.

'Aunt Grace's daughters?' I say, sitting up.

'Yeah. Sorry, we didn't mean to wake you.'

'It's fine,' I say, touching my head unconsciously. 'Where's Aunt Grace?'

'She's gone to Makola Market with Boat. She won't be long.'

'I was hoping to have some time with her–'

'But she will be busy when she gets back,' Adjoa interrupts.

'Of course,' Afua says.

'She wants you to rest and enjoy yourself,' Adjoa continues.

'I'm here for a funeral...'

'But you can't leave Ghana without experiencing it,' Adjoa says. 'Also, we didn't know if you'd want to do your hair and maybe get some new clothes.'

I don't respond at first, not sure that I've understood what she means. I wait for her to explain, but she doesn't. Her sister, Afua, is the one who eventually fills the silence, 'Mum said that if there was anything you wanted to get done, like hair, nails, anything at all...'

'We'll take you to the salon and...' Adjoa says.

'...wherever really...'

Both Adjoa and Afua have hair like the women in the Spanish magazines; chestnut waves cascade down Adjoa's slim shoulders, reaching the middle of her back, while Afua's darker, shorter style curls just below her chin, framing her face and drawing attention to the balls of her cheeks, which she's dusted with a powder that makes them shimmer when the sun hits them. I know my tight little curls can't be forced to fall and flow like theirs without some form of torture and I have no desire to try it out.

'If it's ok, I'd rather not,' I say.

Afua clears her throat and suggests that perhaps we should return to the subject later. She asks if there's anything in particular I'd like to do or see in Ghana. My mind is blank, then I remember that Aunt Grace had mentioned some castles. Afua claps at this suggestion and says it's perfect. We just need to wait for Boat to get back from the market with the car so he can drive us all to Cape Coast. While we wait, we should get some breakfast; we'll go to the Fire of Ebenezer Chop Bar, she says.

After the shock of a cold shower, I dress in a navy blue skirt that comes down to my ankles and a white cotton blouse with a lace trim collar. They're donated clothes that Sister Maria helped me find in the last-minute rush to get ready to leave Holymead. Sisters Alma and Maria agreed with me that it wouldn't be appropriate to travel in my brown and cream Carmelite robes with my age belt wrapped around me. My cousins look less than impressed with the effort I've made, so I can only imagine how they might have reacted to the alternative. I dab a final bit of Vaseline on my lips and I'm ready to leave. Outside, I'm surprised to see how imposing the house is in daylight. It is pale blue and two stories high, with balconies at nearly every window. There are trees along the walls of the compound: some with coconuts and others with large green bananas. Two white bungalows are nestled in the shade of the trees at the far side of the grounds: 'Boys' Quarters,' Afua says. Jewelled women in heavy black cloth enter one of the Boys' Quarters.

'What are they doing in there?' I ask.

'Meetings,' Adjoa answers, leading me out of the compound by the elbow and pulling the gate shut. 'Our father is a doctor, but now he travels and lectures mostly; Kenya, Nigeria, Botswana – or a talk here at home.'

'Yes, it'll be one of those meetings,' Afua confirms. 'His colleagues now hold the meetings here, even when he is not at home.'

On the walk to breakfast, they introduce me to neighbours, shopkeepers and street vendors. 'I'm just now going to your place,' a man in a black blazer says.

'God bless you,' Afua responds, and Adjoa whispers to me about how busy the house has become in recent years as Uncle Samuel's work has grown.

'Should we go back and help?' I ask. Something feels off and I wonder if all of these people might actually be helping with funeral preparations.

'No, no,' Adjoa says. 'We'll get in the way. It's teaching, networking, this sort of thing.'

'While the family is in mourning?' I ask.

The girls look at each other. I think I see a slight panic in Afua's eyes.

'Business stops for no man,' Adjoa retorts and we walk on.

We greet nearly everyone who crosses our path; I am their cousin from the UK. It seems that what I lack in style, I make up for in other ways.

'Just wait until you hear her speak!' they take turns to say.

They spot an old school friend of Afua's across the road, and she runs to him. He's short and stocky, and Afua, who is a head taller than him, covers his eyes and signals for us to join them. 'Black, brown, yellow or white?' she asks. She nods at me. I stare blankly. She nods again.

'I don't know what you want,' I tell her.

'Whoa!' the friend shrieks, starting to laugh. 'Say something else.'

'Like what, exactly?'

'"Like what, exactly",' he says, laughing harder. 'Obroni! Obroni! Definitely white!' He moves Afua's hands from his eyes and looks at me, shocked.

My face heats up and I want to disappear. He shakes my hand and uses his free hand to shield his eyes from the sun.

I'm standing in front of him and, like Afua, I'm at least a head taller than him, so I should be blocking the light. Instead, the sun runs through me. From his expression, he knows something is wrong, but he hasn't worked out what it is. Terrified, I shuffle, trying to get out of the way without drawing attention to myself, so the sun can shine directly on him. Giddy with excitement, my cousins haven't noticed a thing. A brief introduction follows: he's Kwabena, an old classmate. Very pleased to meet me. He will be happy to show me around during my time in Accra. There's something strange about me, familiar, he means familiar, not strange, he didn't mean strange, have we met before? My cousins tease him and ask when did he ever step foot on a plane? They accuse him of changing his voice when he speaks to me. They start chanting *LAFA, LAFA, LAFA*, and Afua explains that he's got a Locally Acquired Foreign Accent. He laughs and his cheeks flash with rose as he blushes. Shocked at how his skin betrays him, I wonder if mine has been doing that all the times I thought I was protected by it. Before he's had a chance to defend himself, and to realise what it is he finds so odd about me, my cousins pull me away to meet the next person. This time, I am more cautious about where I stand.

We stop finally at a metal kiosk with two sets of plastic tables and chairs in front of it. It's set back from the pavement and no one is around. As open as it is, I'm relieved by the partial privacy offered by its roof and three walls. We take a seat at one of the tables.

'Do you want pizza?' Adjoa says brightly, sitting beside me.

'I'll eat whatever you're both having.'

'Pizza?' she repeats to her sister, nodding enthusiastically.

Afua pulls a face, 'You have pizza. I want food-food.'

Adjoa takes a small object from her bag and dabs powder on her nose to soften its shine. Then she adds more colour to her already fuchsia lips.

'Want some?' she asks her sister.

'No, but some fragrance please.'

Adjoa hands her a little blue bottle.

'What scent do you wear?' she asks me.

Afua kicks her under the table.

'I am making conversation!' she snaps. 'No make-up, ok, but nuns can wear perfume, right?'

'I'm not a nun,' I say, more defensively than I'd intended. 'We don't usually wear perfume, no. They're all things ... considered ... related to vanity.'

The sisters share a look and smirk. A waifish girl comes to our table and Adjoa speaks to her in Twi. The word 'pizza' is said by both of them, repeatedly. Adjoa looks frustrated. Afua cuts in. The girl grins, inspecting me through clear-rimmed glasses. Then she turns to leave.

'The dough isn't ready yet,' Adjoa says, irritated.

'So no pizza, kay?' Afua adds, in a voice that sounds borrowed.

'That's fine,' I insist. I hadn't wanted pizza anyway. It wasn't exactly a diet staple at St Teresa's. I'd eaten it once at Harold's house.

'What sort of things do you like?' I ask, trying to repair whatever's broken between us.

'Music, Mariah Carey–' Afua says: / *Carey Mariah, Sammy Davis Jr, Earth, Wind & Fire...* I feel a connection with them as the old bedtime litany plays in my head; ...*Stevie Wonder, Sam Cooke and Samantha Mumba.*

'...Whitney Houston. Toni Braxton,' Adjoa continues from where her sister left off.

'Do you know Samantha Mumba?' I interrupt, trying to manage my excitement.

'Who?' Adjoa asks, screwing her face.

'We like fashion and shoes as well,' Afua says, missing my question.

'The vanity stuff,' Adjoa chuckles. Their conversation races on, talking about other things of which I have no experience.

'We share most things,' Afua says. 'When I can fit into your clothes – I've got our mother's thighs,' she adds. 'My sister is slender like you and our aunties...' she pauses for a moment and then corrects herself, 'like you and our aunty.' There is only one aunty now, Aunt Esi. Afua's cheer evaporates.

'But you got the good skin!' Adjoa chips in, rushing to erase her sister's unease.

Afua looks at Adjoa, disorientated for a moment. Adjoa chatters on, gushing about her sister's smooth, clear skin. Afua eventually joins in, wishing she had her sister's thighs, but her own bottom – because 'no self-respecting Ghanaian woman should have a bottom as small as Adjoa's'. She turns to me and says, 'I notice yours is a little on the small side as well, but it's still bigger than Adjoa's, so you're blessed.'

Despite their talk, there's still a shadow of that previous moment stalking Afua's smile, the shock of forgetting and then remembering that their other aunt, my mother, is gone.

'Are you twins?' I ask, breaking into the flow of their chatter.

They beam, flattered by the question.

'I'm seventeen. This coming year will be my last at SS – secondary school,' Adjoa says. 'Afua is fourteen months older than me. She's already in the university. But lots of people think we're twins. It's quite common that we're asked that question. Especially when I'm out of school and can fix my hair properly, and also now that my skin is clearing up.'

Three plates are put on our table; it all looks heavy, like something you'd eat later in the day. I choose the rice porridge and koose as it seems the simplest and lightest of the three options. The sisters share the rest between them.

An older woman with gold medallion-like earrings walks by; she pauses, looks over at us and approaches our table. I don't understand at first, but then in English she says, 'Dr Samuel's house,' and she brings out a piece of paper with an address on it.

'It's our house,' Adjoa says, getting up and directing her down the road, walking a short distance with her. She points in the direction of the house and the woman thanks her and leaves.

'There are a lot of people going to the house today,' I say to Afua, hoping she'll elaborate.

'And this isn't even a busy day,' she smiles rigidly and remains silent until her sister returns to the table.

'What things do you like?' Adjoa asks as she sits down.

I shake my head, 'You'll find it boring.'

'Come on, we told you ours.'

'I guess, I'm a strong swimmer, and ... I know quite a bit about birds.'

'Birds?' Adjoa says, pulling a face.

Something in me clenches. I hesitate for a moment, then take a napkin and start to roughly sketch a puffin.

'You're good at drawing,' Adjoa says. 'You should draw my portrait before you leave.'

I laugh involuntarily at her self-assurance. 'Thanks, maybe I will. These are the kinds of birds that live near me. They're part of a family called auks.'

'Can you pet them?' Afua asks.

'No, they're wild, and the terns, you wouldn't want to pet. When it's nesting season, they dive at your head if you're anywhere near their nests. They've made people bleed.'

'That's horrible!'

'It's like that old movie,' Adjoa says.

'She likes scary movies and stupid things, don't mind her.' We eat our breakfast as the conversation continues in spurts and almost feels natural.

The Castle

They're wrong to call it a castle. It was built as a fort, Reverend Mother had said. My skin congeals to gooseflesh as the fortress rises in the car windscreen. *It was a day of brilliant light and the place was covered, unblemished in white.* The car stops. We step out and approach Cape Coast Castle. The gleaming white stronghold grows tea-stained as we draw nearer and can see it more clearly; flakes of sepia and grey crack and fall like dandruff from its walls. Everyone ignores the groups of children gathered outside it. One of the boys sees me looking and takes my hand.

'What's your name?' he asks softly, in a lilting voice. He can't be more than nine. His hair is cut close to his scalp and his wiry arms and legs are ashy at their joints. 'I'll write it on a shell for you,' he says, lifting an ivory mottled shell to my face. 'You keep and take home with you.'

Adjoa pulls me away. 'Don't even think about it.' She presses her mouth to my ear and whispers, 'Any money you give him, those men will beat him to take it.'

Down the street, a woman is standing beside a metal table cutting green coconuts with a machete and offering them to passers-by. A short distance from her, two men stand at the corner of the street; when they see me looking, they make a show of being deep in conversation. The little boy releases my hand and sucks his teeth the way Adjoa had done to the children throwing balls at the window earlier in the day.

'Did he just kiss his teeth at me?' Adjoa asks, glaring at his back.

A row of cannons faces over the castle walls. *It's a strong building that protects people from their enemies, Mother said.* I feel trapped in heat and light as the sunlight bounces against the white surfaces of the courtyards and open spaces in the castle. A tour guide takes us around, explaining that the castle was built for administrative purposes, to allow more effective management of the Triangle Trade. Sweat trickles down my back and I search to find and stand in the natural shadows. Did he say the Triangle Trade?

/ The narrator of the BBC documentary said St Teresa's Convent was built on the site of the Cunningham family mansion. The family had built the stately home as a holiday residence and later gifted the land and its buildings to the Carmelites of St Teresa, who were looking to establish a convent in Northumberland. Cunningham, a prominent tobacco baron, and his family made their fortune through the Triangle Trade. You made a mental note to ask Harold to use the Yahoo search engine to find out about the Triangle Trade. But you were so excited to give him your definition of faith and reality, you forgot to ask. /

The tour guide stops at a large black door beneath an archway. Unlocking the bolts, he carefully pulls, and the door opens to the Atlantic. Waves surge in a mass of white fury, mountains of foam roll and return. There is something mesmerising and repulsive about this gateway to the ocean.

'This was the last stop before a Ghanaian ceased to be a person,' he says. 'From here, they stepped onto the slave ships and left home for good.' He points to a sign above our heads: The Door of No Return.

Behind us, another tour begins: 'Built in 1653, this castle, like others in Ghana, was where enslaved people were kept before they were shipped off to the Americas and the Caribbean. The castles were administrative centres, built to manage the Triangle Trade more effectively.' The narrative rises, rolls and repeats.

/ It's a castle, you said.
For slaves, I told you.
Castles are not for slaves! you claimed. /

Out in the waters I see a dark figure. Our tour guide moves to close The Door, and I have to rush to stop him. Adjoa is standing beside me and I nudge her towards the wall and slip out before The Door closes. It slams shut behind me. I slip on the uneven path outside and end up on the ground staring out at the breakers.

'Amarie!' I shout at the figure on the ocean.

The shadow of a woman stands vertical in the water and the waves storm around her. Behind me, The Door opens. 'Miss, you cannot just run into areas anyhow,' the guide says.

Boat and my cousins rush out of the castle towards me.

'Are you ok?' / 'What happened?' Afua and Adjoa ask simultaneously.

'Maybe the heat is getting to me,' I say. 'I thought I saw someone – something.'

Adjoa pulls me up and I steady myself. Her arm is grazed; the skin is scratched and bright red but isn't bleeding.

'Just a scratch,' she says when she sees me looking at it. 'Don't worry.'

'Did I do that? I'm so sorry,' I say, looking at her wound, regretting having pushed her into the wall.

'How are you?' she asks.

'You have a cut as well,' Afua says, reaching for my elbow.

I look at it; similar to Adjoa's, it wants to bleed but hasn't started to yet. 'It's nothing. It's my own fault,' I say.

The other members of our tour look on irritably as my cousins fuss over me. The tour guide tells us that we've wasted enough time and the other visitors would like to complete their experience. Mortified, I apologise again, but he ignores me. Boat takes my arm and we walk back to the group, and together we all follow the guide underground.

The tunnels in the dungeons stretch and constrict. They offer protection from the sharpness of the sun, but the air is heavy and the gloom is oppressive in its own way. Our guide leads us through to an opening; holes at the top of the wall allow a small amount of daylight to sneak in. At the back of the enclosure, three steps lead to a small platform. A man sits there; he's dressed in furs and leather. In front of him are several objects – wood, ivory, something black, round things with feathers, cloth, a blade, beads. They are collected around a centrepiece – a metal pot over a small fire. Two tourists stand watching him. Our group waits a short distance behind, giving the couple time to observe: they take pictures of him and then stand back and watch him solemnly.

Our guide tells us that several hundred slaves were kept in this space. 'An Anglican church was built above so the administrators and managers would have somewhere to worship. They would have been able to hear the slaves and smell their sweat and faeces as they knelt for weekly prayers.' Our guide says that there were no toilets in the dungeons, and gutters had been carved into the ground to collect and tunnel out the excrement when it got high enough to flow into them.

'He's a traditional healer,' the guide says about the man on the platform, when at last we move towards him. 'He says blessings for wounded souls.' The guide turns to the couple who were in the tunnel when we arrived, 'If you offer him a donation, he will give you a blessing.'

They smile and nod, then leave without giving anything. Members of our group step forward and drop money into a container. I feel inside my bag for some money and turn to add it to the pot.

Adjoa stops me. 'It's all for show,' she whispers. 'He was just chanting nonsense. And just now, he was swearing at that couple because they didn't leave him anything.'

'They know we're young and that we're Ghanaians,' Afua says, joining us as we walk back through the main tunnel. 'He doesn't expect anything from us.'

'What's wrong? You look funny,' Adjoa says to me.

'I need to sit down.'

'Let's go back outside,' Afua says, taking my arm. 'You need some air.'

The thought of going back up there to meet the glare of the sun makes me feel dizzy.

'I'll just stay here … for a bit,' I say, working to keep down the panic in my voice. 'You go ahead. I'll be up soon.'

They hesitate for a while, then move to leave.

'The Americans find it really hard, too,' Adjoa says, knowingly. 'Some of them even break down.'

New groups come in and their shadows overlap as their guides talk them through the numbers of enslaved people housed here, the masters' prayers that were said above their heads, and the role of the healer – who sings throughout. I sit, on the ground, out of the way and hug my knees to my chest. A young boy asks his mother if I'm sitting in the place where the slaves' faeces would have been piling up. His mother turns him away from me, chastising him in whispered tones as she does.

When I look up, there are no more groups. The only noises are muffled and coming from beyond the dungeon. The healer is watching me. He speaks. I want to understand. He repeats himself again and rises from his seat. / *He says he can help you through your dreaming.*

He picks up an object from his assortment and walks down from the platform, moving towards me. Unsure of him, I stand and back away. He reaches for me and grabs my wrist. My right hand feels weak in his grip; a sharp pain shoots through it and my index finger begins to throb. He repeats the same words over again, as though through the repetition I might come to understand./ *He says, I can help you through your dreaming. Through your dreaming you might heal. I see the problem and I can fix your dreaming, he's saying.* / But his words are incomprehensible. He flicks the object and then points it at my chest: it's a torch. He stares past me, and I don't need to follow his gaze to know that the torch-light is shining against the floor and the walls, passing straight through me. I pull my throbbing hand out of his grasp and I turn and run. He calls after me, but I don't stop or look back.

The Night Market

After hours driving on dirt roads, we're back in central Accra. The sun dips as we enter the city, but this doesn't reduce the heat or humidity. The roads are choked with traffic and for an hour we barely move. Afua talks continuously; she's been very cheerful since we decided to go to Osu on our way home from the castle.

'The main road in Osu is Oxford Street,' she says, looking at me expectantly. 'Like the one in London,' she explains when I give her a blank look.

After the ferry from the island, Sister Alma had arranged for a car to take me to Newcastle Airport, where I got a direct flight to London. I only saw Heathrow Airport; I don't know any of the roads in London, and if the city's as big as they say it is, I wonder how she expects me to be aware of a specific street. I smile half-heartedly and nod and she seems satisfied with that.

'Over there is Kwame Nkrumah Memorial Park...' Afua carries on. 'He was Ghana's first president ... further down ... we'll pass it just now ... is Osu Castle.'

'Another slave castle?' I ask, tensing.

'It was, but now it's the seat of government.'

'Isn't that ... strange?' I ask, winding down the window, suddenly needing more air. 'Why would the government want to be in a place like that?'

'Don't do that,' Adjoa says, reaching over me and winding the window back up. 'You'll let the heat in. Boat, turn up the aircon, she feels she can't breathe.'

Oxford Street is bustling. The car crawls along as people walk in and out of the road, zigzagging between the nearly stationary traffic. Hawkers at our windows try to sell us crisps, soft drinks, peanuts and more. Afua calls them plantain chips, minerals and groundnuts, and I wonder if the difference is just in the words or if we're seeing different things. Afua waves to dismiss them, Adjoa ignores them completely, and Boat concentrates on the road, waving people away only when they get in his way. We turn into the small lane of the night market; the streetlights are fewer and dimmer than on the main road. There are stalls, musicians, drink vendors, storytellers, something in every direction. I've had this heavy, woozy feeling since being at the castle and I try to shake it off by letting the market take me in. A live band plays at the centre of the street, blocking what I assume is a road during the day. A drummer's sticks pirouette and spin between his fingers before colliding with his instrument in cracks and crashes. An older drummer beside him beats his palms against the djembe nestled between his thighs. A woman with plaits down to her waist purrs and croons about love, holding her own against the drummers, an electric guitar and an instrument I don't recognise.

'Get something to eat and we'll meet back by the tables over there,' Afua says, pointing at seating in the distance.

Adjoa follows her sister and I go with Boat. An aerialist is hanging from an improvised trapeze, fashioned between scaffolding and the side of a building. He glides through the air followed by a trail of white silk. A little way down from him is an old man with salt-specked hair and peppercorn curls; wrapped in red and yellow woven cloth, he's small but stands tall, telling stories to a group of about five. Boat leads me to a food stall between the salt-and-pepper storyteller and the aerialist. He points at the food and at himself and I understand that he wants to order for me. I'm not sure I want to risk it, but our shared language is so limited, and I feel so drained, that there's not much to do but say, 'Yes'. While Boat speaks to the vendor, I watch the aerialist, and the old man's story is audible in the background.

'Anansi the spider man was building his web between two large trees.'

I'm shocked by the mention of Anansi, the trickster spider from my bedtime storybook. I turn slightly to concentrate on what the old man is saying.

'He worked hard to make it brilliant.' / The aerialist swings left and right, and left and right, working hard in motion. / 'Between the trees he had chosen, lay the stump of another. Anansi dived down to inspect it.' / The trapeze artist pauses mid-air and dives towards the ground. He stops inches above a pothole and touches the depression in the land.

The old man's story and the young man's dance seem to synchronise. I wonder if this is a coincidence or choreography or my light head. As I watch, the two performances merge and the old man appears to narrate the young one's dance.

'This destruction of the earth disturbed Anansi. Broken branches and rotting fruit lay spread around the dead stump. The fruit was strange, of a variety that he had never seen before. He tasted it and it was both bitter and sweet. Lying in the remains of the dead tree was a large pod. The trickster had an idea: he would use the serum from the pod and mix it with his own spider's silk to create a wholly new material.

'The next morning, he began. He pulled the sap from the pod and blended it with extracts of his silk. This combination made a stronger material that was more luscious than any he had ever created alone. He had built himself many magnificent homes – castles knitted across the sky – but nothing he'd built, even the most magnificent, was made from silk that was as fine as this. Using this new material, he began to spin his web. He spun day and night and when he'd finished, he stood back to admire his work. He saw how beautiful his creation was and he gasped at his own artistry.' / The acrobat creates a mesh of white with his silks and its pattern against the night *is* the magnificent cobweb from the old man's tale. He hangs in mid-air from a small piece of remaining fabric and looks with awe at his creation. / The old man finishes his tale with the words, 'This is my story, which I share with you. If it be sweet or if it not be sweet, take some and share, and let some come back to me.' / The dancer disconnects himself from the material, jumps down and lands lightly on his feet.

I'm about to clap when Boat nudges me. He carries a tray and signals that I should follow him. A small group beside me start to applaud the old man, and a different crowd claps for the young aerialist. Reluctantly, I leave without showing either of them my appreciation. We walk to the agreed spot and find an empty table. Adjoa appears, picking at snacks.

'Kelewele?' she asks, offering me the container and sitting down. 'You're invited.'

I look at it, reluctantly.

'It won't bite,' she says.

I bring a small handful to my mouth and they are warm, sweet and spicy. 'It's delicious!'

'I know,' she smiles. 'What did you get?' She leans in to see the contents of my bowl.

'Boat ordered it,' I say sheepishly.

'You didn't choose?' she laughs. 'You're going to have to start speaking up. You're not in England now. Quiet doesn't mean polite in Ghana, it means unheard.'

'What is it?' I ask, looking doubtfully at the bowl.

'It's fufu and light soup,' she says.

The soup has meat, fish and whole chillies floating in it and looks anything but light. Adjoa addresses Boat and they both laugh.

'What?' I ask, feeling self-conscious.

'I asked him if it isn't a bit late to be eating fufu. He said where he's from fufu is taken at any time. I reminded him that where you're from fufu is never taken – at all! He didn't seem to mind.'

I look at the soup, and I can feel Adjoa and Boat watching me, restrained mirth tickling their lips.

'You have to taste it to know if you like it,' she says.

Boat speaks to her.

'He says it's what we give to people who need to recuperate,' Adjoa tells me.

'Make you go feel good,' Boat adds, haltingly.

'You can see who he's focused on!' Adjoa teases. 'He didn't consider getting some light soup for me and my pain.' She lifts her arm up to show her grazed elbow. There are a few pearls of dried blood where the skin has opened and started to scab.

'Ma told us your mother was like that when they were young. When she was in a room, the other sisters didn't exist – all eyes were on her.'

I'm thrown by the mention of my mother and embarrassed by the compliment. Boat seems to have understood something of what she's said and he offers her his bowl of soup. She shakes her head dismissively. 'It's too late now. Eat your own soup, Chale!' she says in English before following it up in Twi.

I want to ask her more about my mother, what was it about her that attracted so many eyes? How did she feel about it? But I realise I've missed the moment – its presence was fleeting. Also, I have the feeling that if I'd actually tried, Adjoa would have clammed up, just as Afua did earlier in the day.

My thoughts drift back to the bowl in front of me and I wonder why Boat is giving me soup to recuperate. Did he notice how the sun shone through me at the castle? I tried to be careful, but if the medicine man noticed there was something wrong with me, maybe Boat saw it too. I decide to stop being fussy and wash my hands in the bowl of water on the table. Then I eat the soup as Boat does, with my hands. I scoop the balls of fufu with my fingers, make a small indent in the middle to hold the liquid of the soup, before spooning it into my mouth. It's spicy, but not as hot as I'd feared. The fufu strokes my tongue and slips down my throat before I have a chance to chew it. It's strange at first, but after a while it's kind of nice.

'Where is Afua?' I ask.

'She knows where to find us,' Adjoa says, irritated.

I clean my plate and feel more solid.

I tell Adjoa about the old storyteller and the aerial dancer and I try my best to retell the Anansi story.

'I know that one,' Adjoa says. 'Depending on how it's told, it's either intended to be a warning or inspiration. When Ma used to say it, in her version, when Anansi finds the dead tree stump, he doesn't know what tree it belongs to. He should go to the elders and ask for advice, but he doesn't. When he mixes it with his own silk, initially it is strong and the web he makes is magnificent, and then in time it begins to rot. He doesn't know why because he didn't take the time to understand where the thing had come from. The rot spreads and the whole forest dies.

'When our father used to tell the story, he told it the same way you just did. In the end, Anansi makes a beautiful home and all of the creatures in the forest admire it, The End. His ignorance about what the tree was or why it was so damaged doesn't come into it when Da tells it. I always preferred his version; Ma's gave me nightmares.' Adjoa finishes her kelewele and slaps her hands together to clean the spice grains off them. 'There is also a third version,' she says. 'It's not one you regularly hear. In that one, Anansi consults the elders, who tell him what the tree was and what happened to it. I think they tell him what the fruit of the tree was and what its serum is. Then he uses it and mixes it to make new silk and he builds a magnificent web – like in all of the other versions.'

'What happens to the web in this version? Do the other animals look in awe or does it rot?'

'You know, I don't remember.'

We watch the night market around us and when Afua still hasn't returned, I consider going for a walk alone around the market, as it's not very big.

'It sounds like you're asking permission,' Adjoa says. 'What did I say about quiet voices?'

'I'm going to look around,' I say more assertively.

'Good,' she smiles.

I wander past the women frying chicken, the aunties boiling soups and uncles pounding yam. A young woman with thick braids sits curved over a clay-grinding dish crushing peppers, tomatoes and onions with a wooden pestle. Her movements create a soft percussion. The smell of grilled fish and spice mixes with perfumed bodies and the tang of sweat and people dancing. On the pavement, on one side of the street, are stalls with foodstuff. The band plays in the road in the middle, and there are tables and chairs for dining and craft stalls on the other pavement. Behind the food counters, there's a sheltered area; I move towards it.

'No access, no enter!' a man shouts, blocking my way. At his back is a short wooden divider. Behind it, just metres away from the busy market, a mother sits bathing a baby in a metal tub. *They live here:* embarrassed at intruding, I turn to move back to the street, but before I cross the barrier created by the food counters, I spot Afua. She is backed into a corner, entangled with a boy, who seems like he's one of the people who live in the background of the market. Their kiss looks nicer than what I saw Duncan do to Shannon back at Holymead. I step away to give them some privacy.

Back in the main street, I bump into Boat. He speaks in Twi, and I watch the contours of his face work as he tries to make me understand. His hands wave, and it's the shadow of his movement on the pavement that draws my attention to it: we're standing beside a lamppost, his shadow gesturing wildly on the ground beside us, and next to it is – not my shadow, but a dull spot – a place where I'm blocking the streetlight. I feel light-headed to see it. I'm blocking the light. Amarie still hasn't appeared, but I'm blocking the light. Boat sees it too. He looks at it and says, 'Light soup heal small. Co Dosu, you go stay. Dosu, heal big...' he nods, staring into my eyes, willing me to understand.

On the car journey home, the sisters barely speak. I'm lost in my thoughts. Did Boat's soup really heal me small? I replay his words, trying to make sense of them. What is Dosu? Then Adjoa says to her sister, 'You might as well be in love with an illiterate from the village. When we go to Dosu for the funeral, you can pick up another one there if one nyama-nyama boy is not enough for you.'

Afua kisses her teeth and stares out of the window at the night.

The Funeral

You wear red fabric with black embroidery. The Gye Nyame symbol is stitched as a pattern on it. It means, Except God; I fear nothing except God. Only her family wear this cloth. It distinguishes you as the chief mourners. / I step out of the car and remove my shoes.

'You don't have to do it,' Aunt Grace says. 'My girls will keep their shoes on.'

'I want to.'

The dusty ground is hot on my feet and the gravel scratches. It's uncomfortable rather than painful. A crowd surrounds the car as we get out. There are greetings, hugs and introductions.

'This is your Aunt Esi, your mother's sister.' / 'This is Nana Abena, she's the grandmother of the family.' / 'This is your grandfather, Nana Kofi.'

I lose track of the number of grandparents I'm introduced to – seven, eight maybe more – and the aunts and uncles outnumber the siblings I've been told my mother had. Aunt Esi wears the same cloth as us, red with black stitching and the Gye Nyame symbol embroidered on it.

'You look just like her,' she says. She hugs me a second time and her shoulder-length braids brush against my face. 'Only she was fairer.'

'I keep hearing that,' I say. 'I feel a bit like the step-mother in *Snow White*.'

'They mean she was lighter-skinned than you, you're darker,' Aunt Esi says, 'like me.'

'I thought everyone was saying, "You look just like her, only uglier",' I try to joke.

'Well, it's kinda the same thing,' Adjoa says, and Aunt Grace gives her a little slap on her arm.

Adjoa's shawl slips from around her shoulders and reveals the scrape on her arm from our day at Cape Coast Castle. It's dark grey and wrinkled like spoiled fabric, burnt by an iron. It looks worse than I remember it being. The graze on my elbow is barely noticeable now. Fixated on her arm, I miss what Aunt Grace says to her.

More people arrive. They speak in mournful tones that are somehow also rejoicing. There is a cadence to their words; I don't understand them, but something in me recognises their rhythm. We walk barefoot on the dirt road to the arch of the church. Other than Maame Yaa's house, where we're staying, this is the only brick building I've seen in Dosu since we arrived a few days earlier. A woman stands at the door and opens her arms to receive us. She speaks to Aunt Esi first, then Aunt Grace. Aunt Grace mentions Uncle Samuel; I assume she's explaining that her husband has travelled for work, that they said he would be back in time for the funeral, but he's been held up in South Africa. The woman nods but doesn't look happy.

'You must be Imani,' she says to me in English. 'Your mother was a great woman. I am sorry that I couldn't make it to Accra to attend the wake.'

'I've told you, don't worry,' Aunt Grace cuts in.

'Wake?' I ask.

'It's tradition,' Aunt Grace says, in place of an explanation.

'She lay in wake for a week,' Aunt Esi says.

'Where?'

'It began before you arrived,' Aunt Grace says.

'Why didn't anyone tell me?' I think back to my first day in Accra, leaving Aunt Grace's place for breakfast and meeting all those people who were headed for the house. What had my cousins said was going on? I just remember that they were keen to get away.

'It is a strange custom,' Aunt Grace explains. 'We thought it would be upsetting for you. Even Esi herself didn't stay for the whole period; she just came for the first days and she left before you arrived.'

'You didn't ask me...' the words come out choked and quiet.

'We thought it best,' she says firmly, and the conversation is over.

The church service is a haze; my awareness of what is going on slips in and out of focus. I think back to that first day with Adjoa and Afua; they pull me away from the jewelled women dressed in black and headed to the Boys' Quarters. At the kiosk, Adjoa jumps up and walks away with the woman who is asking for directions – directions to my mother's wake. I should have been more assertive, asked more questions. If I'd only spoken to some of the people we bumped into, something might have come out and my cousins would have been forced to tell me. And I might have got the chance to see her.

The priest's sermon comes to an end. Aunt Esi and Aunt Grace get up to speak. Adjoa and Afua sing a hymn and a song in Twi. An uncle gives a speech, a grandma prays. Finally, Aunt Esi reads. When she's finished, she asks if I would like to say anything. I stare at her, watching the words form on her mouth. I notice we have the same mouth, the same-shaped curve of the top lip and plump bottom lip. I try to get my bearings by concentrating on her features, and I move from her lips to her eyes. They are mine as well, large and coal-black with a circle of fire around the pupils. It's then that I recognise her from the gallery of family photos in the bedroom at Aunt Grace's house. Hers was the face that I'd decided was possibly my mother's, along with one other.

'Imani, I asked if you would like to say anything,' Aunt Esi says again.

I snap out of the numbness and answer as clearly as the lump in my throat allows, 'I'd like to see her.'

Aunt Grace is on her feet immediately. The priest asks something of Aunt Esi, who's standing beside the casket. She responds and a murmur ripples down the pews.

'I'd like to see her,' I repeat, louder this time.

Aunt Grace looks at me, shocked. Aunt Esi addresses her and Aunt Grace responds in English, 'No Esi, it is not our way.'

'Hush, Grace,' Aunt Esi says and she beckons me to join her at the front of the church. A few people shake their heads as I approach her, but my gaze is fixed on the fire in my aunt's eyes and I walk with my head up.

'You should know that this isn't your mother,' Aunt Esi says when I reach her. 'She was a vibrant, beautiful woman. What you will see is, is ... fog...' she shakes her head, 'cloud ... not even a shadow of her former self.'

The murmur from the congregation grows louder. Aunt Esi's words echo in my ears. I picture a decaying face inside the casket. As she lifts the lid of the coffin, I close my eyes before the sight hits me. Aunt Esi puts her hand on my arm, touching the fabric above the injury on my elbow from the day at the castle. The material scratches the sore. This is the cloth that distinguishes me as her family. I am one of the chief mourners. I open my eyes.

Her eyes are closed. They have soft lines at their edges, from smiling I guess, and laughing. I imagine the sound of her laughter, hear it ring with mischief and mettle. She's greyish-black now, like Amarie, more spirit than flesh. Aunt Esi is right: what remains of her is a cloud, a whisper of water. It can't hold my reflection. It's not enough to drink and won't quench my thirst. But also, because of this, I can breathe through it without drowning. So, I thank God for small mercies.

The Interior

At the main square in the village, tables have been laid with food and drinks. I sit at the head table with my cousins and aunts, sweating into black and red cloth. Music begins – bells, then drums, then voice. In the space that has been left at the centre of the square, aunties and grandparents, uncles and children gather. They bend, as though to pick something up, then shuffle their feet, make shapes in the air with their hands and move their hips to the rhythm. Aunt Grace stands and takes Aunt Esi's hand. They walk into the centre to join the dance. It is mournful and rejoicing – grieving and giving thanks at the same time. Aunt Grace looks like she might collapse and Aunt Esi holds her up and slowly sways to the music. Aunt Grace, the younger sister, cries into her elder sister's chest. Beside me, Afua and Adjoa turn away from their mother's tears and wipe their own eyes. This feeling, this force of opposites, is too much. I excuse myself and walk away. I walk out of the square, out of the village and cross over to nearby fields. Covered in brush and tall grasses of deep green and straw, it reminds me of the dune-grass on the sandbanks at Holymead, although the straw-like grass here is softer than the sharp dune-reeds back there. I want to dive into it and disappear, but the heat keeps me searching for shade. Just beyond the field is a forest, and its promise of shelter pulls me in. I cross over to it and settle under the trees. From that distance, I can still hear it all: the music and the mourning, instruments, chatter and clatter. I hug my knees to myself and listen from a safe distance.

❖

Footsteps tread and crackle the tangled undergrowth. Surprised, I turn to see who's there. A man stands a few metres behind me in the denseness of the trees. I stand and take a step backwards. The light that slips through the gaps in the canopy illuminates his face. He looks exactly like Boat, a bit older perhaps. He wears long shorts and a T-shirt with a faded purple tick on it. If he were really a relative of Boat's, he would be at the funeral, dressed in heavy folded cloth. He takes a step towards me. I'm reminded of the traditional healer at Cape Coast Castle and I move back. He stops and backs away too. He picks up an object from the ground and holds it to his chest. It flickers as the light through the trees hits its surface. Something about it pulls me closer. I gradually move towards him until I see my reflection in the object. He holds it steady and I watch myself approach. I stop and stare into it. There, reflected in the mirror's surface, Amarie stands behind me. She waves and I wave back, smiling and crying at the same time.

'Kwaku,' he says, pointing at himself.

'Thank you,' I say. I turn around slowly to see her with my own eyes, careful not to move too quickly so I don't frighten her away. By the time I've turned, she's gone. The trees stand in their own shadows. When I turn back to Kwaku, he's also gone and the mirror lies broken on the forest floor.

Aunt Grace Speaks

'I told you the day you arrived that you must be patient with us. That we will do things wrong while trying to do right. I'm sorry for keeping you away from the wake. There are several formalities related to death; if you are not used to our customs, they can seem strange. I was trying to protect you. But you – you have also made mistakes. I wasn't happy with the way you behaved at the church service; you can't just make demands and disrupt processes in this way. And I'm not happy that you say you want to remain here when the rest of us go back to Accra. What can you know about living in a place like Dosu? It will be so ... so alien to you. I don't know what has possessed you, really. But I accept that you want to know the stories of the family. And with regards to that, I can do my part.

'Our paternal grandmother, your great-grandmother, lived in a town not too far from here – her family had moved there from the North. Our grandfather saw her for the first time when he travelled there to attend to some business, and after that he refused to marry anyone else. The people said our grandmother was the most beautiful woman in all Ghana, Wafaa the Beauty. People said that coming from a town, she would never accept a village boy's proposal. But my grandfather had prospects and vision and she shocked everyone when she married him and moved here. Your mother took after our grandmother: she was fair-skinned with big eyes; she had full, soft hair and a gap in her teeth. She was our father's favourite, they say because she looked so much like his mother. Our father had always wanted a son, though he had only girls. But Dofi, a girl as beautiful as his own mother had been, well, that was the next best thing to having a boy. He used to say that she was twice blessed. He said she was so great, she had two destinies to fulfil in life. He had big plans for her; she would be the first in the family to go to university and not just that, she would go abroad – two destinies could not be fulfilled by staying in Ghana alone.

'Our father decided to move Dofi from the government school she attended to a private school, as he thought it was a better environment to nurture her abilities. At the private school, she met Jonathan, who was attending the neighbouring school for boys. She fell pregnant before she was sixteen. Honestly, I thought our father would kill her – his twice-blessed daughter giving birth outside marriage – heh! He allowed her to remain in the house, but he said to all of us that he would never allow another fatherless baby in his home. During those days your grandfather and your mother didn't speak at all, but when Kisi was born he softened.

'For years no one spoke of the two destinies and Dofi concentrated on being a mother. I don't know when she started schooling again, maybe she told Esi. She'd been attending night classes to get her high school qualifications. I'd returned home after my own graduation, and that's when I was told – Dofi was going to university, in England. Our father had continued to save for her education. He had not offered the opportunity to either Esi or me. He said he had always hoped that Dofi would climb back to glory after her fall. She was the one who was twice blessed.

'When she returned to Ghana after graduation, she interned for some years then set up a small agricultural development institute. Things went well for a time. Then Kisi got sick. In the final years of Kisi's leukaemia, Dofi suspended all work. She travelled throughout Africa and further afield looking for the right medical care. I always believed the travelling was hurting Kisi as much as the disease itself, but your mother wouldn't listen. When your sister died, your mother fell into a deep depression. All that while, your aunt Esi had been in America. When she heard about Kisi's illness and Dofi's depression, immediately she came back. She was the office manager in Dofi's organisation for some years. Where her skills failed, she got the appropriate people to do the work, and she managed them. I do believe your mother's organisation remained solvent in those years because of Esi.

'Dofi was sick for a long time after Kisi's death. In truth, I don't know if she ever recovered, but after some time she did return to work. The cancer developed a few years after that. One of our uncles said that she fought so hard to rid the sickness from her child that she called it into herself.

'I had never heard her speak of the two destinies, it had always been our father's obsession, but on the day she died, she spoke of them. She said she had always believed that one was to be a great mother and have many children. The other was to be a social leader of some sort, to improve Ghana's condition and position in the world. She said she'd made the wrong decision, that she'd tried to go back and make things better, but it was too late. They wouldn't allow it. She called your name, but it meant nothing to me at the time, it was just a word – and she was always unclear when she said it … the effects of the medication, I assume. You see, it was impossible to know what it meant or what it could refer to. Then she started asking for her child to attend her funeral – I thought she was asking to do traditional rites, fetish rituals to call Kisi's spirit back … and these things are not Christian. We are a Christian family. I insisted that we use the church in Dosu and that we do a Christian service and bury her with our parents, but I'd misunderstood. It was when Esi came that we learned more. Esi had known everything. She told us that Imani was the name the nuns had Christened you with and that this was the only information your mother knew about you.'

The Second Born
after Twins

This is your story, which I share with you. If it be sweet or if it not be sweet, take some and share, and let some come back to me:

Dofi Asare was the second born after twins, but not in the conventional sense. She arrived just two years after her twin sisters, and between the birth of the twins and the arrival of Dofi, their mother had had another pregnancy. For nine months her belly grew, and she ate and moved as though she carried a child. But as her uterus opened and its waters ran, the child that should have emerged did not. Instead, her waters rushed on, flooding the ancestral village she had returned to in order to give birth. It created a river where there had been none before. The first born after twins is called Do, in the tradition of her grandmother's people. So, the family named the water Do, in place of the child that should have been born. When another child was blessed onto them one year later, some felt it was only right and proper that she be named second born after twins, and that the small girl should be called Dofi. Others argued that it was wrong to name the child in this way after such a tragic event and to do so would only bring calamity unto her. She was given the name regardless and, of course, after all of the events had come to pass, everybody claimed they had been right all along.

The Weekly Shop

'How come Aunt Grace has an English name, and you and my mum have Ghanaian names?'

'Grace is her Christian name. Our father gave them to all of us. Until I met my late husband, Malcolm, I went by my Christian name as well. He encouraged me to use my African name.'

'Did my mother have a Christian name?'

'Yes, Faith.'

What's the difference between faith and reality? Harold had asked. It was a very grown-up question indeed.

When it was time to return to Accra after the funeral, I asked to stay in the village with Aunt Esi. Boat had told me I should remain in Dosu the evening we visited the night market in Osu. And after hearing the story Aunt Grace told, I was convinced that Aunt Esi would be the only person who could fill in the large gaps of my mother's story. I'd thought my request to stay would be straightforward, but everyone seemed put out by it, although no one wanted to be the first to refuse, so I used that silence to my advantage.

There is something about Dosu: a humility, a calm. It's unlike the pulse and constant noise of Accra. It does not threaten to overtake everything around it or swallow you into its swirling masses. The size of Dosu, its pace, the small mud homes of its central village, they feel manageable to me.

After dinner, Aunt Esi and I sit on stools at the back of her home, which is away from the central village. Unlike the houses there, hers is made from corrugated metal sheets, layered and fitted together; it's blue-grey in parts and red with rust elsewhere. The door is bright yellow and there's a window with a timber frame that doesn't open. As we sit, Aunt Esi washes the dinner plates using two metal buckets – one with soapy water and another with clean. When she's finished, she empties the buckets in the soil around the trees. She returns to sit with me, seeming agitated. She looks in my direction, but never quite at me, and she talks to the air above my head.

'Do you know who named you?' she asks.

I shake my head.

'It must have been the nuns,' she says, 'it's not a Ghanaian name; it's from the east.'

I wonder where in Asia my name might be from. Then Aunt Esi says, 'Kenya, I think. But I guess it's all Africa to them.' And the difference in our geographies catches me by surprise.

'Names are important,' she says. 'They tell you where you came from and how you fit in. They can be small prophecies, dreams for people.' Still looking above my head, she says, 'Your mother's names had lost their meanings.'

'I don't understand.'

'Her name, Dofi, means the second born after twins. She was the second birth but not the second born. The first born died and then my twin died, so then there were no twins and no first born.' She looks baffled suddenly, as though someone else has spoken and she doesn't understand or agree with their words.

'Why wasn't she Faith?' I ask.

'What?'

'You said why she wasn't Dofi, but why wasn't she Faith?'

'You ask too many questions!'

'You talk in circles!'

'Oh! Not such a meek English girl, eh?' she says looking me in the eye at last.

❖

The next morning, I wake to see, lying at the front door: a cutlass, a club, a net and a bag. Aunt Esi says we're going to gather food and if we're lucky, we might find some bushmeat to have with our rice and beans for dinner tonight. For two days now we haven't eaten meat, and she wants to rectify this. I don't miss meat, I tell her, I'm used to a mainly vegetarian diet at St Teresa's. But Aunt Esi insists. Aunt Grace had warned me that Aunt Esi has some unconventional ideas and I should speak up if I feel uncomfortable about anything she suggests. As we both get ready for the day, I begin tentatively by calling her name.

'Yes?' she says.

'I'm not sure I feel … ok about this.'

'What?'

'Hunting giant rats.'

'Well, when you say it like that, of course you're not going to feel *ok*,' she laughs. '"*Hunting giant rats!*" We're just going to get some food. Grasscutter is like young tender chicken meat or fish. It's lean like fish. You like fish, don't you?'

She's bent over, massaging shea butter into her legs; she looks up at me with a smile that feels like a challenge.

'Didn't the nuns ever take you shopping in England? Didn't you go to a superstore…?'

'We got most of our things from the grounds or local farmers.'

'Well, this will be the same as your big weekly shop; think of this as the Ghanaian superstore.'

'The catering for the girls' school came from the mainland. That was from a supermarket, I think, but I never-'

'In England, the nuns took you to Walmart or something like it. Do they have Walmart in England? Anyway, they would have gone to a very big store and bought the food there. They will-'

'No-'

'Most people in England will buy food from one big store that sells everything – food, clothes, electricals. You just have to see this experience as the Ghanaian version. It's not so different.'

'I went to a big store like that with Aunt Grace and Adjoa, last week in Accra. They'd been insisting on buying me clothes...'

'It's exactly the same, then. You'll feel like you're right back in England,' she chuckles to herself.

I'm nearly shouting now, 'That wasn't England! You're not listening to me!'

She continues as though she hasn't heard me. She puts the cutlass, club and net inside a thatched plastic bag and walks out. I follow, slamming the yellow door behind me. Her house rattles with the force of it.

'Even if I'd had that experience at Holymead, I imagine this still wouldn't be anything like it,' I say. 'No other Ghanaian I've met has talked about hunting for giant rats.'

'That's because those other Ghanaians have moved away from nature and from the Motherland,' she says. 'Look, I'm not forcing you to come.' She disappears into the trees and I run after her, not wanting to be left alone.

Aunt Esi picks up a large-leafed plant, 'This is good,' she says, pushing it under my nose. She picks up another, similar leaf, 'This is bad.'

'I'm not sure I can see the difference.'

'Show me everything you pick before putting it in the bag,' she says. 'We can't be too careful.'

We walk for a while in silence, each examining plants and bagging or discarding them. I break the silence first, 'My mother told you about me, didn't she?'

'Keep an eye out for droppings, it will mean there are grasscutters nearby.'

'You didn't answer the question.'

She still doesn't. We continue in silence. I steel myself. I stayed behind for this and I'm not going to leave Dosu without asking my questions. I'm about to ask another question when she looks at me and puts her finger on her mouth. She is stalling. I open my mouth to ask anyway, when she pushes me aside and rushes into the undergrowth.

'Gotcha!' she says, lifting the net to show a large mole-like creature. The thing is tangled in the mesh; its back legs and tail hang out and it thrashes, trying to break free. Aunt Esi bangs the net repeatedly against a tree stump until the creature is too wounded to struggle.

'The club!' she shouts, pointing at the weapon that's sticking out of the plastic sack on the ground.

I reach for the club and hold it up. The animal starts to move slowly. I can't bring myself to do it. I stand, holding the club in mid-air, arms shaking and palms sweaty.

'If you can't do it, give it to me!' Aunt Esi shouts, snatching the club from me and bringing it down on the net. It lands on the creature with a squelch and a jet of blood shoots from the animal onto the leaves beside it. Holding the net with only one hand, she isn't as steady against the final frantic movements of the grasscutter. Before she can bring the club down a second time, the creature escapes from the net and scurries into the shrubs.

'It's injured, we can track it,' she says, pointing at the trail of blood.

'No,' I say firmly. 'I've had enough.'

She glares at me, but doesn't insist. We continue in silence and it takes all my resolve not to demand that we go home.

We've been walking around in silence for at least thirty minutes after the grasscutter incident when Aunt Esi says, 'Your mother was my sister. She told me some things and didn't tell me others.'

'Aunt Grace said you were very close.'

'I was the eldest, I had the responsibility for the younger ones, so I was close to everyone.'

'Responsibilities?'

'When we were at school together, she would take things from people, there would be arguments, I had to resolve them.'

'Why would she take people's things?'

'She didn't really know better. She'd always been given *everything*. Whenever the school sent letters home complaining, our parents would blame me for not looking out for her. It was easier to be with her and prevent things happening than to try and pick up the pieces of the things she tore apart.'

'She tore things apart?'

'Don't look at me like that. I don't mean to make her sound like a monster. She was just ... spoilt. It got better when she left for boarding school.'

'But Aunt Grace said–'

'Grace was the baby, she saw what she wanted to see.'

'She said my mother told you about me ... years before she knew.'

'Careful you're not throwing the good ones away,' Aunt Esi says, picking up a leaf I've discarded.

'Is it true?'

She bends to examine a plant with large open leaves before pulling it from the root, fighting with it until it yields.

'I was living in New Jersey when she came to see me and told me she was pregnant. Unannounced. We talked about it and she made her decisions. There's not a great deal more to say than that.'

The Grasscutter

Aunt Esi is quiet, speaking only when she absolutely has to. The silence thickens and solidifies, becoming a thing between us. We move beside it and around it, without much friction. The noises from outside fill in for discussions we could be having. We wake up to birds landing on the roof, clawed feet settling and scratching corrugated iron, and then their chorus. Sometimes it's the cock that crows from somewhere off in the distance that wakes us. Though he can't be relied on: the first morning he crowed at dawn, then the next day he was mute until mid-morning, and the day after that, he started crowing from 2 am and didn't stop until midday. Once we're up, we walk down to the river to fetch water for the tank. Then we bathe in a metal tub at the back of the house, hidden in the shadows between the water tank and the trees. On the other side of the water tank is a little wooden surround with a hole in the ground and a lid on it – our toilet. We eat millet, then do the morning clean. Despite having mopped, dusted and swept the day before, each new day the house is covered in a new film of red dust. After the morning routine, Aunt Esi goes for a long walk. She invites me each time, but she doesn't really mean it, so I let her go alone. The first time she was out, I just sat feeling sorry for myself, regretting not returning to Accra with Aunt Grace and her family. The second time, unconsciously, I began to meditate. The time after that, for just a moment, I tried to kneel and pray. It felt strange and kind of illicit, like the time the dawn bell sounded for morning meditation at St Teresa's and I'd been lying in bed with my hand between my legs. I'd discovered a warm hollow inside that triggered stars in my head if I touched it right. For it to be hidden in the shadows like that, it was clearly private, and because it was hidden in the shadows, there was a danger Reverend Mother would call it demonic. So I kept it to myself, between God and me. Kneeling to pray in Aunt Esi's home, I have that sensation again, a tentative intimacy. The feeling that I want to, but what if it's wrong? That first time trying, I wasn't able to see it through to the end.

The third night at Aunt Esi's, I can't sleep. It's too hot. We keep the door ajar but there's nothing cooling about the warm dusty air that enters. Aunt Esi moves restlessly beside me.

'Stop it!' she says in her sleep. 'Stop it! Stop it!' she shouts. She screams and jumps up.

A shadow moves beyond my legs. For a second I think it's Amarie, but I sit up just in time to see a hairy mass run across the floor and out of the door. Aunt Esi sits up, screaming and holding her thigh.

'The flashlight – get the flashlight!' she yells.

I look for the torch and stumble as I try to stand up from the sleeping mat.

'Behind my pillow!' she says, rocking as she holds her thigh.

I reach under her pillow to find it and switch it on. Its glow fills the room. Her hand is on her thigh and blood seeps out from the edge of her grip. She points at the suitcase on the floor and I run over to it not knowing what she wants.

'A white plastic box!' she says.

I rummage through clothes, sheets of paper, creams and combs, and eventually locate a small, white plastic first aid box. I hand it to her and she tells me to go outside and boil some water.

'What if it's out there?' I ask, not sure I know what the 'it' actually is.

'Take the torch, it won't come near the light.'

I set the coals to light in the small fire pit dug into the earth. I try to do it the way I've seen Aunt Esi do it over the past few days, but for me the process is slow. When it's finally lit, I fill a metal pot with water from the tank and place it on the fire. As it begins to boil she comes out. She dips a cloth in the bubbling liquid and applies it to the wound on her leg. She grimaces as the hot fabric touches her.

'What was it?'

'Don't be afraid.'

'I'm not,' I lie.

'I think it was a grasscutter. It's strange, though, they usually stay away from us. There must have been something wrong with it to enter a human house like that.'

'Was it the one we tried to kill?'

She smiles, 'I don't think animals have the concept of revenge.'

After cleaning the wound, she applies a serum from the first aid box and creates a bandage with a roll of gauze. We go back to bed, but this time we close the door and put the suitcase against it, so we'll hear if someone or something tries to get in again. I lie back staring up at the metal roof, wondering if it's possible to die of humidity and fear.

The following morning, we get up and go to the river to collect water as usual. But this time, Aunt Esi begins to talk. I didn't sleep much and I'm too tired to ask questions, but her words flow uninterrupted.

'The river was called Fum, and the village Fumsu. But while we were children the water came to be known as Do and so the village, Dosu,' she says. 'It was just Eyi and me then, we were young. We were told we were going to have another little sibling, but it would be more than another year before your mother was born. We played in the grass by the river and were running up and down the valley. Our elder cousin was with us; I think she'd been told to look after us that day. She chased us and ah, we laughed.' She pauses for a moment, 'It was fun.'

But it was also sad. It was the day the baby never came.

When we're back from collecting the water, I take my towel and go to have a bath. As I approach the metal bathtub, I see it: a brown-black thing lying outstretched. Its dark stubbly hair and rope-like tail are smeared with blood and pus. Its head is swollen, as though a second scalp is trying to grow from within the first. Yellow liquid seeps from a wound under its leg. I think it's dead but can't figure out if the heaving is coming from the thing or me. I scream and can't stop screaming.

Aunt Esi runs out, 'What is it?'

I point at it – part-rat, part-mole, part-miniature bear.

'Christ!' she shouts, turning away and crossing herself. She goes inside and comes back with a sheet that she throws over it. I stare at the sheet, fixated on the blood and yellow discharge seeping through the fabric.

'How did it get here?' she asks.

'I didn't put it there! It's the one we tried to kill, isn't it? It's the same one that bit you last night!'

'It's impossible,' she says, not taking her eyes off it.

'You said it yourself, it wouldn't have come into the house unless something was wrong with it – did you see its head? That's what was wrong with it! We have to get your bite seen to; you have to go to a hospital! It could be infected with something.'

'We cleaned the wound last night. I'm fine. You have to calm down; not every grasscutter we see is the same one,' she says. 'What we have to do is get rid of it, not stand here disagreeing.'

'You wanted meat–' I start to say, then I double over and vomit.

She moves away from the splurge and kisses her teeth.

'In Ghana, you don't speak to your elders in this tone. And of course we won't eat this! Are you insane?' She's silent for a while, and when I look up, she's brought me a cup of water and is handing me a towel. I swirl the water around my mouth and spit it out, trying to rid my mouth of the taste of the stomach acid and the smell of the dead thing. Aunt Esi hands me a shovel.

'What's this for?'

'Take it, unless you want to carry the animal?' she says.

I leave the towel and cup inside the bathtub and I take the shovel. Using the bedsheet, Aunt Esi wraps the excess layers around the animal, then picks it up and carries it like a baby. I follow her, gripping the shovel and wondering why we'd do this for an animal we were prepared to kill and eat only a short while ago.

When we reach a spot that she's happy with, she places the grasscutter on the ground, takes the shovel from me and begins to dig. She works for ages while I sit and watch her. Finally, she stops and hands the shovel to me. She's covered in sweat and her hands tremble as she places the tool on the ground in front of me.

'Your turn.'

I continue where she's left off, pulling earth from the ground and throwing it aside. I don't ask questions, but just perform the task. It's not long before my own clothes are soaked through. We take it in turns to dig until she's satisfied that the hole is deep enough.

'We don't want the children from the village finding it – or another animal digging it up,' she says. 'If it's too shallow, even the rainwater can wash away the soil to reveal it.' Aunt Esi places the wrapped grasscutter into the hole. On our hands and knees, we push and scoop the earth back in to cover the creature. When the soil covers the hole, we stand on it and tamp it down, then cover it over with leaves and twigs. She looks around and wanders off, then comes back with a large smooth stone that could almost be a piece of marble. She places it at the head of the dirt covering and stands to full height.

'Come now,' she says.

I get up and follow her out of the forest, half-walking half-running to keep up, not sure what she's planning next. Over her shoulder she says she cannot tell me my mother's story but she's ready to tell me hers and I will have to be satisfied with that.

Pa Kwasi's Daughters

Esi Boahemaa Asare was the first born of twins. She was the daughter of Kwasi and Patience, the eldest of their three girls. Esi and her twin Eyi were bright and loved to play and misbehave. Tragedy visited the family when Eyi died very young. It was an accident on a main road in Kumasi, on a visit to the city from Tema, where the family lived. Eyi had chased a chicken into the street, hoping to catch it and save it from being hit by a car. But while the bird ran to safety, the little girl lay cold on the tarmac.

Esi was just nine when her twin died and her family closed their home to mourn for the little girl. Ma Patience cried throughout the day; Pa Kwasi cried throughout the night; Esi and her little sister cried continually. Esi lost her voice and did not speak for many months, and while she withered, Pa Kwasi's youngest daughter developed the abilities and faculties of the sister who had passed away. This meant she became ambidextrous, and could write with both her right hand, as she had always done, but now also her left, like her dead sibling. She developed an interest in cooking, alongside her existing love of eating. She would remain in the kitchen with her mother, insisting that she help with food preparation, much in the way her departed elder sister had done. She demanded she be given tasks that were too challenging for such a young child.

One night, as Esi tried to sleep, her little sister called to her, 'Sister Esi, are you sleeping?' Esi did not respond immediately but recognised that the younger sibling spoke with the voice of her dead twin.

'Why are you putting on that voice?' Esi asked, speaking for the first time in months.

'I am Eyi,' the little sister answered.

'Stop it!'

'I've come to tell you something, Esi, listen–'

'I will hit you if you carry on with this!' Esi chided.

'You must start speaking again, ok?'

Esi's pillow grew wet with tears.

'Come back, Eyi. I promise never to argue with you again.'

'You must speak, Esi. Otherwise your tongue will rot in your mouth and when we meet in death, you will not be able to talk to me.'

Esi continued to cry.

'Ok, Esi? Do you hear me? You must speak to Pa and Ma and the little one.'

Esi cried harder.

'We will meet again and then, ahh, we will talk and we will laugh. Ahh, Esi, the things I will have to tell you. But for now, you must talk so you will have stories to tell me also, ok? Esi? Esi?'

'Esi? Are you ok?' Pa Kwasi sat on the edge of his daughter's bed and held her in his arms.

She cried into his chest, 'I miss her so much.'

After that night, several priests were called to the home to see the little sister. They were asked to exorcise the ghost of the elder sister from her. The last to be invited to the house was a traditional healer. When he arrived, he spent hours with the young girl, asking her questions and telling stories. At the end of his time, he said he would not perform an exorcism. The spirit that had spoken to Esi had been there only to pass on a message and what remained in the little sister was not the spirit of the dead girl, but all the hope and potential she had not fully realised. The medicine man told the family that the little sister was now twice blessed and had two destinies to fulfil. Pa Kwasi asked why the ghost of the big sister had not blessed her twin with her essence and her promise, as they had been so close. The medicine man said that they had been too close, and the weight of such a gift on someone who already shares part of your essence would be too great a burden. Esi would not have been strong enough to receive it.

In time, the little sister became the middle sister, as a younger girl was born to Pa Kwasi and Ma Patience. Everyone gave the middle sister special treatment; after all, she had two destinies to perform and no one ever forgot this, least of all Esi, who remembered that she was too weak to have been given the gift. Halfway through her secondary studies, the middle sister was taken out of the school she attended with Esi and enrolled in a private boarding school. Esi missed her sister, but she studied hard and looked for the right career for herself, something lucrative and appropriate for a woman. She decided to get into management and to focus on business administration. She left school with excellent grades, many friends and no enemies. The family was proud, and she went on to university. After completion of her studies, Esi secured a job as an office administrator for Ghana's national bank.

Meanwhile, her middle sister, who had been sent back home from boarding school when she'd fallen pregnant, gave birth to a little girl, who became the family's crowning glory. Everyone who met her loved her at once, and the middle sister settled into her role as a mother. Years later, the middle sister gained her secondary school qualifications and the family sent her to England for further studies. In truth, this angered Esi. She had also worked hard, but the family had never offered her this opportunity. Esi decided she too must go to abrokyire, but she would go to a bigger abrokyire than that of her sister. Through her links at the bank, Esi made friends with people in prominent places, as this would guarantee her a smooth visa application process. She applied to colleges in America and successfully secured a scholarship for a Masters in Business Administration. When the time came, the family drove Esi to the airport with her suitcases and they kissed her goodbye. The biggest tear Esi shed was for her niece, the middle sister's child, whom she loved very much.

During the first year of her master's degree, Esi met Malcolm Small, a young Baptist minister. Malcolm called Africa the Mother Country, and although he had never visited, he said Ghana was its beating heart. He had vivid visions of life in Ghana, and he'd tell her stories of the rich and prosperous Motherland. At first their friendship was combative and she challenged his views often. But in time, neither of them knew exactly when, their ambivalences converged and together they created a Ghana that was her homeland and his birthright. They took comfort in this shared fiction and sheltered beneath it. They were blessed with several happy years together, but one day, Malcolm's heart failed and Esi was left alone. That same year, she received a letter from home, informing her that her beloved niece had leukaemia and the middle sister, who by then had returned to Ghana from university in England and started her own organisation, had been taken by a mental sickness due to her grief over the child's condition. Esi knew she would have to go back.

On her return to Ghana, Esi worked in the middle sister's business in Accra. She kept it afloat until her sister was ready to return to work. When that time came, Esi picked up her things and moved to the remotest, most beautiful place she could remember from her childhood; her grandmother had taken her for walks there when she'd visited their ancestral village of Dosu. When she found this place, she built a house of iron and wood and made it her home. She was back in Ghana, but this time she would build the Ghana she had created with Malcolm. During those first weeks, she slept under the trees at night and built her home during the day. When at last her home was finished, she cooked herself a meal and slept inside it for the first time. That night she cried. With no clocks and nothing but the movements of the sun and moon, she could not be sure if her tears had lasted days or weeks. Sleep and tears came and went until, like lovers, they settled into each other.

Storms

Tin. / I replay the things Aunt Esi has said. / Tin, tap. / Lay them beside what Aunt Grace told me. / Tin, tin. / Moving the pieces around, I try to fit them together, to make sense of it all. / Tin, tap. / I had a sister. / Tin. / Kisi. / Tin, tin. / Kisi. Kisi. Kisi. / Tap. / I play with her name; imagine her features. / Tin, tin, tap. / Trying to recall the pictures on the wall in Aunt Grace's house, I wonder, have I seen her already? / Tin, tap. / The soft strum of dew falling from the trees onto the roof draws me from my thoughts. The rhythm speeds up, then the drops start to pelt. The walls tremble as the wind picks up. I sit up from my sleeping mat to see Aunt Esi cross-legged with a book in her hands. But she's not reading, she's watching the walls as they shudder.

Barely speaking a word between us, we pack up the contents of the house in seconds. It all fits into a thatched plastic bag and a brown leather suitcase. She asks if I'm ready and I pick up my rucksack, which I'd never unpacked. She throws a sheet of tarpaulin over us and picks up her luggage. Under the tarp, we head out into the rain.

'He wanted me to move to the city. He's in abrokyire now and he has big city ideas,' Maame Yaa says. I'd met Maame Yaa when we came for the funeral. She was one of the many grandmothers I was introduced to. But although we'd stayed at her house when Aunt Grace and my cousins were in the village, she never seemed to be around much. So when she opens the door to let us in from the storm, it feels like we are meeting for the first time. Maame Yaa's home is like a palace in comparison to Aunt Esi's. It has four bedrooms and the living room has a five-piece suite in a peach textured fabric. Each of us has a sofa to ourselves, and we sit on them as though marooned on separate islands.

'I'm a village girl,' Maame Yaa says, 'and I always want to be a village girl. At my time of life, you don't decide to change – you decide to stay the same.' She gulps down her malt and her plump outline quivers in satisfaction. The weather booms beyond the walls, but the brick house makes the elements feel a safe distance away.

'He was my favourite,' she says. 'My nephew's eldest boy, one of the many children I've raised.' She has watery grey eyes and skin that is smooth but weathered; both young and old at the same time. 'He was one of the few that appreciated it, you understand?'

'I appreciate you!' Aunt Esi says defensively.

'I don't speak about you! How could I still have so much time for you if I didn't know that you appreciate?' She turns back to me and takes another gulp of the drink and holds the bottle neck in her teeth for a few seconds. 'With his first big job in abrokyire he sent me money to get my teeth fixed. You see here,' she points at her mouth. 'My front teeth were gone; for many years I didn't have any here. He paid for me to travel to Kumasi and get it all done nicely.' She smiles wide, showing off a row of gleaming white teeth. 'He moved from England to take up a job, a big man's job in Germany, but he still used to contact the old woman in the village. It's why he's my favourite – one of my favourites,' she says looking at Aunt Esi from the side of her eyes. 'You're allowed to have favourites with grandchildren. After my teeth were fixed, he kept insisting I move to the city permanently – so it would be easier to care for me. But no, I am a village girl. In the end he had to give in – the old woman knows best.'

'He never said that, did he?' Aunt Esi asks.

'It's my story!' she says, patting the back of her small afro and giving me a wink. 'So instead he sent me the money to have a place built right here. He's been to visit, twice … no, maybe three times. He still made mention of moving to Accra or Kumasi, but I'm deaf when I want to be. It's the age.'

When we stayed for the funeral, I didn't spend much time in the communal areas of the house, but I take it all in now as I listen to her. She sees me looking at the rows of books on the wall.

'I keep them for your aunt, she's eating them.'

'I'll eat you, old woman!' Aunt Esi says, reaching across the divide of the chairs to grab her. The older, larger woman moves quickly and is more sprightly than I'd expected – she is out of reach in a second and batting Aunt Esi's hand away with a cushion.

'She reads them as others drink water,' Maame Yaa says.

'I came back to Ghana under particular circumstances,' Aunt Esi says. 'I wanted to be here, but I felt I'd lost something.' She strokes her braids absentmindedly. She tells me how she borrowed American books from the public libraries in Accra when she first returned, to feel closer to the place she'd left. 'When things were ok with your mother, the business was under control, she was dealing with her condition, I decided to move out here. I had fond memories of this place from our childhood…'

'Then ask her why she didn't move into the village, why she lives on the outside of it?' Maame Yaa says.

Aunt Esi continues, ignoring her, 'Once I was settled here, I needed my books.'

'She needed books because she's not living with the people.'

'When Maa found out about it, she told me that her grandson is always trying to send her things from abroad that she doesn't want.'

'More things to dust,' Maame Yaa says, shaking her head.

'She told him I was going to teach her to read.'

'They like to take you for a simpleton, the ones with abroky-ire ideas. He never bothered to realise that I read quite well, so I played with this ignorance.'

'We told him we wanted books by specific writers: Zora Neale Hurston, Toni Morrison, Langston Hughes, Maya Angelou, many … but black Americans, mainly. He sent them and kept sending. My place is too small, so we keep them here.' She says that they've tried to read the books together.

'Yes, but I don't understand them,' Maame Yaa says.

'That's not true.'

'I like stories with music,' Maame Yaa says. Thunder rumbles over our heads as if in response. 'I need music you can nod your head and shake your buttocks to. These books don't wear their hearts where old women can see them with ease. And they talk about things that shouldn't be discussed publicly.' She shakes her head in disapproval.

'Maame Yaa has some traditional ideas.'

'Didn't you move back here for traditional ideas?' Maame Yaa snaps. 'I prefer when Esi tells me the story of the book. Then I tell her I don't want to hear about that, tell me more about this bit. Then I hear the Ghanaian voice come through. With some of them, it's like eating chicken bone – you chew and chew, and maybe it's nutritious, you have to believe it because they tell you it's good, but there's so much work and not so much flavour. You have to snap it and suck and suck until the marrow comes out, and now that's the good stuff, finally. I'm old; I don't mind making that effort for food but not for stories.'

We eat two rounds of fufu with goat and palm nut soup. Maame Yaa has a small paddock at the back with goats and chicken, so the meat is fresh and reared right here. Aunt Esi eats with relish and tells Maame Yaa how I spoiled our opportunity to eat meat because I was too scared to kill the grasscutter. She doesn't say anything about being bitten or how we went into the forest to bury the dead animal. I let her keep her omissions. Maame Yaa laughs and tells me not to mind my crazy aunty, nobody goes out hunting grasscutter unless they know what they're doing.

Maame Yaa teases Aunt Esi that her obsession with black American writers is no different from the abrokyire worship of the others, always looking west, never seeing the value of their own. Aunt Esi disagrees and they argue in loud, abounding tones scattered with laughter and exclamations.

'You don't understand because you've never left,' Aunt Esi complains. 'There is a lot ... something changes with the journey. You're a Ghanaian, you knew that, but suddenly you're there and you're ... an African and you're Black...'

Fade from Brown to Black. Open. Close. Open. I'm shocked to hear it – her transition to Black was also unexpected.

'...And as a woman, you know, as with all of these things, you're noticeable, you stand out, but you're silenced, so it's like you're very visible and invisible at the same time. I'm not describing it well. You have to have experienced it.' She says this last part facing Maame Yaa, who's screwing her face up and shaking her head. 'It's like you're the object that is touched but never allowed to touch. You're the bearer of the feeling, of the lion's portion of the feeling – and pressure – but without the right to release it ... or have it heard. Do you know what I mean?' She looks between Maame Yaa and me.

'You don't even know what you mean!' Maame Yaa taunts.

'Look, Ghana is far from perfect, it has its problems, but that particular one – America gave me. So, I found a home with its writers – in a way that I didn't find in the place itself ... until I met Malcolm.'

'You went there and developed western sadness. You like to shed too many tears for yourself,' Maame Yaa says.

Aunt Esi looks emotional, and I'm not sure if they're still joking or if the tone of things is changing. I want to say something, to show that I understand – or that I understand something like it, but I don't know where to start.

'With some forms of touch and sight, you can be both,' I say.

They look at me, surprised by my sudden contribution to the conversation. I rub my hands together in front of my face. 'Which hand is being touched?' I ask. 'Which one is the object?'

They don't respond immediately; they just watch me.

'They do it together...' I say nervously, not giving them enough time to answer. 'Collectively ... it's unified t-touch,' I stutter, trying to repeat what Amarie had told me all those years ago on the sand-banks at the causeway. 'Perhaps there's a bit of that in everything – every object also perceives ... it perceives its perceiver ... maybe not to the same extent, it's not allowed. Maybe, not all of the time, but in time, and perhaps it can grow. Both can see both, in time, if allowed. I don't know, it was just a thought.'

'You know what you mean, so say it!' Maame Yaa challenges.

'I was the object at St Teresa's, put upon but never allowed to say how I felt or what I saw. But in time, I began to see anyway, more and more, and all that stuff ... it had to go somewhere.'

'What did you see?' Aunt Esi asks.

'I'm not sure. Maybe that things were not what I was taught they were.'

'And then?' Maame Yaa presses.

'Aunt Grace from Ghana called and invited me to my biological mother's funeral, and here I am.'

We sit in silence. I am stunned by the sound of my own voice; I feel I've barely spoken since arriving in Dosu. Maame Yaa coughs, breaking the silence first; it sounds like she's choking but then it becomes laughter. Aunt Esi is laughing next and finally so am I. The laughter is loud and filling and cleansing. When it subsides, a hush takes over. I feel shaken, but also lit from within. Aunt Esi holds herself on her sofa-island; the rocking of her laughter becomes a different kind of sway – slow and weary. When her first tears fall, they are silent and it's a while before Maame Yaa and I realise what's happening. Aunt Esi folds further into herself. When she sees, Maame Yaa leaves her couch and goes to sit with her. She holds Aunt Esi close, but lightly enough to let her continue rocking. I go to them and I put my arms around Maame Yaa, who is wrapped around my aunt. Aunt Esi didn't cry at the funeral. It's the first time I've seen her cry. My cheeks are wet before I know it. The three of us sit wrapped and rocking together.

How Lion Discovered
the Mirror

I wake up to find Aunt Esi asleep on her sofa. Noises are coming from the indoor kitchen, and I walk through to find Maame Yaa cleaning dishes at the sink.

'Let me do that,' I say, taking the sponge from her. She moves out of the way and pulls a tall stool over to sit beside me. I wash and she dries.

'Have you realised that you do not have a shadow?' she says.

I turn to look at her, shocked.

'When did it happen?' she asks.

'When I left the island.'

'You had a shadow there?'

'Yes. When I left she disappeared.' / *And yet, I've never left your side.* / 'When I first left the island, I couldn't even block light, but now I can.' I turn and stretch out to show Maame Yaa what I mean. In the dimly lit kitchen the shadows hang like portraits, but beside me there's only a pale smudge. Maame Yaa's face is neutral, impossible to read. 'The traditional healer at Cape Coast Castle saw it, too; he grabbed me and...' Panic builds in me as I remember him; my breath grows short and my right hand, which is holding a plate I'm cleaning, feels tender. 'He said something to me ... I couldn't understand...' I put the plate down out of fear that I might drop it.

'Don't mind them! They are all charlatans – there to perform for tourists,' Maame Yaa says.

He said he could teach you that through your dreaming you might find me.

'Do you know about shadows?' I ask, tentatively.

'Ask and I can see if I know.'

'Is it normal for them to ... hurt people?'

'What do you mean?'

'If they hurt people, is that normal – or does it mean they're something ... demonic? Like, could they kill someone?' / *Demonic?*

'Well, it's part of you, so it can't kill someone without you yourself being implicated.' Maame Yaa screws up her face as she says this, like she's trying to make me out through fog. 'Do you believe she killed someone?'

'I have this strange memory.' / *Then document, now dream; that curious dance called memory.*

My ears tingle as though tickled by breath, but Maame Yaa is sitting too far away for me to feel her breathing. I pick up the plate and try to continue washing it, but my hands shake and they still feel fragile. I've never told anyone what happened that day or about the night terrors I had afterwards that left me disorientated and confused when I woke up.

'I think she, she might have wounded someone – severely.'

Maame Yaa doesn't react; she looks serious, but only leans closer to listen.

'I've tried so hard to remember exactly what happened. I think I was returning to my room, it was late, and she was holding ... a severed hand or a finger. I think she was holding it – but sometimes it feels like I was the one holding it. I've had nightmares about it for years. But sometimes I can't separate what I remember of the nightmare from what I remember from that day. I don't know whose body it was from or where the rest of the body was. I remember being terrified.'

'But that wasn't the last time you saw her?'

'No, later, I'm not sure if it was days or weeks or longer, she came back, slowly at first. And little by little, I started to feel ok with her being near again. I don't know how long it took for us to be ok with each other after it happened. We never discussed what happened. Then I started getting the nightmares and thought perhaps I'd dreamt the whole thing.'

'She is capable only of what you yourself are capable of. If you were six or seven, it's unlikely you would have been able to really harm someone in the way you're describing.'

'She always felt older than me, though – could she be older than me?'

Maame Yaa takes my hands and turns me to face her. 'If she is this fearsome being that might have killed someone and then cut off their finger, why would you want her back?'

It's an impossible question to answer. I am afraid, and maybe I've always been afraid of Amarie. But the fear also feels like a betrayal. What if she is the best and the darkest of me, and losing her – the complete loss of her, if it becomes irreversible – what if it is the loss of some essential part of myself? As hard as I try, in the moment, I can't form these feelings into words to share with Maame Yaa.

We finish washing and drying the plates in silence. When we're done, Maame Yaa leads me out to the back garden and we sit at the wooden picnic table and chairs. She sees me looking at the metal fence and says, 'It's to keep the yard in and the forest out. They do it in abrokyire.'

'I feel good here,' I tell her. 'Aunt Grace thought I was crazy when I said I wanted to stay longer, but I felt like being here might … answer some questions, not just about my mother, but also about me – fill a hole … do you know what I mean?'

'Don't mind your Aunt Grace. You have come back to fetch your essence.' She says it matter-of-factly, as though it's a daily task, like washing the dishes or going to the river to collect water. 'This is between you and Nyame.' / *The one who knows and sees all. I spoke his name to you once, back on the island* / 'So you don't mind what any of them have to say,' Maame Yaa says. 'Did anyone ever tell you how Lion discovered the mirror?'

I think of Kwaku and the mirror he held up to me; how I saw Amarie reflected in it. 'No,' I answer, and she begins.

'This is my story, which I share with you. It may be sweet, it may not be sweet, take some and share and let some come back to me.'

Lion sat staring into the river at his reflection. It had been many years since he had seen himself and he was pleased to see how he'd grown. Frankly, he was beautiful. He decided he should carry his own image with him always. So, he needed to look for a way to take the river water with him wherever he went so he could keep a part of himself, with himself, forever. That day, Lion walked back and forth across the river, the savannah, and the forests, looking for a container he could easily carry. If only he could find this thing, he would never feel alone again. Lion attempted to use a split coconut shell. Although it held water, it didn't give a good reflection and he struggled to carry it when he moved. He tried a banana skin, and though he could carry it very well in his mouth, it did not hold water well at all. He tried half the skin of a passion fruit; this did not hold the water well and was not so easy to carry. By the end of the third day of experimenting, Lion lay down by the river with a headache. As he hung his head over the edge, he looked at his reflection in the water and it eased his pain. Anansi the spider man emerged from the trees, laughing. Lion turned around, preparing to pounce on the trickster, but before he could spring onto him, Anansi jumped into the trees and hung upside down, just out of reach, on the highest, thinnest branch.

'Little Lion, what have you been doing? If I told people the things I've seen these past few days, your crown would be taken from you. King of the Jungle? Ha! You have behaved like a servant toad, a curious baboon.'

'Go away, spider man. Your trickery is not welcome here.'

'What were you doing? Maybe I can help.'

Deflated, Lion told Anansi his story, 'I recently left the pride, and the lions I grew up with are no longer my family. I will have to create my own pride now. It is our way, but it is a lonely path. I came across my reflection in the river and thought I should carry it with me, for as long as I am able, until I make my own pride. I was looking for a container that would hold the river water and allow me to carry myself with me – always.'

Still hanging upside down, the spider man smiled wide, 'Lion, Lion, Lion! I should have come to your aid much sooner. Had I known what your foolishness was about I could have helped and put an end to your silly search, quick-fast! Take the leaf from the cocoa tree, fold it carefully in half and dip it in the river water twice then let it dry. Once dry, place it on the red dirt path at the outside edge of the forest and roll it three times. Then walk to the darkest corner of the forest, where you will find a lake fortified with silver particles and salts. Dip the leaf into it, but only for a very few seconds, then leave it out to dry in the sun for five days. You must do everything precisely – any variation might cause an error in the results. When you have finished, you will have a surface that will allow you to see your own reflection. It will be thin and light and you will be able to carry it in your mouth or I can put a string through it, and you can carry it around your neck.'

'Can I trust you?' asked Lion.

'Do you have an alternative?' smiled Anansi.

Lion did as Anansi instructed: he found the leaf from the cocoa tree and performed the actions as he was told. He folded it, dipped it twice in river water, and rolled it thrice in the red dirt at the edge of the forest. When he finally brought the leaf to the silver-fortified lake, he heard Anansi's words, 'You must do everything precisely – any variation might cause an error.' But

Lion couldn't remember how long Anansi had told him to dip the leaf in the silver lake, was it five seconds or four or perhaps it was three?

'Anansi!' he called, wanting to ask the spider man.

No one responded.

Holding the leaf in his mouth, Lion dipped it into the silver pool and began to count: one, two, three, four. Finally, he pulled it out. Nothing bad happened. He was pleased. He would leave it to dry and come back to fetch it in five days.

When Lion came back to find his leaf, Anansi had made a little hole at the top and tied a string through it, and he stood holding it out.

'You've done it,' Anansi said, placing it around Lion's neck, where it hung like a large medallion. Lion looked down at it and tilted the mirror to face him with his paw. He saw his reflection and smiled – he had done it! But then, the strangest thing happened: his reflection opened its mouth and let out a deafening roar. The sound made his eyes water. Lion ran around, trying to get away from it, but the noise followed him everywhere he went. He tried to take the thing off his neck, but it was stuck. He hit it against tree trunks and stumps, but nothing worked. He came to a rock and beat the mirror against it until it shattered and the sound of his own roar finally stopped.

'Anansi!' growled Lion.

Anansi was dangling upside down from a thin branch on a tree just above Lion's head. 'Don't blame me, your Highness. I told you to keep it in the silver lake for a precise number of seconds; three is the best, but you chose four. Three would allow you to see your reflection – anything else will allow you to see what you need to see,' Anansi chuckled.

'I will do it again, this time for three seconds.'

'Sorry, Lion, each of us can use the silver pool only once every seven years. So, you can either sit by the river and look at yourself for seven years or go out and make your pride.' With that, Anansi vanished into thin air and all that was left behind him was a silk thread, dangling from a branch, blowing in the breeze.

Two Sisters

'She is capable only of what you yourself are capable of. If you were six or seven, it's unlikely you would have been able to really harm someone in the way you're describing.'

'She always felt older than me, though – could she be older than me?' / *I have been here all along. But this particular me – this moment of 'two hands touching' – this us that we are, this came to be at your conception. Then I, like all the others of my form, I was with you and also, everywhere.*

This is our story, which I share with you. Is it sweet? Is it not sweet? Take some and share, and let some come back to me.

The blue jay squawked at the passing traffic on Melrose Avenue. A steady stream of cars rumbled along the residential road, taking the shortcut home to avoid the traffic of the main streets. But this convenience for them congested the residential road, creating traffic that didn't belong there. The bird, sitting on the windowsill, shrieked at the cars as if telling them off. Its cry, though reproachful, blended with the chug-chugging of the vehicles creeping along. And so the cars and the bird created their own harmony – belonging to each other as neither could have imagined.

On Melrose Avenue stands a blue house with a white roof that looked very much like the doll's house Pa Kwasi brought back from Singapore on his first and only trip to sea. The doll's house was a gift for his daughters when they were still too young to think of destinies and lost souls; when the twins were still twins and Faith was still called the second born after them, still the youngest and not the middle sister. Before tragedy had touched the family. Before anyone had ideas of studying abroad; before babies were left in countries that grew cold enough to snow. Back then, before all the befores, everyone in the house at Tema, Community 12, was enthralled by the blue doll's house with its white roof. The neighbourhood children would come and peer through the window to look at it – 'You see the big toy from abrokyire?' they would say. But in this time, in New Jersey, USA, in a real blue house with a white roof, in the attic which some-one has had the self-assurance to call an apartment and rent out to a young preacher and his new wife for more than they can comfortably afford, Esi, Pa Kwasi's eldest daughter, sat on a brown leather sofa looking at her sister, not quite believing she was in front of her.

Faith seemed fake, like something Esi had dreamt up. Like she might melt away with the breeze if only Esi could get to the window and open it to let the air in. Faith's hair was wrong, the weave didn't sit right on her scalp; her clothes, her breath – none of it fitted. The song of the blue jay, the sound of the rush-hour cars, Esi's breath – all of these things had come to work in time with the place, creating their own rhythm. Faith sat cross-legged, hands clasped in her lap, breathing out of time.

'I need your help.'

'I heard you the first time,' Esi said.

'Then why are you just staring at me?'

'I told you my answer on the phone, and you still came. It's a long way to travel to make me repeat myself.'

It had been nearly three years since they had last seen each other. It was that day at Kotoka Airport when Faith had left for London. Kisi, her daughter, had cried so much she made her eyes swell. The only way Esi could calm her niece down was by promising that her mother would stay in London only briefly, that she would be back in no time at all. Esi also had to promise that she, Esi, would never go away. She promised that she would always be there, right beside Kisi and Pa Kwasi and the family. At the time, Esi didn't know that these words of comfort would become a lie so soon; that she too would leave her niece and her family not more than a year after her sister had gone.

'I hoped you'd change your mind,' Faith said. 'I thought if you saw me … I thought we'd be able to think of something, together.'

'You're not a child.'

'You've grown so cold. Has America done this to you?'

Esi smirked, 'Don't give America all the credit.'

'If Pa could hear you.'

'Then go, go tell him your situation. He told you never to bring him another grandchild out of wedlock.' Esi moved to the window and opened it. The blue jay turned on the sill to look at her.

'What do you want from me?' Faith asked.

'Grow up!' Esi shouted.

The blue jay jumped from the ledge, hovered in mid-air looking back at them, then flew down towards the snaking traffic. Faith picked up her bag and coat.

'Where will you go?' Esi asked.

'Does it matter?'

Even after she had left, Esi felt Faith was still in her home; something of her lingered. Esi poured herself another whiskey and drank it in a single gulp. She opened the top drawer of the sideboard and took out the envelope. She read it again and willed the tears to come. They wouldn't. When Malcolm came home, she was sitting curled on the sofa with the letter on her lap and an empty glass in her hand.

'Will you stop looking at that thing?' he said, pulling her up towards him. The letter fell to the floor.

Esi buried her face in his shoulder, partly for comfort and partly to hide the smell of alcohol on her breath.

'Everything we need, we've got,' he said.

She forgot herself and kissed him hard on the cheek, 'They'll say that you shouldn't have married me. That you're too young to be stuck with such a woman.'

He pulled away at the smell of her breath, 'You've been drinking.'

'I had an unexpected visitor.'

'Who?'

'A relative.'

'What did they want – to stay for six months with free room and board? Someone to marry to get a green card?'

'Stop it.' She turned away from him and he pulled her back into his arms.

'I'm just playing. But that one cousin of yours, though – eesh!' He squeezed her tighter and rocked her slightly. 'So, who was it?'

'It doesn't matter, I didn't give them much time ... I'm not sure if I did the right thing.'

'You did what you thought was best.'

'You know, in Ghana, we don't really have the idea of family in the way you do here.'

'Yeah, that's right. It's more of a community feel: "It takes a village to raise a child", right? I love that approach, much better than how we do it here.' He started to talk about the ways of the Africans, how they were far superior to that of the Americans. She had stopped challenging him recently. She tried to let the rhythm of his clichés and hopes cleanse her wounds. She let him talk and didn't finish what she'd started to say – that sometimes in Ghana if a woman finds herself pregnant and unable to look after the child, members of her family take on the responsibility of raising the child as their own. She let him talk about the beautiful, noble ways of Africans, while lying on the floor was the letter that told her she would never have children of her own.

The Build

Sheets of corrugated iron and splintered wood litter the ground and entrap the bushes. 'You can stay with me,' Maame Yaa says. 'For as long as you need – permanently!'

'No.' Aunt Esi shakes her head. 'I will build it again.'

'The storms are becoming more frequent, and stronger. Will you build each time?'

'Better each time,' Aunt Esi says.

'It will need to be *much* better,' Maame Yaa says.

'I'll help,' I offer.

'You're supposed to leave tomorrow,' Aunt Esi says, dismissively.

'I'll take the tro-tro another time. I want to stay and help,' I insist.

'It takes time to build. More than a week or two.'

'The visa is for three months,' I tell her, 'and my return ticket isn't booked.'

Aunt Esi is quiet for a long time, long enough for us to take her silence as agreement.

'So, she stays,' Maame Yaa says finally. 'You will both stay with me until the building is finished.'

Aunt Esi looks like she might argue, but Maame Yaa waves her hand and it's decided.

'First, we must choose what to build with,' Maa says.

'The same as before.'

'Where will you get the materials?' Maa asks.

'We'll go to Kumasi or even Accra. We can take the tro-tro tomorrow as planned, yes that's it – we'll go to Accra and we'll use the time to also tell Grace that Imani is staying here to help.'

Maame Yaa turns to me, 'Your aunty wanted to live the

traditional Ghanaian life, but she came to the village and lived outside it. Then she built a home like the shanty huts in the city slums.'

Aunt Esi pulls a face.

Maame Yaa pulls out an iron sheet from its entanglement with the bush, 'Do you see the people in the village living like this, in tin cans?' She shakes her head, 'You want to be traditional, use what we have.'

'Dust?' I ask.

'Why not?' Maame Yaa says firmly, 'And the forest. What is my home built from?'

'Bricks,' Aunt Esi replies.

'Weren't they dust once? In the village, houses are made with mud and roofed with palm leaves. When I was a child, all homes were built this way.' From the ground, she picks up a handful of copper-coloured dust and lets it fall through her fingers, 'That's tradition. Not your Accra-style metal hut.'

We need a measuring stick; a long blade; a cutlass; buckets – several of them; a hoe; water; red soil; the grey soil found under certain bushes in the centre of the forest; grass – dried out; muddy hands; and wet feet. We walk to the village to ask for buckets and tools and when people hear what we're doing, they offer to help. The storm left most of the village unharmed and what damage there was has already been fixed. The boys bring water from the river in borrowed buckets and stay on to help, and later others arrive. The older women who don't want to get involved in the dirty work bring food throughout the day. Kukua, a young woman, stays with the elders, providing refreshments. She's been told not to get involved, not just because she's pregnant – that's never a reason for a woman not to work – but because she's lost three children already and if she loses this one her husband will be forced to take a second wife.

My first job is to cut the long grass, bring it back and lay it out to dry. Once it has all turned yellow, I have to mix it together with soil and water. There is some dispute about whether the dried grass should be added or not, but Maame Yaa insists it's better that way.

'She's following foreign practices,' a woman in a green head-scarf says, not so quietly.

'Foreign?' Maame Yaa shoots back, 'Akan nations have used grass for centuries, and in the northern region the people there still use it today. Don't speak nonsense to me because you don't know your history!'

The woman in the green headscarf responds that we rarely use grass in this area, but the white woman told Maame Yaa to use it, and ever since then she must always use grass as the whites instructed.

'What white woman?' I ask.

'Nonsense,' Maame Yaa says, and as she walks away, she shouts something back in Twi that makes the woman in the headscarf bow her head. But Maame Yaa doesn't come back to the build for the rest of the day. In the evening, back at her place, I ask what it had all been about.

'Don't mind them,' she says. 'Not all stories are good. Some stories are a curse on the teller, the told, and the one who cries for the lies that have been set down as the truth!'

After she's said that, it is difficult to ask any more.

The next morning, as we walk to the building site alone, Aunt Esi explains that there was some bitterness in the community about how close Maame Yaa had got to missionaries in her youth. They had favoured her and taught her to read and write and speak English. The sister of Betty Akwetey, the woman in the green headscarf, was Maame Yaa's age-mate and she had passed her bitterness to her younger siblings.

'There's still a lot of envy from that time,' Aunt Esi says. 'And now she has that big house, there are new reasons to be jealous. Maa says I isolate myself from the people, but I have my reasons. You see it now,' she says, shaking her head.

We moisten the ground with water and start to pile the grass and earth mixture to create the outer walls. It is slow, dirty work, but satisfying. We'd previously marked out the floor space and had decided we would build Aunt Esi a bigger home. Nii Boakye, Kukua's husband, suggests having an internal kitchen that opens out into a courtyard, so Aunt Esi can cook inside but the smelly stuff can still be prepared outside. Maame Yaa says we must have a gate, to keep the yard in and the forest out – like hers. I'm waiting for the outer walls to be completed so I can create a mural on the side, although I haven't decided what it will be and I haven't mentioned it to anyone yet. Everybody has suggestions about the build and, besides me, no one is shy about sharing them.

We come home early to cook for those who will join us for dinner after the day of working on the build. I'm chopping okra and waiting until it is just me and Maame Yaa in the kitchen. When my moment comes, I ask, 'Maa, do you remember the conversation we had a while ago … about my shadow?'

'Yes, do you feel her coming near?'

'I don't know.'

'In time.'

'But you said that before.'

'And it didn't stop being true.'

'Nana, can I help?' a voice says and someone steps into the kitchen.

I don't turn around, keeping my back to the person who has entered; I make a show of concentrating on the chopping.

'Don't call me Nana,' Maame Yaa says, 'I'm too young to be Nana. Please help Comfort pound the yam outside. She looks tired. If she sleeps too tired this night, she won't be back in the morning to build.'

There are always people in Maame Yaa's house these days and there is never any privacy. I slam the knife into the chopping board with each lunge, taking my frustration out on the vegetables. The door rattles as the person who entered leaves.

'Boat said something to me the night they took me to the Osu Night Market,' I say, trying to begin the conversation again.

'I didn't know the boy spoke English.'

'He doesn't. A little. He said Dosu would heal me.'

'And is it not doing so?'

'Yes, but I thought he meant something … *more*.'

'Give it time,' she says, and I want to scream.

Each morning, we have no idea which of the people from the village will turn up to help with the build, or when. We don't know whether they'll stay for half or the whole day, and we don't know who will stay on for dinner at Maame Yaa's afterwards, or who will stay after that and sleep over. One day I said goodbye to Nii Boakye, Kukua's husband; he'd stayed the whole day and had come back for dinner. On his way out he said, 'See you tomorrow,' but he didn't turn up again until the following week. This takes me some time to get used to. Aunt Esi seems less frustrated about it than me, but not altogether happy. She's started complaining of nausea and headaches and I think it's an excuse so she can continue to sleep in a room by herself without having to share her bed with the various people who decide to stay over each night.

I should find my own coping strategy. Despite my frustrations about the coming and going, we are never short of hands to help and the food in the evenings somehow always stretches to whoever is there. In this way, with the constant ebb and flow of people, Aunt Esi's new house slowly takes shape.

A Prayer

Aunt Esi and I had gone for a walk. She'd wanted some air because she felt a headache coming on, and I insisted on going with her. She was quiet initially, but after a while she recovered herself and we wander and talk without a destination.

'You should let me do your hair before you go back to Accra,' she says, looking at my head disapprovingly.

'Since I arrived in Ghana, everyone's always trying to do my hair or buy me new clothes!'

She laughs. Aunt Esi has had her braids changed three times since I first arrived, and I can't imagine going to that sort of effort to do my own hair.

'I've been thinking.'

'About hair and clothes?' she asks.

'About being here, and what happens when the build's finished...'

She stops walking and drinks from the bag of ice water she's carrying. She nods for me to continue.

'I've been thinking about staying on – or, I mean, coming back.'

'Here you mean?'

'Yes ... permanently.'

As we arrive back at Maame Yaa's house, I hold my breath waiting for her response to what I've said. But there is a note on the door and her focus is on that. She pulls it down and as she reads it, her face falls. It says that Kukua has gone into labour and Maame Yaa has gone to assist. Aunt Esi and I hurry to Kukua's home. When we reach the circular mud-house there is a crowd of about thirty waiting outside and Nii is among them. Those gathered are silent and all of the noises come from inside – shouts, screams, cries, calls – but not the sound of a baby.

Maame Yaa's face appears at the small window. 'Come inside,' she says looking at me.

I turn to look behind me, 'Me?' I ask.

'Hurry up!' she shouts and I half-stumble, half-fall into the house as I'm pushed by Aunt Esi and a dozen other hands.

The room smells of salt and bog. Five women huddle around Kukua. Her face is wet with sweat and her eyes are large, tired and bloodshot. She's propped up on the floor with her legs wide; there is a mess of brown, and tendrils of red dangle and weep from between her thighs. Something hangs from between her, like the limb of a broken doll. I look at Maame Yaa, my breath caught in my throat. What can she possibly want from me in this situation?

'Lay your hands on her and pray,' she says, beckoning me to come close.

I look at her dumbfounded.

'Put your hands on the girl's head and say a prayer,' she says tersely.

'I c-can't. I don't know if … if I believe any more.'

Maame Yaa kisses her teeth, 'Don't make me lose my temper with you.' After a deep intake of breath, she says, 'Your faith is not important right now. It is what she believes that matters. Hurry up and don't make me repeat myself – or you will regret it.'

I put my hand on Kukua's head; her hair is wet and spongy to my touch. She looks up at me with hope and adoration. I'm terrified. I try to call the words. Nothing comes. I was never taught to pray aloud. Mother, the Bishop, senior nuns, they prayed out loud – the rest of us did it silently. I think of the salt-and-pepper storyteller at the night market, how the rhythm of his words had made me feel. I remember the story Maame Yaa told me about the lion. The night market teller and Maa both used a similar invocation; I try to remember it, and say it silently to myself: This is my story, which I share with you. If it be sweet or if it not be sweet, take some and share, and let some come back to me. Then I begin: the words tumble out like folklore, sure and steady of their own weight, moving towards their own conclusion. Maame Yaa nods in approval and pats my arm. She speaks gently to Kukua in Twi, and I realise I've never actually talked to Kukua. I'm not sure she even understands English, which makes the situation even stranger, but I continue letting the words come.

Kukua screams. My hand remains on her head, wet with her sweat. I close my eyes and the prayer keeps coming. She jerks back and forth and my palm follows her, moving with her rhythm. Maame Yaa consults one of the other women. I sense movement from the other side of the room, but I don't open my eyes. Kukua sobs and rocks beneath my palm and I plead in prayer for her, and for her child: Let them be ok, please.

The cry of a baby cuts through the noise and heat, and relief surges through the room. I open my eyes to see Maame Yaa easing the small bundle out of Kukua. They're still attached, and some-one is separating them.

/ What's an umbilical cord?

It's what links you to your creator, Mother had said. /

As the umbilical cord is being cut, Kukua's head falls back and away from my palm; she lands on her side and convulses. Her pupils slip backwards, making her eyes appear white. The woman between Maa and Kukua finishes cutting the cord and another woman struggles to put a pillow under Kukua's head to stop her from repeatedly hitting it on the ground. Maame Yaa, who is still holding the baby, signals and someone appears from the shadows to escort me out of the house. I'm no longer wanted.

Outside, the sun has set and the crowd has thinned. Aunt Esi stands by the door with a small number of others. Heads poke out of the windows of nearby homes as we emerge. They look disappointed to see it's only me. The woman guiding me out hands me over to my aunt like a sack of overripe fruit. Aunt Esi takes me to a nearby bench. The few remaining people return to their homes and Nii joins us on the bench.

Hours later, we're still there. Nii has collapsed into an uncomfortable sleep, and Aunt Esi and I rest on each other, staring at the round house.

'If we'd been in the city, they would both be alive,' Aunt Esi says.

'You think they're…?'

'I guess,' she says. 'If it was good news, we would have heard them jubilating by now.'

Nii, who looked like he was sleeping, lifts his head, 'It is not true, Aunty,' he says in slow but sure English. 'She will be very fine. The sister from abrokyire prayed for her.'

Aunt Esi puts an arm around him and apologises for what she's said.

'It is dawn,' Nii says, 'and miracles happen in the morning time. Kukua will be fine.'

'I pray she will,' Aunt Esi says.

The three of us sit, keeping vigil over the house.

Aunt Esi stands. Nii and I had both fallen asleep beside her on the bench and we wake and stand up, disorientated.

Maame Yaa comes out of the house and crosses over to us.

'Nana?' Nii calls, desperation in his voice.

'I've told you people before,' Maame Yaa says, 'I don't want to be called Nana just yet. Mother and child are both fine.'

Aunt Esi hugs her. Nii cries out and falls to his knees. I reach for him and wipe tears of relief from my cheeks. Our noise breaks the quiet and the dogs start to bark from left and right, in people's houses and maybe even the wild ones from the bush. The barking grows; people come out to see what the noise is about and the jubilation Aunt Esi expected begins. We are fed and celebrated by everyone, as though Aunt Esi and I had personally delivered the child with Maame Yaa and the others. Every time we try to leave, someone finds a reason for us to stay; we must come and greet this person, so-and-so wants us to drink something at his house, Aunty such-and-such wants to feed us. There isn't a full-on party – not because Aunt Esi was insisting that the mother and child need to sleep, but because Maame Yaa said we would not enjoy the party well enough if we were tired. It would be best to rest now and plan the party properly, so that we can all really enjoy it. Then finally we are allowed to leave. As we say our final goodbye to Kukua and Nii, he smiles at me and says, 'You see, Sister, I tell you, morning is a time for miracles.'

Traditional Rites

I swirl the river water in the bucket and use my hands to wash the mud off the sides before pouring it back out into the stream. The build is nearly over; we have only the gate to mount. We've come to the river to clean the tools we no longer need. Everyone is by the river, then I notice Aunt Esi and Maame Yaa sitting in the distance on a cluster of roots that link two large trees. I pick up my bucket and run towards them, desperate to have a few minutes alone with them.

Maame Yaa smiles as she sees me approaching. 'I was just discussing you with your aunt. That perhaps we should arrange something for you before you leave.'

I sit on the grass at her feet.

'Some sort of initiation, to help with the healing you keep talking about.'

'Look at her,' Aunt Esi says, and I think she's talking about me, but she's looking past me, at someone by the river; it's Kukua – she has Baby Akwesi wrapped around her back and is bending over to help Nii clean tools in the water.

'She's doing all of that work and it was just a few days ago she gave birth. Me, when I get my headaches, I have to take the whole afternoon off.'

'That family is secure now,' Maame Yaa says, nodding happily.

'Is it true, then?' I ask. 'I heard there was talk that he would leave her if she wasn't able to have this child, but I didn't believe it.'

'He wouldn't have left,' Maame Yaa says. 'She's had three miscarriages, but he wouldn't have left her.'

'He might have taken another wife,' Aunt Esi says, and Maame Yaa doesn't contradict her.

'The pressure was from his mother,' Maa says quietly. 'Anyway, we gave him a son, so now he'll stay forever.' She chuckles.

Aunt Esi doesn't respond, and I suspect it's because she has too much to say and not too little.

'You see how she carries him?' Maame Yaa says. 'We do this for three main reasons – the first is for touch; touch is essential for infant development. The second is that his position at her back, where his head is placed, is actually very close to her heart. The beat of the heart calms the baby and it gives him rhythm. This is why all Ghanaians can dance, because in their first years they moved to the rhythm of their mother's heart.'

/ *She's got rhythm, Mrs O'Shea said. All black people have.* /

'The third reason, and this is most important for girls, the third reason is that the way they have the baby's legs when it is on the back, it helps for the proper development of the pelvic bone. This is necessary for childbirth, to allow birthing without complications. It's why we have so few caesareans in Ghana.'

Aunt Esi is staring at the young family, but she doesn't say a word.

'You said something about healing, Maa?' I ask.

'Yes, first I was thinking we could do something straightforward, like pour libation. Because they didn't pour libation for you when you first arrived – to ask the ancestors to bless your path. But then I started thinking, perhaps something more specific to your stage of life and being a woman. So I'm thinking Bragoro,' she says.

'What's that?'

'This is not Christian, Maa, these things are not Christian,' Aunt Esi says.

'It's tradition,' Maame Yaa responds.

'But … there are some issues, no?'

'What's Bragoro?' I ask again.

'It's a rite into womanhood,' Maa says. 'The women gather,' her voice falls into the rhythm of her storytelling, 'there is an older woman – me – and a mother figure – you,' she says pointing at Aunt Esi. 'And there will be others, too. We bring you here, to the river, and wash you – three times – and we cream your body with shea butter. On the ceremonial day, you're seated with a bowl of food in front of you. We give you pepper.'

'It symbolises adversity,' Aunt Esi says, half-heartedly.

'It's for life's difficulties that will surely come. We give you salt, for the times when things taste as they should. Each time we give you, you take a little, three times. We give a boiled egg, you swallow it, you must not chew. It is your womb. The rest of the food is left in the bowl and we place cloth over your eyes. Then we call the children to come and eat. As they approach the bowl, you must try to catch them, and they too must try to run away. The number of children you catch and the sex, that will be the number and sex of the children you will have in life. Then later, we will examine you.'

'For what?'

'To make sure you're still,' she says the final words with care, 'intact.'

'A virgin,' Aunt Esi says bluntly.

'We must check. Then you will be ready to present to the world, to take a husband.'

'What if I don't want to take a husband?'

'Maa, do you hear all this? It sounds...' Aunt Esi begins.

'How will you know if I'm a virgin?'

'Did they teach you nothing in that place?' Aunt Esi snaps, her irritation turning on me. 'What did they do with you in that monastery?' Then she turns to Maame Yaa, 'It's old-fashioned! Nobody does this any more!'

'Maybe we could do something that mixes tradition with something new,' I suggest, trying to offer a third way.

'It's tradition,' Maame Yaa insists.

'But maybe there's a way to choose pieces of the tradition and add them to new things…'

'You don't pick and choose your heritage!' Maa snaps.

'Look at us, neither of us had children…' Aunt Esi says, gesturing between them. 'The custom shows that a woman's only worth is to be a mother; do you agree with that?'

'Speak for yourself!' Maame Yaa says, 'I have been a mother many, many, many times over. I have grandchildren and great-grandchildren in this world, all over the world!'

'Yes, but you've sacrificed many things, too,' Aunt Esi says, gently now, as though choosing her words with care. 'You weren't permitted to love who you wanted to love. Were you?'

Maame Yaa's face turns stony; she is silent for a moment and then she stands. 'You have no right to question an elder, understand?' She moves as though to walk away and then turns back to Aunt Esi, 'You say you came back here for tradition, but you look down your nose at it. In the city, they are dying from the illness. They get pregnant when they've barely stopped being babies themselves. We didn't have the illness when Bragoro rites were observed. Nii's mother, she told me yester-night that nearly all of the young ones from her father's village have gone, dead! When we maintained these things, they regulated our lives. If the tradition is too rough for you, look in your books and find your answers there, but don't talk about my life or my sacrifices as though you understand anything about them!' Maame Yaa turns abruptly and walks to the river where the others are gathered.

It took a few days for things to be ok between them after the disagreement. I never said anything, because for once I knew what they were talking about. Gifty, Kukua's younger sister, had mentioned it to me before. Being the only girl in the village who goes to boarding school in Kumasi, Gifty speaks the most English. It's a point of pride for her that we spend the most time together and she acts as my translator when Aunt Esi and Maame Yaa are busy with one thing or another. Gifty told me what she'd heard, that when Maame Yaa was young she'd been in love with someone she shouldn't have loved. When the elders found out, they forbade it. After that, Maame Yaa swore never to marry or have kids, and that's why she raises other people's children but has none of her own. Gifty said it was so long ago that the people who were there at the time are either dead or so old their memories fail them, or they were so young at the time that they didn't understand what was going on. Now, there are different stories about exactly what it was that happened. The children say the person she loved was a man from another village, but Gifty knows that's not true. She believes it was a white man. The words hang before me, 'White Man'. I guess Reverend Mother and the sisters would be White Women. I'd never thought of it before.

Gifty said she'd even heard someone say once that the person Maa had loved was a White Woman. She paused after she said it to look at me, waiting for a reaction. A word comes back to me from a forgotten place: 'Lesbian'. Harold's mum said it was when a woman kissed another woman. Then he got in trouble at school when he tried to look it up on Yahoo. I asked Gifty what's wrong with a woman being in love with another woman? She looked at me for a moment, then laughed as though I was joking. When I saw her reaction, I decided not to ask my other question: what's wrong with someone from the village loving a white person? I remembered what Maame Yaa had said about some stories being bad for the teller, the told and the person the story was about. This was probably one of those occasions, so I changed the subject.

Her Grandmother's Face

This is our story, which I share with you:

The village looked like a toy model of itself in the baked afternoon heat. No one was around. The circular clay homes that Dofi had known from childhood visits were always busy with life, but now they stood abandoned. Chickens wandered through the courtyard pecking at grains in the dirt and giving each other a wide berth. There was a repetitive bang, smoosh, bang, smoosh that Dofi recognised as the sound of someone pounding fufu or yam. She walked out of the shade of the tree, her left hand resting unconsciously on her stomach, and made her way towards the noise. Maame Yaa stood in the shadows of the houses, sweating profusely as she pounded the fufu alone.

'Aunty,' Dofi said as she approached the older woman. She was relieved that the only person around was the one person she had hoped to find. Maame Yaa was the elder cousin of her father, Pa Kwasi. As an unmarried woman, she had assisted in the care of most of the children of the family. If there was anyone who could help Dofi in her current predicament, it was Maame Yaa.

Yaa stood pounding fufu and berating her relatives in her head. The entire village had gone to the neighbouring settlement to enjoy their harvest festival celebrations. Yaa's brother, now the big man in the village, insisted that she remain behind to continue preparations for when it would be their turn to receive the neighbouring village. It should have been left to one of the young girls to do this, but her brother had insisted it should be her. First with flattery – 'No one pounds fufu as you do!' – then with a look in his eye that threatened harsher forms of persuasion.

Sweat poured down the side of Yaa's face, and she wiped it with the back of her hand. She ran her tongue along her empty front gums; they felt swollen in the heat, every part of her felt like it was sweating or starting to swell. When she looked up, she thought she saw a ghost. She crossed herself and mumbled a quick prayer.

'Wafaa?' she said. / 'Aunty?' the ghost called.

Yaa held onto the pounding stick as if it were a weapon, poised ready to defend herself if necessary. They both stood looking at each other. The ghost came nearer. It walked with its hand on its stomach.

'It's me, Dofi. Pa Kwasi's middle daughter.'

'Dofi?' Yaa said, relief coursing through her. 'What are you doing here? I thought you were in abrokyire.' Maame Yaa smiled tentatively, revealing her bare gums. 'You look so much like your grandmother, I thought I was receiving a vision from beyond the grave.' Maame Yaa crossed herself again.

Dofi tried to smile, but it only made her look more tired. Yaa set her pounding stick down and motioned for Dofi to sit.

'Tell me what it is – Pa Kwasi and Ma Patience, they're both in good health?'

'As far as I know, yes, yes, there's nothing to worry about with them.'

'Then?'

The two women sat on the dusty floor. Dofi hesitated for a moment, not wanting to dirty her dress, but she felt she needed to humble herself if she was going to ask Maame Yaa to help her.

'How is Kisi?' Maame Yaa asked, enquiring after Dofi's daughter.

'By God's grace, she is well, Maa.' Dofi looked at the ground; she started to pinch the red dust, playing with it absentmindedly as she spoke.

Maame Yaa noticed how Dofi had arrived calling her Aunty and had now switched to Maa, which meant there was mothering to be done.

'Maa, you remember when I was pregnant with Kisi? The trouble it caused? Pa told me never to return home again with a fatherless child?' She continued to look at the ground and pinch the dirt as she spoke.

'But in the years since, I've seen how proud you've made him. He loves Kisi, he has accepted her, everybody sees that. But yes, at the time it was a bad business.' Maame Yaa had an inkling about where the conversation was headed.

'Have you visited your family since you arrived in Ghana, eh?'

'No,' Dofi said.

Pa Kwasi was like a junior brother to Maame Yaa. He had always treated her well. But her feelings for that side of the family were complicated. When Pa Kwasi's parents had first left the village for the city, she had been their house girl. His mother, everyone said, was the most beautiful woman in all Ghana. Her fair-skin, good hair and the gap in her two front teeth drove men to distraction. But the woman was mean.

'You look so like your grandmother,' Maame Yaa said. 'It is only now, seeing you here, that I realise how striking the similarity really is.'

'Thank you.'

'And just now, as I think about it, perhaps your father named you after her.'

'Pardon me?'

'Her name was Wafaa, it means faithfulness. And your Christian name, Faith, it makes you her namesake, no?'

'Yes, I suppose so; I never realised.' Dofi's fingers continued to fidget and unsettle the dust. 'I need help, Aunty, Maa, please.'

Maame Yaa felt tempted to ask who the father of this new child was, but she resisted the urge. Don't get involved, she told herself. Dofi, sitting, weeping before Maame Yaa, should have incited feelings of sympathy. Maame Yaa's tendency to rescue and protect should have been flared by the sight of this young woman in need.

But Dofi really looked too much like Wafaa and instead Maame Yaa kept thinking that she should really get back to pounding the fufu.

When the whites arrived in Dosu there was a lot of excitement and tension about their presence. They talked about building a school and improving the infrastructure of the village, but some of the elders had their suspicions. Wafaa, for all her beauty, was slow to learn. Maame Yaa, a teenager at the time, was the younger and less beautiful of the two, but she was quick and clever. The whites showed favour to Yaa and gave her preferential treatment concerning some matters. Wafaa was not used to being favoured less and didn't take to it well. Maame Yaa didn't know if it was spite that made Wafaa do it, but she went to the village elders and told them she had seen Yaa in a compromising position with a white. No one asked Yaa if it was true – Wafaa the Beauty had reported it, therefore it was as good as gospel. The elders unanimously agreed that Yaa should be punished. When her father said he could not to do it, the responsibility was passed to his brother. Yaa's mother insulted her husband for his inability to perform his duty; she called him a coward and insisted on staying in the room to watch her brother-in-law beat her daughter. Yaa had believed that her mother's actions were borne of shame and a desire to make sure her daughter was adequately punished. Later, Yaa realised, her mother had done so to protect her child. During the beating, her uncle displayed a violent nature that was previously unknown. He beat her so badly that he knocked out her front teeth and left her bedridden for months. Had her mother not been in the room, the beating could have gone much further.

'So, Maa, will you take the baby?' Dofi asked.
Looking into her face, Maame Yaa could see only Wafaa's eyes,

Wafaa's cheeks, Wafaa's complexion, a lopsided weave sitting awkwardly on Wafaa's head. Then she said to Wafaa's granddaughter, 'You have your grandmother's beauty. She was coddled in life. Everyone looked after her. Our side of the family, your grandfather's side, we're not like that. We meet the consequences of our actions and we stand on our own feet – I hope you take after us in this regard.'

Return

The wooden gate looks like it's grown from the earth to surround Aunt Esi's plot of land. It does the much-needed job of
keeping the house and yard in and the forest out, and it is the
last thing to be completed. We gather together to eat; there are
sixty or so people sitting inside and outside the confines of the
gate, which is open to allow for the coming and going that's happening. Some of the older boys from the village have brought
drums and play beyond the gate; a small group dances beside
them. Maame Yaa weaves between people, sharing a moment
with one, telling another person off, teasing everyone as she
goes. Aunt Esi has been missing for some time; she'd been feeling nauseous so went to lie down. Now that everyone is here,
and just as I get up to go and find her, she reappears and says
she's feeling better. Maame Yaa sees her and immediately clinks
her glass with a spoon to get people's attention. The drummers
take a while to notice, but an aunty shouts for them to be quiet
and everything falls silent. Maame Yaa thanks everyone for
coming. She says a prayer of thanks for Baby Akwesi, Kukua
and Nii's first-born son, and she prays that God blesses them
with more children. She continues in Twi and then switches
back to English, thanking God for bringing me, her granddaughter, safely to Ghana and allowing me to spend time in my
ancestral village. She says that with every day that passes she
sees my spirit strengthen. She thanks everyone for welcoming
her daughter, Aunt Esi, back to the village and asks that God
bless them all abundantly for helping her to build a new sturdier
home in the traditional way. She then turns to address Aunt Esi
in Twi and Aunt Esi shakes her head.

'No, no, I can't Maa,' she says in English. 'I've been feeling unwell all day.'

Maame Yaa insists, and Aunt Esi reluctantly says a few words to the crowd. They explode into cheers in reply and Maame Yaa seems about to demand that she says more, but Aunt Esi cuts her off, 'What I would *really* like is if you would tell some stories, Maa.'

Maame Yaa beams at the request and forgets what she had been about to say. The sun sets with Maame Yaa telling stories to those gathered within the gate; some in English, for my benefit, and many in Twi, which I listen to for their music.

'Sit in front of me,' Aunt Esi says. She is sitting on her bed with a cushion on the floor between her legs.

I sit on the cushion obediently. Aunt Grace, Afua and Adjoa arrived in Dosu two days ago with Boat. We'll travel back to Accra together later in the week and then I'll leave for England a few days after that. The thought of going back feels strange, like returning to someone else's life. This afternoon might be the last time in a long while that Aunt Esi and I are alone together, so I do as she asks and I sit in front of her; trying to make the most of the moment. She brings out a comb and a bottle of Pink Moisturiser and begins to pick at my hair. I flinch from instinct and move away.

'I don't like people doing my hair.'

She pulls me back, 'I'm not people.' She picks at the bottom of my hair with the comb, adding a blob of pink lotion to a small patch, before picking at it some more. It softens the hair and she teases larger sections out easily as she goes.

'You can wear your hair as you like in Dosu, but you're going back to the city and the rules are different there.'

'No one said anything before.'

'Are you sure?' she asks, and I can hear the smile in her voice. 'You were a foreigner then. Now you've been here long enough to know better. And you've been living with me, so people will judge me as well.' Her fingers knead my hair and I'm surprised that it isn't painful. 'Have you thought about what you'll do when you go back to England?'

'Get another visa and come back.'

She laughs.

'I'm leaving because Aunt Grace says I have to.'

She tugs the back of my head gently as she untangles a thicket of curls. 'Grace is right – you can't just stay like that. Even if the visa wasn't an issue. You have to see the sisters; you don't just disappear from people like that.'

'But I can come back, right?'

'Of course. You need to consider what you will do – will you study in one of the cities? Work? You must think everything through. Keep your head still,' she says, nudging my head back into place. 'You will always have a home with me. I'm only telling you to think through your plans and lay your foundations well.'

With the comb, she separates out a new section of my hair, applies another dollop of pink lotion and works her way through my hair gently.

'There's an American writer–'

'An African American?' I ask.

'No, a white American, Raymond Chandler – in a letter to a friend he wrote that we should not try to build castles on cobwebs. He was talking about the tendency to want things quickly, not taking the time to ensure that you're building on solid foundations. You've had a nice time here, ok, we all see that – but think through the situation and plan properly. Grace, in her own way, is saying to you don't rush, make sure you're building on something solid.'

I sit quietly as she finishes plaiting my hair, taking in everything she says. When she's finished, she puts a small mirror in my hands and holds it up to my face. She takes another mirror and moves it around behind my head. I turn from side to side to see the back of my head reflected through both mirrors. My features look more defined, better framed by the new hairstyle. I thank her.

'You're welcome,' she says, standing up and moving to tidy things away. I reach for her arm to stop her.

'What you said about spider webs and strong foundations…'

'Yes?'

'You're right, a spider web is not a solid foundation, but only if you see it in a particular way. If you look at it differently, it's the most solid thing there is.'

'You can't just choose how to see things – some things merely are.'

'The spider's web is flimsy,' I tell her. 'You swat it and it's gone. It doesn't hold anything heavier than a fly. The castle is big and strong, and it might not even be just a castle, it could be a fort to keep enemies out … or a place to enslave people. But, in another way, the castle is just a home or a fort or a prison. The spider's web is its home, and it provides food because it's how the spider catches its prey. For particular species, if they make their web beautiful enough, it will help them attract a mate. Some male spiders produce a sperm web that gets them ready to mate – it actually makes them fertile. Sister Maria teaches a whole term on arachnids.

'Then there are the spiders that eat their own webs when they're tired, when they can't take any more – and it gives them strength. The spider's web is made from itself; you can find its DNA in its web because it's made of the silk from its own, its own body.' The words trip out unevenly, hurrying forward before she interrupts to explain why I'm wrong.

'So, yes – yes, a castle is big and strong with bricks and stone and metal, and spider webs are flimsy … but then, if you think about it a different way, the cobweb is the best foundation ever: it's versatile, it's for love, new life, family … and … and personal reju-venation, and it's from the self, it's of the self, so perhaps building a castle on these foundations or, or building a castle like a spider builds its web, perhaps that would be the most amazing thing in the world and not stupid at all.' I look up at her, nervous about what she'll say next and how she'll go about proving me wrong.

'You can blame those nuns for a lot of things,' she says, 'you can say the education they gave you had many holes in it, but you can never say they didn't give you words. Eh, you and your words!'

Afua picks at the nail polish on her fingers and squints when a piece breaks off and flies towards her face. 'You were meant to stay for one week and then come back to Accra!' she says.

'Five months – who stays in the village for five months?' Adjoa asks, scandalised.

'I told myself, if she asks me to extend the visa one more time, I will refuse,' Aunt Grace says. 'But now I see you, I see it was good for you – you're a proper Ghanaian now.'

In Aunt Esi's yard, my cousins and aunt sit around a plastic table borrowed from a family in the village. A little away from them, I clean a grasscutter so we can offer some meat to our guests. I hold the limp animal over the hot coals and its fur hisses as it burns. The smoke curls and wafts through the yard and over the gate. The smell is acrid and makes my eyes water; this is why Aunt Esi refuses to do this part in her new indoor kitchen.

'That stinks!' Adjoa says holding her nose.

'You get used to it,' I say, wiping my eyes with the back of my wrist. When did I get used to it?

Aunt Esi steps out of the kitchen with a bowl of water. 'Adjoa, what have you done to your face?' she says.

Adjoa's skin is yellowed with dark patches under her eyes that she's tried to cover with make-up, but it's started to flake at the soft pockets of her eyes.

'Thanks!' Adjoa says. 'You're looking beautiful too.'

'I'm not insulting you. Really, I want to know.'

'Oh, don't mind her,' Aunt Grace says. 'You know these girls, always experimenting with cosmetics.'

'You should be careful,' Aunt Esi warns. 'Some of these things are no good.'

'I'll be careful with *your food*,' Adjoa replies. 'I'm not eating that thing.' She nods at the grasscutter in my hands.

'You have to taste it to know if you like it,' I tell her with a wink, echoing the words she'd said to me at the Osu Night Market several months before. She looks at me blankly, not remembering the reference.

'I'm just cleaning it, that's why it smells so bad. It'll smell better once it's cooked.' I pull it off the fire and scrub the charred fur off in the bowl of water Aunt Esi has put in front of me. Then I hand it to her to gut and season before cooking. 'I'm still too squeamish to do that part myself,' I tell them, and my aunt takes it into the indoor kitchen to begin the next stage of preparation.

Aunt Grace follows her inside, and as she's leaving Afua shouts, 'They spread disease!'

'Rubbish!' Aunt Grace snaps, turning back. 'These children stay in the city and they pick up rubbish ideas. I should send you back here to live with your aunt for a few months like your cousin – then you will learn.'

'She's not completely wrong,' I say. 'If they live by contaminated land or water, they might have something, but the land here's good and the river's clean.'

'See!' Aunt Grace says before disappearing into the kitchen.

'It's very lean meat,' I say to Afua. 'So you can eat plenty without gaining weight.' I say this pointedly, remembering she was concerned about her weight.

Afua sticks her tongue out at me, but I know I've been heard.

'We don't *have* plenty,' Aunt Esi calls from the kitchen. 'We have one between six – at least! Maame Yaa is coming and who knows how many she'll bring with her.' She sticks her head out of the kitchen door, 'If you want to make yourselves useful, you could go to Maame Yaa's and pick some plantains from her tree. If she's not home, pick extra because it means she's in the village and she will bring everyone with her.'

Adjoa pulls a face, but Afua nudges her, they both get up and we all move to go.

'If you walk around that side of the house, you'll see the mural Imani did, it's really wonderful!' she says and then her head vanishes back inside.

'We don't have to walk that way,' I say.

'I want to see what you've done,' Afua says.

'Yes, I'm intrigued,' Adjoa agrees, walking ahead of me.

While Adjoa's ahead of us, I quietly ask Afua how things are going with her boyfriend, the boy who lives at the back of the Night Market. She looks surprised by the mention of him, as we'd never discussed it before. She looks uncomfortable, and whispers that they're no longer together, so I don't ask anything more. Adjoa skips in front of us unaware; she's wearing a duck-egg cotton dress that stops at her knees and has thin floral straps. It billows a little as she gambols along.

'You're admiring my dress?' she says, pleased. 'I actually bought this for you. It has that prim look that you always have, but it still manages to be stylish. I thought it was so cute I decided to try it on and then I had to keep it.'

I laugh at her honesty. 'It looks good on you.'

'We have the same shape – tall, slim, not so curvy – so it would suit you, too. We can do more clothes shopping when we get back to civilisation. One full week in Accra is not enough time to properly shop, but we'll make it work.' She spins around so I can fully appreciate the dress.

'Your elbow still hasn't healed,' I say, noticing her arm.

The graze on her elbow from the day at Cape Coast Castle is a shock of black, like scar tissue from a much bigger accident. It's smudged with blood as though it's recently bled.

'Oh, it's fine,' she says, waving my comment away.

'It's been months ... mine's completely disappeared.' I lift my elbow to show her where my scratch had been.

'It's the creams,' Afua says.

'Shut up!' Adjoa snaps.

'...skin-lightening creams.'

'Why would you try to lighten your skin?' I ask, and the answer comes to me as the question leaves my mouth, and I feel stupid for asking, and guilty. I remember my surprise each time I caught sight of my own reflection at St Teresa's, and it was not a completely neutral feeling. It had something in it, like disappointment. But Adjoa's not on a tiny island where she's the only person that looks like herself, she's surrounded by people who look like themselves in the most magnificent ways. Aunt Esi with fire in her eyes and her braids flowing down her back. Maame Yaa's full afro and her assortment of silk headscarves that she matches to every outfit she wears. Aunt Grace with her skin that shines like marble. Even Afua and Adjoa with their hang-ups are unapologetic in the way they flaunt the things they're proud of, and the sudden realisation that there's something in her reflection that she doesn't like leaves me winded.

Adjoa hasn't responded to my question, and it's Afua who breaks the silence, 'We're the children of a doctor, so we know more than most, those creams thin your skin and if you use them too much, it takes the longest time to heal from even the smallest thing.'

'Is this your mural?' Adjoa says, looking up at the thing I've created.

'Yes,' I answer, feeling the threat in her voice.

She walks towards the wall and looks at all of the little faces carved into the side of the mud-house.

'You did this?' Afua says with awe. 'It's amazing! It's like a jigsaw puzzle made up of lots of little individual pictures.'

'Aunt Esi thought a similar thing,' I tell her.

'So, it's the faces of everyone from the village?' Adjoa says.

'That's what I tried to do.'

'Where are you?' she asks.

'Erm, well, Maame Yaa said...'

'I'm not asking what Maame Yaa said or what Aunt Esi thinks, I'm asking you – where are you in your own picture?'

'No, you're right, I'm not one of the individual faces – no,' I concede, trying to defuse the situation.

'You are very good at looking and seeing others, but can you even see yourself?' she says.

'Leave her, Adjoa,' Afua pleads.

Ignoring her sister, Adjoa continues, 'Why don't you come back and ask me about my elbow when you've figured out what's going on with your whole self!' She walks off, leaving Afua and me standing at the side of the house. The direction she's going in is wrong, but there's no point trying to tell her that.

The scent of hot meat, chilli and ginger fills Aunt Esi's yard, replacing the harshness of smoked hair and skin from earlier in the day. Just as the grasscutter is done, Maame Yaa arrives holding Baby Akwesi; with her are Gifty, Kukua, Nii and his two brothers and two older women from the village. Maame Yaa hands the baby to me. 'Your son came to say goodbye,' she says.

It's a nice evening. It isn't a party – I'd made it clear that I didn't want a party-party – but soon enough Boat arrives with his mother, who he's been staying with in the village since he drove in from Accra with Aunt Grace and the girls. Gifty and Kukua's parents arrive, then others from the village drop by, and soon everyone's there.

The Ecstasy

I walk back to the interior, to the spot in the forest where I sat during the day of my mother's funeral. I tread back to the place where he appeared. I've glued together the pieces of the broken mirror, using the mud and straw mix from the build. The mud has seeped and dried in the cracked places, making a criss-cross effect; it's not neat, but it holds together. When you look in it, pieces of yourself are cut off from each other by lines of earth, but you're still all there.

His footsteps crush the foliage. The crunch pulls me out of my thoughts. I know it's him even before I've turned around. He smiles as I approach. I leave the mirror on the ground between us, then walk back to my original spot. He moves towards it and picks it up, raising it to his face. He says something, but I don't understand. He points at himself, 'Kwaku,' he says.

'I know.'

He turns the mirror to face me, as he'd done before. With so many mud-lines crossing it, and from the distance between us, it's hard to see myself in it. I move closer. Amarie isn't there. It's just me. I point to my reflection: 'Imani.'

I watch my name form on his lips: 'Imani.'

I step towards him, moving slowly, until we're standing in front of each other with the mirror between us. His breath touches my face and I smell its heat. I trace his cheek with my fingers. He doesn't move, letting my hand settle on the side of his face. Despite the canopy, there is a glow around him. *He appeared to be one of the highest types of angel who seem to be all afire.* St Teresa's words come to me. I see her vision and recognise the feeling. He touches my mouth, nudging it open as he strokes my bottom lip with his thumb. He moves his lips to mine; *he seemed to pierce my heart several times so that it penetrated to my entrails. When he drew it out, I thought he was drawing them out with it and he left me completely afire with a great love. The pain was so sharp that it made me utter several moans; and so excessive was the sweetness caused by this intense pain that one can never wish to lose it, nor will one's soul be content with anything less.*

A New Dance

There's a whisper. Someone's lips brush against my ear. I wake up and it's dark, but a silhouette is outlined in the gloom.

'Amarie?'

She pulls me up and I follow, still half-asleep.

'Is it you?'

'Take your rucksack,' she says. I reach for the bag that's lying at the corner of the room. 'Careful,' she whispers, manoeuvring me around the sleeping bodies on the floor. 'This way.'

'Where are we going?' I mumble. 'Where have you been? Is it really you?'

She leads me out. 'Who is Amarie?' she asks.

'Aunt Esi?'

'Yes. Who is Amarie?'

'I must have been talking in my sleep.'

'Maame Yaa and I were talking and we came to a decision – concerning your idea, about putting pieces together and coming up with something new. We wanted to do it before you leave for Accra in the morning and we thought you would prefer it if it was just the three of us.'

I nod, because, yes, I always prefer it when it is just the three of us. She leads me away from the house and in the direction of the village. For some reason, I keep expecting to turn into the forest, but she takes me towards the river instead. We stop a few metres away from it at the top of a slope that descends into a small valley. The land dips to reveal Maame Yaa sitting at the bottom with a drum and an assortment of objects spread around her. She reminds me a bit of the medicine man from Cape Coast Castle. We walk down to meet her.

'You're welcome,' she says, standing and bowing.

I bow back, deeply. Aunt Esi asks me to contribute something to the collection of things on the ground. I look in my rucksack and pull out the scarf I wore on the day of my mother's funeral, the red and black fabric worn to identify me, us, as her family. My hand brushes against a small jewelled pen. It had been in the rucksack when Melia left it for me. I pull the pen out and add it to the collection. Maame Yaa begins to drum. The rhythm is like the Adowa beat I heard at my mother's funeral. Aunt Esi starts to move to the music. Her hands make shapes more joyful than the ones from the day of the funeral. Her hands scatter seeds, then become birds in flight, rivers in flow, an offering, a receiving. Each movement tells a story. I want to ask what I should do, but I know they'll tell me off – this, after all, was my idea. So I follow, mirroring Aunt Esi, copying her flow and flight. I am driftwood on her river, wind for her birds to glide on, the response to her call. Maame Yaa sings. I join in and my voice surprises me. I kneel beside her and Aunt Esi circles around us.

Maame Yaa takes the drum under her arm and stands to dance to the beats she's creating. Kneeling on the ground, I sing as they dance. I think I see the flicker of Amarie in their movements. Aunt Esi grabs a piece of cloth and swirls it around. Hesitantly, I stand and reach out for the drum. I hold it cautiously, then strike my hands against it – listening to the sounds I make. Again, I catch sight of a shadow shimmering just before me. I blink and she's gone. I drum and I dance and accept that she will come in her own time.

Aunt Esi, Maame Yaa and I are so absorbed in our piecemeal ceremony that when the rain comes, we barely notice it. Our stamping feet create a mud storm in the valley and the wet earth rises to dance with us. Raindrops fall in my mouth as I sing, and we keep dancing. I throw my head back and drink it in, and we dance. I sing out louder, and we dance. I close my eyes, and we dance. My lungs pulse with new energy and my entire body tingles, and we dance. I feel a flash of light beyond my eyelids; it glows bright brown, ochre. I open my eyes and see her then, as clear as I've ever seen her, Amarie, dancing among us. And we dance. Thunder rumbles in the distance and we dance. I beat the drum harder and harder, and we keep dancing and dancing and dancing.

❖

At the top of the incline, we've made a little camp. Maame Yaa has dug a fire pit, for light rather than heat. We sit looking out at the river beyond and the flames flicker in front of us. The glow of the sun leaks from just beyond the horizon; dawn is coming. My heart is still racing; Amarie was with us, she danced with us. I saw her. I can't see her now, but I sense her presence.

'It's the dance,' Maame Yaa says. 'It does something to you. But, Esi, you were never a dancer before.'

'Every Friday after work, Malcolm would take me dancing,' Aunt Esi responds. 'Saying no to him just wasn't an option, so we danced.' She falls silent for a moment. 'That was one of the hardest things about his funeral – there was no dancing.' Her eyes search for something in the distance. 'He knew that we dance at Ghanaian funerals, and he wanted that for himself. We'd even discussed it – when we thought it was a plan for a far-off time. Then, when he passed, the funeral was this sober, quiet thing. No dancing. Nothing like he wanted. I suggested it, but the pastor said it wouldn't be appropriate.'

'Tonight we danced for him as well,' I say.

'We did.' She takes my hand and gives it a gentle squeeze. 'In the old days, with him, I could have danced for hours. Now, with my age and these headaches, one good dance and I'm done.'

'With your age? What about mine! I'm past eighty and everyone still thinks I'm a chick and they haven't yet started calling me Nana.'

'Nobody thinks you're a chick, Maa, and everyone has tried to call you Nana, but you won't have it,' Aunt Esi says.

Maame Yaa continues, ignoring Aunt Esi's comment. 'This headache business you keep complaining about – every few days, "I feel nauseous, I have a headache" – what is this?'

'Do you suffer from migraines?' I ask.

'Don't bring western sickness to our door,' Maame Yaa says. 'She doesn't suffer from migraine, whatever migraine is!'

'It's a real thing! Sister Alma used to suffer from them terribly.'

'Well, your Terribly Sister Alma can keep her migraine to herself!' Maame Yaa responds.

Aunt Esi lies on her back watching the sky, listening to us argue and trembling with laughter.

'He would have loved to meet you both,' she says. 'He would have been your son,' she says to Maame Yaa, 'and he would have loved to have been your father.'

I squeeze her hand back in response. 'Did you ever … know who my father was?'

She shakes her head, 'Someone Dofi met in England, that's all I know.'

Maame Yaa sighs, 'So many questions we haven't been able to answer for you.'

'Maybe it wouldn't have made any difference,' I say half-heartedly. 'What would you have named me, if you'd raised me?'

'You wouldn't have been raised here, you'd likely have grown up in Accra,' Aunt Esi says.

'But what would my name have been?'

'It would have been your mother's choice,' Maame Yaa says.

I look between them both, frustrated.

'You would have been named after the day of the week you were born,' Aunt Esi says, offering some response. 'I'm Esi because I was born on Sunday and Maa is Yaa because she was born on Thursday.'

'No I'm not, I'm Yaa because I'm named after my mother's mother, who was Yaa. That's why I'm also Maame: it means mother. So it shows I'm Yaa because my mother's mother was Yaa. But if I was born on Thursday, I would also have been Yaa, but I wouldn't necessarily have been Maame. Understand?'

I nod.

'Because of her age, by now we should be calling her Nana, but – as you know – she doesn't like it,' Aunt Esi says.

'Nana is for very old women. I might not be a chick and I might be old, but I'm not yet very old.'

Aunt Esi laughs at this; the sound is fragile.

'I don't know which day I was born on.'

The birds chatter in the distance.

'I would have called you Faith,' Maame Yaa says finally. 'After your mother.' She pauses. 'She came to me, you know? She told me she was pregnant and she asked me to take the child. I'm the one who takes the children when people in the family are struggling. But at the time, I was also struggling; I carried a lot of … bitterness – I couldn't. When she asked, I could see only the past looking at me and I couldn't be kind to her–'

'Maame, stop it!' Aunt Esi says, sitting up. 'Imani, she's saying this for me. This is my story. Faith came to New Jersey first, I told you that before. What I didn't say is, she asked me to raise you and I refused. I could have been your mother and I refused.'

They both look at me with regret in their eyes, as though seeking absolution.

'I could have done my part,' Maame Yaa says.

'It's on me,' Aunt Esi insists. 'I should have been the one to take you, no one else.'

I stare straight ahead, not looking at either of them, not knowing what to say. Trying to understand what their rejection meant for my mother and for me. To have a past that you're so committed to that it drives your choices feels almost like a luxury. My past has always felt like a blank space. What would I have refused to countenance if I had known my past?

Maame Yaa opens a small pouch and gives me a flask. 'Akpeteshie,' she says, 'drink.'

I drink and the sweet-sour liquid warms my throat as it goes down. I cough slightly and Aunt Esi pats my back until the cough subsides. I turn to look at her and tears fall. She touches my face and wipes them away with her thumb. We hug. We come out of the embrace and Maame Yaa hands her the flask. Aunt Esi drinks.

'It's good for you,' Maame Yaa says. 'It warms the sunsum.'

'Can I live with you now?' I ask.

'Of course, of course,' Aunt Esi rushes to say. 'I explained before, you have to go back because of your visa. You need to sort out your paperwork. But once that's done, if you want to return, you can. This is your home – it always will be.'

I nod and take another swig of the flask. 'What is sunsum?' I ask Maame Yaa as the drink trickles down my throat.

'It's spirit … character. Colour. Your flame. The piece of God within you,' she says.

'Your soul,' I say, handing the small flask back.

'I didn't say soul, I said spirit,' Maame Yaa corrects. 'What you're calling soul is okra.'

'The Akan idea of the body and soul is tripartite,' Aunt Esi says. 'A bit like the Christian idea of the Father, Son and Holy Spirit.'

'No it's not!' Maame Yaa snaps.

'Tripartite means three in one,' Aunt Esi tells her. 'I was just explaining.'

'I don't need you to explain. I can explain myself very well. It is not three in one,' Maame Yaa crosses her arms. 'She spent some few years in America and she forgot her own story. The spirit is the sunsum, the okra is the soul; they are not the same and it is not tripartite.' She reaches into her pouch and pulls out a small cloth-covered notebook that fits in the palm of her hand.

'I wrote it for someone once, to explain.' She flicks through the pages, squinting. 'Here it is.' She pushes the book at me, 'Read it, my eyes are not so good in this light.'

I look down at the small page; written on it is:

Okra (noun)
1. Soul
    a. The enlivening essence
2. God
3. Breath

Different from Okra – the foodstuff.
    See also Sunsum – spirit and Honam – body.

I read it aloud to them and smile at the small note at the end.

'What's the difference between sunsum and okra?' I ask.

'Okra is the God in us. Pure divinity. Sunsum is the spirit, it is also God, but it has your character, fire, destiny in it. It is spirit, *spi-rit*, you understand?'

I look at her blankly and she continues, 'Think of it like you said yourself – you remember the day of the storm? You rubbed your hands and said they were no longer separate; they were touching together.'

'Unified touch,' I say, wondering if Amarie is still near, if she can hear our conversation.

'Yes, yes, exactly,' she nods deeply, satisfied, and unfolds her arms. 'Think of honam, the body, and okra, the soul, as two hands together in unified touch. And the bit in between … the touching itself, that is sunsum.'

'Which is both and both,' I offer.

'Eh-hen! Exactly, exactly! That *bit* is the sunsum. So, you see why it isn't tripartite? It is not three in one. The two that touch are both, and the piece in the middle, the touching itself, it is also both. How can it be three in one if they're all both, eh?' She laughs loudly. 'You can have it,' she says, gesturing to the book. 'Take it back to England with you.' She drains the last drops from the flask and smiles wide before lying back.

'I have something for you as well,' Aunt Esi says. 'Where is my bag?'

Maame Yaa pushes the bag across to her. Aunt Esi rifles through it and produces another book, a standard-sized book, bent and dog-eared and well-thumbed.

'An African American?' I ask, holding it in both hands.

She smiles, 'This one is a Ghanaian. It was the favourite book of your Uncle Malcolm.' The writer's name is Ayi Kwei Armah and the book is called *The Healers*.

'Read it while you're away from us,' she says.

On the banks of the river, we lie, watching the colours of the sky change. I doze off with a feeling of total peace. When I open my eyes it's lighter and the heat, for once, feels fresh and bearable. Maame Yaa is sitting up and Aunt Esi is still asleep.

'We should go back,' Maame says. 'Grace and the girls will be waking.'

'Maa, I wanted to ask you something – the day Akwesi was born, I saw this light between him and Kukua. When they were cutting the cord, the light flowed to him. Was that sunsum?'

'It is likely.'

'Is that why she had the fit – because she was connected to it as well and it was leaving her?'

'It's hard to say. Any number of things could have been happening.'

'When you were describing sunsum, I wondered if that's what I'd seen.'

'Some people are blessed and they can see it. Perhaps you have seen it.'

'Do you see it? Is that how you saw that I didn't have my shadow?'

She smiles but doesn't confirm or deny my assumption.

'I saw her tonight; I felt her with us when we were dancing.'

'Then our ceremony served its purpose,' Maame Yaa says, giving me a wink.

Aunt Esi lies between us, facing the sky, her features resplendent in the leftover moonlight.

'It's time we went back,' Maame Yaa says, cutting off my chance to ask more about sunsum. 'We should wake her.' She touches Aunt Esi's shoulder and rocks her gently, but Aunt Esi doesn't open her eyes. Maame Yaa shakes her, firmer this time. Her braids move like limp reeds. I touch her face; it's clammy. I put my hand just above her nose and a faint breath meets my palm. The birds in the distance start to sing their chorus.

The Hospital

We'd been at the hospital in Kumasi for two days by the time they told us we could see her. Aunt Grace and I camped there as though her life depended on us physically being on the grounds. Neither of us has slept and my body doesn't feel like it's my own; my right hand aches and my index finger has developed a strange tingle. Everyone else has gone to various family members' houses in the city to get some sleep. The doctor looks as tired as we do when she comes into the waiting room. She tells us Aunt Esi is awake and can see guests. We jump up together. The doctor says it's advisable that we go in one at a time, in order that we don't tire her out.

'She's asked to see you first,' she says pointing at me.

Aunt Grace sits back down, deflated, but nods for me to go ahead.

'You look rough,' Aunt Esi says as I walk into her private room.

'Holding vigil in a hospital isn't the best beauty routine.'

She smiles; it's not her normal smile.

I've missed her; in just two days of not seeing her, I've missed her so much. I take a seat on the chair beside her bed. Over the past forty-eight hours, every thought imaginable has been through my mind. I've practised a million times what I would say to her if she would only wake up. But now, sitting beside her, my mouth dries up and the words disappear.

She looks almost grey – more spirit than flesh. I try to open my mouth to speak, but only a small breath comes out. Then, slowly, a single word bursts forth, 'Sorry,' I splutter. Then I say it again, 'I'm so, so sorry.' I keep repeating the apology until other words come to back it up. 'There's something in me … a darkness that follows me. It makes bad things happen and I can't always stop it.'

The need to atone is strong inside me. I saw the darkness while we danced. It was mine and coming back to me, because I had been calling it. I had spent most of my time in Ghana looking for it in one way or another. And when it was returning to me, it entered Aunt Esi and wounded her.

'I'd seen what it could do, but I ignored it.' / *I have been with you for so long and still you do not know me.* / 'When I left the island, I thought it was gone, and because I didn't understand what it was, I thought that being without it meant I was incomplete.' / *I was as close to you as the air in your lungs.* / 'I'd been trying to get it back, but when it came back, this happened, it's my fault.' / *You who have seen me have seen the face of the One who sent me – and yet you do not trust your own eyes.* / 'When we danced, I felt her, *it* – I felt *it* getting closer and I even danced with it. But I am prepared to do it now, to say that it is evil, to renounce it and turn away from it. I pray that you'll be ok. I pray to God that you'll be ok.' Tears stream down my face and my body shakes as I finally have the opportunity to say the words I've been practising for two days.

Aunt Esi reaches for me and wipes my tears away. 'What are you saying?' She shakes her head at me as though regarding a confused child. 'You don't have to renounce anything.' Her voice is gentle. 'The doctors say I've contracted a strain of rabies. It's from the grasscutter bite, I believe. The headaches and nausea these past weeks – they were symptoms.'

Before I can respond, she's shaking her head in response to words I haven't spoken. 'It would not have changed anything. There's no cure. I had cleaned it very well and even if we had immediately come to the hospital afterwards – as I know you suggested – the doctors would not have been able to do much more for me. In fact, they say, I've been blessed that I've lasted so long; we've been blessed that we've had so much time together.' She takes my hand in hers. 'I don't feel afraid. My faith tells me I'll be with Malcolm very soon. For you, I want to tell you as much as I can before I pass. You should know that your mother wanted you – she went back for you. After Kisi died, after she herself had recovered from her depression, she travelled back to England and asked to have you back. I always judged her harshly, and finally now, I understand what it is to make a selfish choice and live regretting it.'

Broken Pieces

For as long as I can remember I've gathered things: shards, fragments, feathers, stones, cracked shells and sea glass, colourful morsels to place on a wall or plant in the ground or press in a book. I had a knack for making them fit beside things they didn't know they could belong to – in fact, it was easier to do that than try to repair a broken thing. How do you understand something that appears to be part of you but is also foreign?

I was taught, that in the beginning was the word. The word was with God and the word was God. If the word was with him and the word was his name, perhaps I should start with the name: Amarie. 'A' as a prefix means not, without, the negation of: *a*typical, *a*moral, *A*marie. Without Marie. Marie from Mary, from the Virgin Mother. A-Marie. Without Mary. The opposite. The antithesis of Mary. The enemy of the Holy Mother. The fallen angel in female form. A Black Madonna?

I have a human finger, she said. What was I to understand from that? Was it meant to be a gift, like Mr Bojangles, Sister Alma's cat, bringing her a bloodied rat that he'd caught in the grounds and dragged to her bedroom as a trinket followed by a trail of red? Each time, Sister Alma tried not to scream and would never scold him. She said he didn't know any better, that it was his nature.

I have a human finger, she said.

I try to grasp the memory, root it into something solid, but the past spirals. Dark patterns come and go, spinning like dervishes; moments layer and knit, confusing logic. They all happen at once, fractal and recurring, falling further out of place. Dislodged, I want to run and hide in the shadows until I am ready to be seen in the light, but darkness is no longer my friend.

My aunt has gone and now, once again, I am without a place or person to belong to. I stood at the river and watched the light play with the stream. I wanted to dive in and float. I missed being in water. I wanted to lie on my back and watch the slow transformation of clouds overhead. I stood on the heat-soaked banks of the River Do and my bones and skin were hungry for that water. Everything hurt and only the water that fills the depressions in the land has the ability to wash away that kind of pain. I needed the river. I stepped down into it. With care. It wasn't hurried or desperate or unthinking. I wanted to be part of it; part of its ripples and part of its dance with the lazy sun.

The water on my skin was warmer than I was used to, but that feeling of being weightless on a natural stream was as familiar as breathing. To be carried by something that knew how and where and why. I longed to disappear into it. To simply not exist in this form. I wanted to become the touch of light on liquid, the ripple and fold of the river caused by the push of the boggy wind. I wanted to be the moment when two elements touching become both and everything. The water held my back and the sun warmed my face and I longed to become imperceptible.

The peace is broken. Footsteps and yelling and splash-ing and pulling. The sunlight is harsh now and the voices are sharp. Hysterical. I am dragged onto the shore's rough, hard surface. The earth assaults my senses, stealing the feeling of calm and closeness, of being and not-being. Of being carried. Held. Hugged. Of belonging to, and then vanishing into, with, everything.

Someone is crying.

I was just floating. Only floating.

In the burble I hear Maame Yaa. The crying is getting nearer.

I went in to float. Just a nap on the water.

Adjoa is the one crying; she's beside me, she keeps asking me why. Her tears and face blur but that one word cuts through the mist that is growing, 'Why?'

Book Three

Undersong

Undersong
Noun

1. The burden of a song;
   a subordinate melody;
   the refrain.

2. The ambient sounds of a place;
   the underlying murmur of land.

3. Accompaniment.

Gumbo

Aunt Esi's face always shone when she spoke about her dead husband. 'It was always gumbo with Malcolm. Don't get me wrong, his gumbo was the best, but it was *always* gumbo,' she said, smiling. 'Before we got married, when he wasn't cooking gumbo, it was junk food. There was no in between.

'"Gumbo takes time," he used to say.

'"Does it have to take the time that you put into it, though?" I used to ask. Then he'd start with one of his stories. His favourite was about his grandmother.

'"My grams was from New Orleans," he'd start, though I knew it well enough. "And southerners, we take these things seriously."

'If there was ever anyone new in the room, or even just someone who hadn't heard him tell that particular gumbo tale five hundred times, then he'd begin, "So gumbo was originally like the leftovers, all the things the masters didn't wanna eat – the chicken heads, chicken feet, leftover bits of pork and whatnot, all the mess. It was cooked up by the slaves and they ate it, and that's how it came about. But then it was passed down from generation to generation. People moved and took the recipe with them, added a little something of the flavours from their new home, and it evolved like that and kept evolving, and now you'll pay a month's rent to eat it in Bellman's on the Upper East Side. And it's basically Louisiana's signature dish."

'"Where'd you find the chicken feet?" I asked the first time he cooked it for me.

'He laughed. "We don't use chicken feet no more! No more scraps. When my grams used to make it, she'd go to the market and she had her one guy who sorted her out with all her meat.

She'd buy cuts from the pork she knew had been fattened all year for that purpose; she'd buy chicken that had been reared on corn alone; and freshwater shrimp the size of your hand. No more scraps for Grams. She used to say that you can't cook gumbo without knowing where it came from ... gumbo is how the world absorbs darkness and keeps moving to the light."

'I'd watch him talk and cook and get lost in his words,' my aunt said.

Yahoo Mail

Dear Harold,

I hope you're well.

I'm sorry I haven't been in touch. I'm ok. I'm doing a degree in architecture in Accra, Ghana, where I live with my Aunt Grace and her family. This year, I'm on a study abroad programme as part of my degree and I'm living in Rochester, New York, in America.

Rochester has a river running through it and I realised the other day that, in one way or another, water has been a constant in all of the places I've called home – although these days, I've lost the impulse to dive in and swim. One of my favourite things about the university here is its underground tunnels; they thread beneath the campus and link all of the buildings. They're full of murals and useful for avoiding the light.

I have two jobs here: the first one is at a sandwich shop called The Sandwich Shop. The man who owns it is not very imaginative. He would never spend a day staring at the clouds, and even if he was forced to, he wouldn't see that sometimes a tractor can turn into a dragon- fly. I work at The Sandwich Shop three times a week and in a laundromat in town for two shifts at the weekend. My college fees and accommodation are covered by money left to me by my aunt who passed away (it's a story I will tell you in person). But there isn't quite enough for everything. It turns out that if you want to create buildings like a spider makes it webs, you have to do a lot of things that have nothing to do with the main aim – like ironing other people's underwear or making them a fresh sandwich because you accidentally put margarine on the first and they absolutely loathe marge.

I don't know if you'll remember Melia; she visited St Teresa's a few times. She lives here in Rochester. When she came to see us, I took her to Pilgrim's Café for tea and Singing Hinnies. Last weekend she took me to the Genesee Brew House for hot dogs and cream ale. We got a balcony seat overlooking a waterfall – it's a bit more dramatic than the view from the window seat at Pilgrim's Café which faces the post office wall.

Tell me about you. How do you spend your days? How are your parents? Do you ever see the sisters at St Teresa's? Do you see Dr Trewhitt? I hope you're well. I hope you're all well.

I miss you loads and sometimes I even miss the window seat at Pilgrim's.

Lots of love, Imani xx

Hi Imani,

I am fine. It made me happy to read your email. I am doing some nice things. I did college and it was ok. My mum and dad were happy about it. Now I go to the day centre four times a week. It is on the mainland and I have a girlfriend there. I like her a lot. We go to the cinema together by ourselves. Sometimes we go to the pub. Our workers come with us when we do that. I don't see the sisters. Dr Trewhitt still comes to see me. I miss you. My mum and dad say hello. Say hello to Amarie for me. You didn't come back soon like you said you would. You are still my friend, though.

Love, Harold x

Dearest, dearest Harold,

It was wonderful to get your email! It made me cry – in a happy way. I'm really glad that you're doing well and congratulations on completing college! I can imagine that your parents are extremely proud and, if I'm allowed to be, I'm also very proud.

Amarie isn't with me anymore. When I first arrived in Ghana, I kept trying to figure out how to get her back. Since being in America – it's not that I've forgotten her, but I've just learnt to live around the feeling of her not being there.

I'm sorry I didn't come back soon like I'd promised. One day, I'll visit and I'll explain everything. Thank you for still being my friend, even though I've been unreliable with my promises. I'm glad you have a girlfriend and that you're going to nice places together. Perhaps there's something in the air – Melia has started dating someone and a customer from The Sandwich Shop asked me if I'd go for a coffee with him. I'm not sure if that counts as a date, but I'll let you know once it happens. Please send my love to your mum and dad.

I miss you and love you loads,

Imani xx

An Old Friend

I sit at a corner table at Slayer's Bar watching the door open and close. With every new entry, I straighten up, expecting it to be her. But it's not. Perhaps something's happened and she's not coming, I think. Just then Melia walks through the door. She scans the room, notices me, and gambols over. She pulls me into a hug, her fleshy, diminutive frame locking me in warmth. Together we work out that it's eight years since we last saw each other, and I tell her it's been four years since I left St Teresa's.

'You look fantastic!' she says, appraising my hair and clothes.

I touch my braids self-consciously. 'I promised my cousins back in Ghana that I wouldn't come to America and embarrass them. They made me swear I'd get my hair done every six to eight weeks and only wear the clothes that they'd approved.' I laugh, thinking about the rules Afua and Adjoa had set out before I left Accra. 'But getting your hair done here is really expensive, so I'm thinking I need to find a longer-term solution to braids.'

Over beer and nachos, we reminisce, and she marvels at the alchemical fact that I am sitting with her in a dingy bar in upstate New York in waist-length braids and skin-tight jeans.

'Didn't fancy marrying the Big Guy then, huh?' she teases, and I tell her that the Big Guy and I have been estranged for some time.

'So, why Rochester?'

'Lots of reasons. The course mostly … but also this…' I pick up the oversized rucksack and hold it open to reveal the label stitched to the inside pocket: *212a Waverley Place, Rochester, New York State. Melia Karystinou.*

She yelps, 'I thought you would have thrown that old thing out a long time ago!' She refuses to take it back, saying that it belongs to me now. I run my fingers through the inside pocket, feeling for the ornate little pen: a trinket that she'd left behind which I also want to return. My hand brushes along fabric, but encounters nothing else. I pull the rucksack onto my lap, reaching deeper, in case it's fallen out and into the main pouch – but it's not there. I search the other pockets, feeling for the contours of the pen and the veins of its filigree design. Buds of heat blossom on my neck as confusion and panic mingle. I definitely picked it up before leaving my room. I remember putting the pen in the top inside pocket and zipping it shut.

'I had something else for you.' Heat burns my cheeks as I tell her about the pen and that I'm not sure what's happened to it. She waves away my concern, telling me she's not worried about an old pen, she's just pleased to see me.

'But it looks expensive, as though it would have sentimental value.'

'I don't remember it, so there goes the 'sentimental value' theory. And we produce plenty of pens in America, so honestly, it's no big deal.'

An old fear stirs, its embers beginning to kindle. 'Maybe the beers are getting to our heads,' Melia says, looking at me with concern. 'Let's order some proper food.'

Melia tells me about her job; she's recently been promoted to team leader at the biggest supermarket chain in Rochester. I try to listen but struggle to concentrate: she says something about managing staff and a DIY nut butter machine.

'Why don't you tell me a bit about Africa,' she says, interrupting her own flow. 'Tell me about life in Africa,' she repeats, when I stare blankly at her.

'Ghana.'

'What?'

'I wasn't in all of Africa all at once.'

She laughs. 'Welcome back! I was scared I'd lost you for a second there. So how was Ghana?'

I tell her about the first year: my mother's funeral, living in Dosu, Aunt Esi – and how I was after it all.

'And are you ok now?'

'Mostly,' I nod, a little too emphatically. 'I still have my moments … they're not quite panic attacks. And I sometimes still get the dreams.'

'Nightmares?'

'Not exactly. Vivid, weird dreams. I had one last night actually; maybe that's what confused me … making me think I'd put your pen in the bag when I hadn't.'

'What was it about?'

'It's one that I've had a few times. I'm in Cape Coast Castle. My cousins took me there when I first got to Ghana. In the dream, it happens as it did back then: this traditional healer grabbed my wrist…' I hesitate, wondering how much to tell her. '…He was trying … trying to talk to me. He was speaking in Twi, though, and I couldn't understand. But in the dream, I know what he's saying; he tells me he can help me connect through my dreaming. He keeps repeating it.'

'He can help you connect with what?'

I pause. 'My sunsum.'

'Your what?'

I explain in words I hope she'll understand. 'Imagine the soul is a brilliant cut diamond, the body is white light that passes through that diamond, and the spirit is all of the colours refracting out. All of those colours, they're who you are and who you're meant to be – so your spirit, sunsum, is character and colour and destiny, and the soul is … it's a pure jewel.' I stop short of telling her that I've witnessed my spirit hurt people: attack them, hold their severed limbs in the palm of her hand, and once I even believed her capable of causing my aunt's death. The lump that has formed in my throat grows sharp and cuts into a soft, warm place in my neck.

A waitress comes over with fresh drinks and the food that we've ordered. My burger looks fine, but Melia's food looks like a mistake.

'It's a garbage plate.' She smiles at the expression on my face. 'It's a Rochester specialty.' She hands over her fork, offering me the first mouthful. Her plate is stacked with layers of indiscernible meat, pasta, cheese, cubed potatoes and on top of it, splatterings of different-coloured sauces. It looks like someone has vomited over the meal. Hesitantly, I take the fork and bring a mouthful of the food to my lips. The indistinct minced meat and assortment of sauces taste better than they look, but I'm not sure I'd ever order a plate of it.

'What made you start coming to St Teresa's?'

'I'm adopted,' she says. She continues eating and seems in no rush to say any more. After a while, I go to ask another question – with my mouth open – and before I speak, she continues. 'Years back, I'd been helping my mom clean out the basement in my folks' old place. In a box, I came across this magazine with an article about unmarried girls in the UK secretly having babies in these convents. Inside the magazine, beside the article, was this book, a pamphlet really, *A Philosophy of Faith*, no more than thirty pages, written by Michaela Berwick.'

'Reverend Mother,' I whisper, bewildered.

'Yeah.' Melia moves her empty plate aside. She takes out a green rolled packet from her bag and unravels it on the table. Laying a small, thin sheet of paper in front of her, she concentrates on spreading tobacco evenly across it. 'I was raised Greek – Greek Orthodox. But as soon as I was old enough, I let everyone know I didn't believe in anything, and I wouldn't be going back to the church – any church – any time soon.' She looks up, halfway into rolling the paper up, a question in her eyes – am I sure I want her to continue? I nod at the silent gesture, encouraging her to go on. 'Reverend Mother's book wasn't mine, and my parents wouldn't have had it for spiritual purposes. So why was it there?' She lights her cigarette and continues, not waiting on a response: 'When I was a kid, some older cousins told me that my birth mother was from the UK. I don't know where they got that idea from, but I always remembered it. So, I put two and two together and came up with ... something more than four.' She inhales on the thin cigarette. 'In the magazine article, one of the women had given birth at around the time I'd been born. She thought her kid had been adopted and taken to America. I read that story and was convinced that she was my birth mom. I became a bit obsessed. I tracked her down to St Teresa's and those visits were about getting close to her.'

'Reverend Mother?' I ask, holding my breath.

She shakes her head. 'Sister Magdalene.' Wisps of smoke escape from her nostrils.

Relief surges through me. 'Sister Magdalene was your mother?'

'She's someone's mother. With the whole cloistered thing, I could never get close to her. That last year, I saw someone walking through the halls one night; I thought it was her. I followed her and ended up in the library. It was Reverend Mother. She was sat in front of the fireplace by the time I got to her; she was looking up at that tapestry that I'd brought.'

'The Black Madonna?'

'She looked kinda mesmerised by it. I sat with her and we talked. I told her about the magazine article and how it had led me to them. She knew what I was talking about right away. She said the article had been a big mistake. She'd agreed to be involved along with a few other convents, hoping any attention they got might help them raise funds for maintenance, but she felt the journalists had taken advantage. They focused too much on Sister Magdalene, and made it seem like St Teresa's Convent existed solely for those purposes, which wasn't the case; Sister Magdalene's experience had been an anomaly. The magazine had also included *A Philosophy of Faith* as an insert without Reverend Mother's consent. She'd pretty much forgotten that she'd written it and the contents caused a lot of controversy among the heads of the diocese council. It was after the article that Sister Magdalene became cloistered. Reverend Mother nearly lost her position at St Teresa's.

'I told her about my adoption and she said, if I was looking for my mother at St Teresa's, I had the wrong convent. She said I had to come to terms with things myself, otherwise finding my birth mother would probably make things worse.

'Some convents might not have accepted Sister Magdalene because of her past, but Reverend Mother's book was all about … it was sort of like Josephine Baker's Rainbow Tribe, only with religion. She tried to include different identities and different ways of seeing things and knowing them. The way you were talking about souls and spirits before, and the difference between them, that's her bag right there. You open your mouth and you can just see that you're her child.'

I jump to correct Melia, to say that the soul/spirit distinction is Akan not Christian, that I learnt about it from Maame Yaa, not Reverend Mother. But the fact that she calls me Reverend Mother's child throws me off. I want to say I'm not hers, was never really hers, but there's a part of me that's also relieved that someone still thinks I am.

'In the book,' Melia continues, 'she talked about identity and particularly gender. The church hasn't exactly been a trailblazer in the feminist movement – she implies that God could be a woman, the Ultimate Mother. And she wrote about sexuality. I found her fascinating, this woman who wanted to create a community where everyone could find their way of believing on their own terms. I mean, why would a lesbian want to join a convent?'

'Mother's a lesbian?' I ask, bemused.

There it was again, that word. Like Black, it explodes into existence, creating impacts I never fully understand.

'I'm not saying that; my point is, if she were, if any of them were, what would it mean? According to her, you take a vow, commit to God and forsake parts of yourself, like sexuality – so then gay, straight, whatever, the words lose their meaning. But then who are you? I was intrigued: if you could just chop off part of yourself, maybe I could chop off this obsession to know who my birth mother was. But I was also curious, right; didn't that go against her whole idea that you build your relationship with your faith and incorporate who you are – past experiences, everything – into your spiritual life?' Melia grows animated, starting to gesticulate and copy Reverend Mother's tone and phrasing. 'She told me that when you accept a particular reality, it always involves releasing aspects of yourself – just letting them go. I disagreed. She used the example of becoming a mother, not a religious mother, a mother-mother. She said that when you become a mother, you must think about someone else; it involves stripping away aspects of the person you once were. I said that's why I never want children. She laughed at that. My feelings about kids are pretty similar to my issue with God – how do you know this being that you're sacrificing so much for is actually gonna turn out to be worth it?

'We were talking for the longest time and then she said it had been truly lovely to speak to me, but in the morning I needed to pack my bags and I wasn't to come back. She didn't give me the option to say any goodbyes.'

'In this vision, where everyone has a choice about how they believe, what was my choice?' I ask.

'I never quite figured out how you fitted into it all. I got as far as thinking that maybe she'd always wanted to be a mother and perhaps that was the one thing she couldn't sacrifice.'

'Why does that feel like shit?'

'Language, Imani!' Melia says, feigning shock. 'What would the Reverend Mother say? You know, my yaya – my grandmother – used to say, "Swearing is coarse, but if you assign it to an animal, it's *National Geographic*."'

'Chickenshit – why does that feel like chickenshit?'

'Yaya would approve,' she says, blowing smoke out of the corner of her mouth. 'Look, honestly, I don't know. I guess if you commit to something, it might be too hard to accept all of the sacrifices it involves, right? Like not expressing sexual or relational needs – not becoming a parent; maybe there are parts – of each of us – that … that you just can't deny.'

'She wasn't a mother, though, so it wasn't something she was denying.'

'But she could have been.'

'So I had to sacrifice knowing my real mother so she could play at it?'

'Mother-daughter things are a fuck-up – I learnt that the hard way.' She stubs out the remainder of her cigarette in the glass ashtray.

'Did you ever find your birth mother?'

She wags her finger at me, 'I don't have the head for that right now.'

The Journey

There are cars racing by on either side of us as we turn onto the highway and take our lane. The weather has been uncertain, but the dark clouds have faded and drifted into the distance. In my mind's eye, New York City looms: it is still several hours away, but it feels like the promise of a reunion. It was her city. The first place she lived when she arrived in America, before she married Uncle Malcolm and moved to New Jersey. I hope to see what she saw, walk where she walked, find glimpses of her rebellious heart in its monuments and parks.

'Do you mind if I smoke?' Melia asks.

'While you drive?'

'Yes, I need one to start a long journey.'

'You had two before we got in the car!'

She pulls out the paper, filter and tobacco from the dashboard. She holds the steering wheel with one hand and uses the other to roll the cigarette, all while the car charges along the fast-moving road. I reach into my bag in an attempt to distract myself from the near-death situation Melia is creating. I pull out a notebook. As I do so, the small cloth-bound book from Maame Yaa falls out of the bag and lands at my feet; the mouth of the rucksack gapes, revealing *The Healers*, the novel that Aunt Esi gave me. I take all three books and place them on my lap. Maame Yaa's little dictionary is on top, and I peel open its pages with care.

Assemblage (noun)
1. A gathering or collection of objects or people;
2. A work of art;
3. Archaeological artefacts that support a theory

concerning a particular culture.
Bucolic (adjective)
Relating to a beautiful rural setting.

Written beside the definition of 'Bucolic' is the sentence: **sound like disease**. I smile at Maame Yaa's large letters. They have been corrected by someone. Before 'sound' is written 'It' and an 's' has been put at the end of the word. A little arrow between 'like' and 'disease' points to something, an 'a'. So, the collection of words together, from Maame Yaa and her English friend, reads **It sounds like a disease**.

I flick through and find a page that begins with Maame Yaa's words:

Akwaaba: welcome
Obroni: foreigner/white man
M'adamfo: friend

On the following page, in smaller writing, but still in Maame Yaa's stout script, is written:

Okra (noun)

   1. Soul
     a. The enlivening essence
   2. God
   3. Breath

Different from Okra – the foodstuff.
   See also Sunsum – spirit and Honam – body.

I wonder what Maame Yaa would make of the diamond and

white light analogy I had used to describe sunsum to Melia. I could never place her beliefs and she never named them. I'm sure Reverend Mother would be suspicious of Maame Yaa's ideas. A smile tugs at my lips as I imagine them discussing their respective views of the world. I hadn't seen Mother lose an argument, and I'd never witnessed Maame Yaa walk away from one until she'd made the person, who thought they were winning, feel like they'd been turned inside out.

Melia finishes rolling her cigarette and smokes as she drives. She asks me to tell her another story about Dosu. Thinking of Maame Yaa has given me the appetite for a story, so I tell her the final part of the tale of building Aunt Esi's home.

'Everyone had ideas about the design and build – if there would be an indoor kitchen or not, perhaps an indoor bathroom, or an indoor toilet – there's no real plumbing there, so these things are big decisions. Then the night after we'd finished, I felt like you could see a piece of everyone in that house, but I wasn't sure if you could see me. I got up and started carving faces into the outside wall. It took a few days to complete, but I put everyone on there. When Aunt Esi saw it, she got out an old picture of Uncle Malcolm and asked me to include him on the wall beside her. She said, "Each face is a piece of the jigsaw puzzle and we all fit together."

'Maame Yaa came and brought, well, everyone. They all commented on how I'd drawn them, and Nii, Kukua's husband, said I should have made his head more prominent. For a long time, Maame Yaa didn't say anything at all, which isn't like her. Then she said, "Imani has made a self-portrait." No one understood. Then slowly people started to squint and turn their heads to different angles to try to make it out. Aunt Esi said she could see it, how all the faces together made up one big face, which looked a lot like me – but I look a lot like Aunt Esi, so I said it could be her as well. But they all agreed that it was definitely me and not her.

They started to tease me, saying I'd used all of their faces just to make a big picture of myself. Aunt Esi said perhaps my father had been a Ghanaian after all, and maybe he came from the North, because it's the people in the North who decorate the outside of their homes with patterns and pictures.'

I'm reading *The Healers* when the car swerves, the book slips out of my hands and we come to an abrupt stop. Melia has pulled over onto the hard shoulder.

'Snack break,' she says, passing me the plastic bag full of food that she's brought from work. She immediately starts to roll another cigarette.

Vehicles speed past and our stationary car shudders each time. 'Do you consider this a problem?' I ask.

'What?'

'Your addiction to nicotine?'

'Only if you make it one – which would be incredibly ungracious of you.'

'If we make it to New York alive, I'll remember to be grateful.'

She lights the cigarette. 'What if it's hereditary – then it's not my fault, it's in the blood.'

'Perhaps. You never told me what happened with your birth mother.'

Melia pulls a face. The car sways gently as several cars pass in a row. 'I don't know what to tell you. When you speak about Holymead or Ghana … even when you talk about things that … they must have been awful, you make it sound … so whimsical. And you always get something out of it, a precious relationship with a relative you never knew you had, money to study, a moral – some insight. I don't know how to tell you about my life in some cutesy way to get a Pollyanna-type of moral out of it. I just don't.

'After years of dead-end jobs, I've just about graduated to be more than a checker at Weggies – now, get this, I manage the checkers! And for as long as I can remember, I've felt like a loser, but I thought if I found my birth parents, something would make sense. Then I met my mom, and Reverend Mother was right, nothing got better. It made things worse. The end. How did I do? Was it adorable?'

'How did you find her?'

'You're not going to drop this are you? Fine.' She sighs. 'I always thought it would be some sort of betrayal of my mom and dad if I came out and asked them about my birth parents. Then, one day, I did it; I asked my mom and she said she had my birth mother's name, address and number – and she gave it to me. That simple. She'd had it all along. She said she knew the day would come when I'd ask. She said she was surprised it had taken me so long, but she had to wait until I was ready. She'd let me go on this wild goose chase, let me make up this whole fucking blockbuster of a movie about British nuns and tidal islands in England. She knew what I was doing, but never once tried to stop me. She said I had to follow my own path – what utter bullshit!

'So, I've got my birth mother's address and her number. I call and then I go to meet her – in Detroit. First thing is, she's black. Light-skinned, but definitely African American. So hello, I'm black. Huh! Crazy! I grew up Greek Orthodox! Christ! Folks call Greeks olive-skinned, right? At school they used to call me Kalamata, cos the olives from there are both brown and green, and that was me, right? Kalamata. But then you find out you're black and not just a little bit brown. You've been "passing" as Kalamata this whole fucking time,' she laughs – a dry, raspy sound with no joy.

Fade from Brown to Black. Open. Close. Open.

'Black has a way of sneaking up on people.'

She laughs hard, as though I'm joking. Melia tells me her birth mother's story with no feeling, like it's a sequence of unfortunate events that happened to someone she'd heard about once. She ends by saying they didn't meet a second time.

'So, when I ask you to tell me about Africa, I'm not trying to be ignorant, I really want to know.'

'Why don't you go and see her again? If you want to know about your history, the best place to start is with her.'

Melia finishes her cigarette and says nothing.

I'm not sure what to say to her, and then a story comes. 'This is my story, which I share with you. If it be sweet, if it not be sweet, take some and share, and let some come back to me.

'Anansi the spider man was such a trickster that when it came time for him and his love to have a baby, he didn't want her to go through the pain of childbirth. He decided he would fool Mother Nature into giving her a child in a painless way. So, he stole her womb one night as she slept, and he put it in the body of another woman. He let the other woman look after the baby until it was ready to be born. When the child arrived, she was a combination of all three parents. She spent most of her time with Anansi and her life-mother, and she visited her birth-mother only occasionally. None of them realised that the birth-mother had fallen on hard times, and there came a period when she had to sell some parts of her body to get by, like her arms and her legs, her head and her stomach. At some point there was so little of her left, the remaining parts laid down and became the dust. The pieces of her enriched the earth, feeding the soil. When the daughter came to visit, what she found was wild bush flowering with heather and fern, nourished by the scattered dust in the soil.'

'The Reverend Mother will freak out if she hears you telling stories like that,' Melia laughs. Tears fall down her face and she seems to be both laughing and crying at the same time. Later, when we're back on the road, with her eyes staring straight ahead and both hands on the steering wheel, she tells me that it's the first time she's cried about her mother.

Dream:
The Seventh Castle

You crouch down so your head doesn't hit the ceiling. The water is above your knees and from the smell of it, it's not just water. It's dark and the corridor is only wide enough for you to walk in single file. You're aware of people ahead and a woman behind, but not much else.

'Don't slow down, Sissy, we have to keep up with the others,' the woman behind you says. She strokes your back but is also pushing you forward. 'I know you're scared, Amma, but everything will be fine.'

You've tried to tell her your name isn't Amma, but just now, when you open your mouth to speak, nothing comes out.

Your thigh hits something that's floating. You stop to move it out of the way. It's the size of a football; one side is furry and the other is the texture of wet leather.

'Don't touch it,' the woman from behind snaps. 'Keep moving.' She gives you another little shove.

You drop the thing and let it float away or drown.

'Don't break the line, keep behind the others,' she says. 'Amma, please, I beg. You walk as though you've changed your mind. Don't make me regret bringing you with us.'

The rumours have always existed. They say that beneath the castles built along the coastline there is a network of underground tunnels. If you count from the northernmost castle southwards, the seventh castle has a tunnel that exits away from the building. It leads to a jetty on the water, under a cave. There, freed brothers and sisters wait in a boat to take you home. You didn't tell anyone that you were born in the castle; you weren't recently taken; you don't know what home you can return to. But even so, you came.

'Amma, don't slow down.' Her hand nudges the base of your spine. 'Come on, not one more day of walking and we'll be at the seventh castle. Not one more day. Be strong for me now, Sissy, be strong.'

Your legs are tired, your back aches, you want to stop and sit, just for a moment. Instead, you stand as straight as the tunnel allows and force yourself forward.

'That's right. That's good, Sissy,' she says from behind you.

'There it is.'

In front of you all, far in the distance, a bright light shines. You hold hands with the woman behind and together you run towards it.

The Rhythm

Aunt Esi had wanted to be cremated, but cremation is not a Ghanaian thing. Several family members were upset by the request. Her wishes were followed, but only just. One day, a small group of us were at a crematorium in Kumasi. The next morning we were scattering her ashes in Dosu, and a few people had travelled to join us. That evening, the relatives who had travelled returned home to their cities. There was no fabric made to show that we were her family, no mournful dancing, no real ceremony at all.

I don't know what made me do it, but the night before we scattered her ashes, while everyone else slept, I crept into the sitting room of Maame Yaa's house and took the urn off the mantlepiece. I opened it and poured some of Aunt Esi's ashes into a blue snuff box. I filled the small container, sealed it and returned the urn to its place. Then I crawled back into bed beside my sleeping cousin.

'I think this is it,' Melia says as she steers the car into the small parking lot at the back of a red-brick church. No one is around. As we get out and walk through the grounds, Melia lights a cigarette and takes a few nervous puffs, but before we've reached the front of the building, she's stubbed the remainder on the ground, with less than half of it smoked. The church has a green door with a crucifix above it. On the opposite side of the building are rhododendron bushes that obscure the entrance to a churchyard.

'It must be back there.'

We walk through the gap in the bushes to a paved area with five or so headstones. Beside Uncle Malcolm's commemorative plaque is a rosebush. We stop. An unexpected peace settles in me. I say a few words to him; I thank him for making my aunt so happy. I tell him I wish I had met him. Then, by habit rather than intention,

I recite scripture – the Lord's Prayer, Psalm 23, 1 Corinthians 13. Beside me, Melia is silent; her arms are knotted behind her back, legs crossed as she stands, looking like she regrets having thrown away that last cigarette. I open the snuff box and spread Aunt Esi's ashes along the top of the rosebush and on Uncle Malcolm's headstone. The dust floats down. I rest some of it in the palm of my hand, watching it in the light, then I scatter it at the foundations of the roses, kneading it into the soil. I kiss the traces of earth and ashes left in my hand and blow them to the ground. I take out the copy of *The Healers*, the novel by Ayi Kwei Armah; it was one of Uncle Malcolm's favourites. I open it at the section called 'The New Dance': the white men have brought different groups of blacks to Ghana to fight each other, but instead, for a time, the West Indians use the Europeans' instruments to create unusual melodies. All of the blacks dance to it – the Opobo, the Hausas, the Ada, the Ga, the Fantse – everyone, they all dance along as the West Indians create new rhythms, and together they make new movements and become a new whole. When I reach the end of the page, I place the book on Uncle Malcolm's grave. I want to dance for him and Aunt Esi, to give them the dance ceremonies they were denied at their own funerals. But there's no music. I turn to Melia, thinking she might be ready to leave, but she takes my hand and turns me around. Then she does it again, and this time she hums a tune. I move my hips and twist to the rhythm. As her hum grows, words slip out – 'Mr Bojangles, Mr Bojangles, come back and dance, dance, dance, please dance. Mr Bojangles, Mr Bojangles, dance, dance, dance.'

And we dance, around the grave and the rosebush. I join in with the few words of her song, singing low in accompaniment. We move cautiously, self-consciously, both trying to give in to the rhythm that all black people are supposed to have; I close my eyes and twirl. I dance for Uncle Malcolm, who was almost my father, for Aunt Esi, almost my mother, for Maame Yaa, my kind-of grandmother. I dance for Adjoa and Afua, for Aunt Grace, Uncle Samuel, Boat and Kwaku and everyone in Dosu. I dance for Melia and Reverend Mother, for Dofi-Faith, my birth mother. And I'm dancing for myself. I squeeze my eyes tighter and move with more courage.

In the car, there's a strange energy between us. 'What was that song?'

'You'd read that beautiful passage about dancing and I felt like that's what we should do. It was the only thing I could think of at the time and I could only remember that one line!' She lets out a self-conscious little laugh.

'We have a black cat back at St Teresa's called Mr Bojangles,' I tell her. 'Where's the song from?'

'I think about a million people have sung it. The definitive version, in my humble opinion, is Sammy Davis Jr's.'

Before I can stop myself, the words roll out '…Sammy Davis Jr, Earth, Wind & Fire, Etta James, James Brown…'

'What are you doing?' she asks, laughter curled around her mouth, but she holds it back – just.

I tell her about the list I had as a child, black people with rhythm, compiled from the information Harold found on Yahoo.

'You still remember the whole list?'

'Yeah.' And I begin: 'Michael Jackson, Eric B & Rakim, Curtis Mayfield, Carey Mariah, Sammy Davis Jr, Earth, Wind & Fire, Etta James, James Brown, Stevie Wonder, Sam Cooke and Samantha Mumba.'

I say it through once and then repeat it a second time and a third.

Melia laughs openly this time. 'They're all Americans – but

who's Samantha Mumba?'

'I never knew who any of them were.' I start to recite it again.

'When you say it on repeat like that, it creates its own rhythm.'

'I know! I used to say it all the time to make that effect.'

'And you know she's not Carey Mariah, right?'

'Yeah, I learnt that in Ghana. But it doesn't sound right if you say Mariah Carey – I've tried.'

She starts the car, with me chanting the bedtime litany over and over. I stamp my feet and she slaps the steering wheel to the rhythm of the names of people, black like us, who all have rhythm.

Dream: Silk

The trees are dense, but through their canopy slivers of light creep in. Somewhere in the distance the crows call out a warning. A spider man hangs upside down. He's above you. You're a baby. His baby. You lie in a cradle of silk, suspended from a branch. Your lips part as he drops warm, sweet milk from his mouth to yours. When you're full, he stops. He hums a song that softly stings as it removes the wax from your ears: when they're clean, his hum fades and you fall asleep.

You wake up; a dazzling light blinds you. You open your mouth to cry, but something soft is pushed inside and your voice is trapped. You look for him, searching desperately, but you can't see through the glare. Silhouettes appear: three of them, women, dark against the light. They wear cloaks. Beneath their hoods, more light streams out, shining where their faces should be. Two of them hold onto a rope. There he is: hanging upside down, tethered to a thick branch. A cord has been fastened to his spinneret; the third woman holds the end of it; when she pulls, it tugs at his nipple and serum shoots from his teat and lands on the ground. He screams. You try to cry out in response to his pain, but your voice is smothered.

This goes on for some time: two of the women hold him upside down while the third one milks him. The serum that pours from him falls to the ground and solidifies. It creates a base; a full foundation then forms into walls. He howls each time the cord is pulled. Silk walls grow and connect to each other, creating a roof and finally spires. Lying on the ground, mute, you recognise it at last – it is the shape of St Teresa's Convent on Holymead Island.

The building is complete. Drained, the spider man closes his eyes and hangs limp. The two women in the distance lower him down.

His body sways, lifeless, as it descends. A drop of blood from his swollen nipple falls and lands on your cheek as he sways in his descent. Then his body finally meets the ground. The woman with the cord walks towards you and takes you out of the cradle. She wipes the blood from your face with the brown cloth of her habit. Where her face should be is the glare of a thousand suns – a blinding white light. Holding you in her arms, she coos gently and lulls you back to sleep.

A Spider Web Tapestry

We buy coconut waffles with maple rum butter and eat them in Central Park. We walk through Times Square. At the Empire State Building, I observe its lines and angles, the sharpness of its protrusions, its art deco influences. Inside the Museum of Natural History, on the Upper West Side, we find, hanging from the ceiling, a curtain of gold. It floats in mid-air, luminous.

'It's made from spiders' silk,' an attendant tells us.

'It's gorgeous.'

'It took more than a million spiders to make this tapestry,' he informs us.

'Where did they get all the spiders from?' I ask, feeling odd about this new piece of information.

'Africa,' he says.

'Where in Africa?' I ask.

'She likes it when people are specific,' Melia tells him.

'Madagascar,' he responds.

'Is that Africa or Asia?' I ask.

'Erm, I don't know ... I guess, I thought it was Africa, I might be wrong.'

'What happened to the spiders?' Heat rises in me as I wait for his response.

'Excuse me?'

'She's really inquisitive,' Melia says, still staring in awe at the fabric.

'I don't know what happened to the spiders.'

'You took the silk of a million spiders and you don't know what happened to them?'

The attendant looks at me confused, 'I didn't take it, the artist did … and they're spiders!'

Melia apologises to him and steers me away from the exhibit. 'What's gotten into you?'

I want to go back and rip the tapestry from the ceiling. Burn it. Raze the whole place to the ground. Rage courses through me, exploding like a Roman candle.

On the car journey back to the motel, the radio fills in for our chatter. I feel angry with Melia, but I can't explain it to her; I'm not sure I understand it myself.

'Why did you bring the tapestry to St Teresa's?' I ask.

'What tapestry?'

'The Assumption of Mary – with Mary as a black woman.'

'I did it … for you, I guess. I'd been coming there what, three, four years, at that point. You were, like, desperate to see yourself reflected in something. You used to obsess over any little thing that might be black or brown enough – those magazines from Spain.'

'Sister Maria brought them.'

'Yeah, and that one woman you showed me, you said she was dark and nearly as dark as you, it was kind of … heart-breaking – she looked nothing like you. Then I brought the purple rose to try to get near to Sister Magdalene because she took care of the rose garden, and you got obsessed with that as well – you told me in the right light the petals look like black skin. It was…' She shakes her head. 'You were hungry for something, anything, in that world that reflected you back to yourself. I wanted to give you that, in some small way. I figured they wouldn't let me just rock in with magazines like Sister Maria. I guess she got away with it because she was part of the community.'

'I'm not sure anyone else actually knew about it.'

'Well, there you go, she definitely got away with it because she was part of the community. I was practically strip-searched every time I came near the place. I wouldn't have been able to sneak *anything* in. The tapestry felt legit – it was a holy image, the Mother of Christ ascending to heaven. To be honest, I never really thought it would be a problem. They were a bunch of women raising a black child – who knew they would have such an issue with the image of a black woman.'

I stare out of the window at my side of the car, blinking away tears.

'Why did you go bat-shit crazy back there? There was no need to behave like that – was that another one of your *moments*?'

I'm quiet for a while. Then I answer: 'I recently realised that some lives are disposable; their sacrifice is deemed worth it for the price of someone else's comfort or the cost of an ornament. I haven't always known this – but once you know, you can't stop seeing it everywhere.'

Melia doesn't respond and I'm glad. I look out of the window, away from her. She steers into the motel car park. On the radio is a sad love song about not wanting to hear any more sad love songs.

Incorruptible

'Shit, my eyes!' Melia says as she passes her reflection in the mirror. A streak of black runs from her left eye to her cheek. She'd been in the shower for over half an hour and came out looking like she was wearing warpaint.

'You should never just say shit, it's coarse,' I tell her, handing her a roll of toilet paper as she stares in disbelief at her reflection. 'Assign it to an animal, remember?'

'Whale-shit!' she says, breaking off the loo roll and scrubbing at the mascara trail on her face. 'Donkey-shit!'

'Whale-shit is actually very precious. Once, I found a lump of it on the sands when the tide was out. I thought it was a funny-looking rock, but when Dr Trewhitt saw it, he recognised it. He sold it on the mainland, and we used the money to finally put a new roof on the parish church.'

'Pollyanna's got nothing on you!' Melia says.

'Who's Pollyanna?'

'A cousin of Carey Mariah.'

I throw a pillow at the back of her head; she ducks and it flies past her hitting a small table where I'd put my belongings. Everything falls on the floor. I rush to pick them up: E45 cream, Vaseline, Maame Yaa's makeshift dictionary and the gold, jewelled pen.

'Here – I found this while you were in the bathroom.'

'Who knew that waterproof mascara was so waterproof?' she says with her back to me.

'This is the infamous pen,' I say, holding it out to her.

'Keep it, really.' She turns to look at it; her mouth drops and she takes a step away. 'Where did you get that from?'

'You left it in your rucksack back at St Teresa's.'

'It's not a pen, Imani. It's a reliquary: inside it is a human finger.'
/ *I have a human finger.*

There was a dream I used to have, a recurring scene of running through the causeway holding a bloodied finger, trying to but never reaching the mainland. / I was six or seven and made to stand in the cold with no gloves. I'd done something wrong. Not me – Amarie had broken the Holy Mother and Child statue. / I was left outside. / My hands went numb. / I try to remember that day, those nights – search the edges of the dream and the memory to push them apart so I can see them more clearly: Sister Magdalene is arguing with Reverend Mother, accusing me of things. / *She is not like us.* / *That shadow of hers, this demon – whatever it is – is proof of that.* / *Her people ... worship ... darkness ... do ritual sacrifices ... kill people ... cut off their limbs ... they keep severed body parts ... keep them to give to their unclean gods.*

Melia sits on the bed, her eyes never leaving the thing in my hand. 'It's the Incorruptible Finger of St Teresa,' she says. 'A religious relic. Inside the case ... is St Teresa's finger.'

I want to drop it, but it remains fixed in my grip.

'Her left hand ... is somewhere in Spain – that is her right index finger.' Melia speaks slowly, clearly unnerved. 'They say that when they dug up St Teresa, after her death, her body was completely uncorrupted, so they kept parts of her because it was considered ... pure or holy or whatever. You should know more about this than me – how come you didn't know?'

'It was in your bag; before that I'd never seen it!' I realise I've been holding my breath; I exhale, choke on my in-breath and start to cough.

Melia gets a water bottle from her bag and gives it to me. I drink a few sips.

'What do you know about it?' I ask, the grotesque ornament still in my hand.

'I found it at the bottom of the wardrobe in the postulants' cell,' she says. 'It was really early on in my visits, like maybe the first one. I didn't know what it was. Sister Maria and I had been friendly until then, I guess because we were the closest in age. When I showed it to her, she freaked out. She said it had been kept inside a small bust of the Virgin Mary that used to be in the chapel. Then one day the statue broke, Sister Magdalene saw a golden light and the silhouette of a holy being holding it, and then they both disappeared – the angel ascended to heaven taking the Incorruptible Finger with it. So, if the finger was sitting getting dusty in my wardrobe, that meant it either came back from heaven, which would be received as a bad omen – or someone had lied, also not so good. Or someone was mistaken about what they'd seen – again, not the best news. Sister Maria said I should tell Reverend Mother about it, but she didn't want to have anything to do with it herself. After that she avoided me and basically looked the other way whenever I was around. Her reaction spooked me … I … I had my own reasons for being at St Teresa's and causing a religious scandal wasn't part of the plan.'

They saw me beside you and cried Demon. And you believed them. When they saw me beside the finger of St Teresa, they called me Angel.

I drop the finger. It makes a dull noise as it hits the carpet.

'Did you hear something?'

'I get that you're in shock,' she says. 'I was freaked out, too.'

'A voice? Did you hear a voice?'

As your aunt lay dying, you disowned me. Accused me of the worst possible thing.

'There! Did you hear that?' Of course, Melia couldn't hear her.

This graceless world that taught you to hate yourself while hiding its own culpability. This world that taught you to look at me and see something dark and view darkness as abhorrent. It kept you from appreciating that nature is something seamed, connected, deep, into which one must dive, going dark. You were educated to split and search for the light; to cut yourself away from knowing; to turn me into A and Marie: reading 'A' as negation; making me the shadow self of Marie, Mary, Mother of God. The irredeemable darkness to her perfect light. But there are different angles of analysis – other ways to read. Amarie, cut differently, is Ama and Rie. Ama, an African word, the Ghanaian name for a Saturday-born girl child. Rie, an Asian word, meaning logic and blessing in Japanese scripts. Or A, as the prefix need not mean negation – without, opposite, other. It could be the inseparable particle, meaning on, in, into or from – like alive, ashore, anew, afresh, akin, aware. Marie, from Mary, in cultures that you do not know, meaning 'sea of sorrow' or 'rebellion'.

All night Amarie speaks. I work to listen, then fall into fretful dreams where she continues to talk and will not let me rest.

Dream: Amarie

Do you remember how the pollack died – that silver-finned baby fish swimming in the blue beneath the afternoon sun? You picked him out of the rock pool and threw him 'to freedom'. Then a bird sucked him up like a leaf in a hurricane. There was nothing we could do to save him. You were twelve. I was older than you could understand. Do you remember what you asked of me? To listen to your confession and absolve you. I couldn't; not in the way that you wanted. I had to do it the way I knew. Do you remember your suspicions?

What am I? What am I? you asked. And you thought you didn't know. But thinking is only one path to knowledge. Is she Darkness or Light? Neither but Both, I tried to explain. What am I? They asked. My shadow, you said.

Follow me to the places where your other selves linger, resting in the shade from the glare. Gather them together across continents. When they meet, then you will know me. You'll remember at that moment, that the sea that you love so much swallowed those who came before you. Delivered others away from their land into bondage. But don't be afraid to swim. Their bodies are sediment now, dust in water and part of the seafloor. They are about to be forgotten. Unsettle them. Hold their grains in your palms. Then fly through the blue unfettered, knowing that the ground beneath the waters you swim through also holds you up. And swim, free.

I am the Sun and the Sum. The Son and the Total. Child and Mother. Sunsum. I am not the left hand touching the right or the right with a finger on the left's palm. I am not the object to their subject. I am both touching at once. Both and both. Unified. Not body or soul, but spirit. I am the moment they meet. I am ancestor.

I am your colour and character and destiny. I hold your past. I am what has come before and what will come to pass. I am the connection between them; the knot that they have become and the code for their unravelling.

You've Got Mail

Dear Imani,

There was an accident. Sister Alma got hurt. You should come back now.

Harold x

Twenty-five

I'm back. I stand at the bottom of the mound looking up at the castle-fort. It's winter again. Time has folded in on itself to confuse me, offering reflections then snatching them away. I start up the incline and there she is: Reverend Mother, finding the baby in the snow. It is a day of brilliant light. *The island is covered, unblemished in white.* She walks carefully down the hill and crosses my path. Goose pimples come. I smile at her back, with some melancholy, and follow behind, letting her move ahead and disappear. This is my story.

Walking through the village is my nineteen-year-old self, leaving the island for the first time, with Melia's rucksack and the Incorruptible Finger inside. 12 bumps into me carrying a pile of books. She drops one, snatches it up and walks on. I follow her, nearly running to keep pace. She stops at the gates of St Teresa's Convent – I'm not expecting it, but suddenly it's there. I'm at the door, standing in front of Sister Alma; our words cross and collide in the awkwardness of family members who have become strangers. She settles me in with fuss and ceremony. Mr Bojangles sneers at me and walks away with his tail in the air. If he comes back, I'll sing his song to him and maybe even dance – he'll hate it and skulk away.

'Reverend Mother will come soon,' Sister Alma says. 'Imani, promise me something?' Her eyes are bright and determined as she addresses me, 'Don't blame her. You mustn't blame her, ok?'

'If you don't blame her, how can I?'

'I'm fine. You can see that with your own eyes.' She starts fussing with the cushions: more to-ing and fro-ing. She says she has errands to run on the mainland and leaves me to rest. Alone, it feels like there is suddenly more oxygen in the room. I'm glad she looks ok. I'd been worried. Harold's email had been brief, but long enough to cause concern.

Reality

In the library, I nestle in my favourite chair with the Black Madonna looking down at me. The chair sags with my weight and I give in to jetlag. I have the dream that I've had many times before: running in the dark, on the boggy causeway, clasping a bloody finger as someone chases me. I wake in a fright; hot and sticky, my back aches.

I wander down the hallways. The colours are more muted than I remember, the halls narrower; the whole place seems – less, somehow. My eleven-year-old self sits in her room with Spanish magazines. She stares at the dark-skinned woman wistfully, with her box of fragments sprawled out beside her.

There's a tap at the window. 11 ignores it. Another tap, and again, and again. She gets up, sees Harold jumping up and down beyond the convent walls. I follow her out and into the grounds where we dance in the falling snow and petals.

I walk through the grounds and my past selves wander by. I hear Amarie's voice: *Follow me to the places where your other selves linger, resting in the shade from the glare. Gather them together.* I call them to me: 19, 12, 10, 14. It becomes a mantra, a new litany: 11, 13, 15, 16. I keep calling: 6, 7, 19, 12, 10, 14, 11, 13, 15, 16. They cluster together, overlapping and becoming nearly one – and there she is, at the centre of the blend: the layer of darkness where the past selves meet. She is the contrast to their light. I always preferred the warmth of darkness; it's where you can hide until you're ready to be seen. I call her name and my selves tremble and pack closer together, making her shape more defined at their core. I move towards them and step into their midst. A flare rises from between us, like white light refracting into rainbow as it passes through a diamond. The North Sea breeze sprays and salts my lips; *We give you salt, for the times when things taste as they should, Maame Yaa had said.* The light settles and, as it fades, my shadow stretches out on the ground before me. I move my arms and she follows. I approach the convent and she crawls up its walls.

'Amarie?'

No response. But she is defined and she is there – and perhaps that has to be enough. Suddenly she moves – without me: her shape on the wall descends until it is touching the ground. I rush to my knees to catch her. Then realise – it's the walls that have moved, not her. The convent melts away and I am left on the ground surrounded by rubble and the redwoods.

Epilogue

Faith

'What are you doing?'

It's been so long since I've heard her voice, but I recognise it instantly.

'Get up. You're getting dirty,' Reverend Mother says.

'I came back to touch the doors and walls and put my face against its bricks.'

'And instead, you're kneeling in its ashes?'

'If that's all that's left.'

'Stand up, you're making yourself filthy.'

I stand, but touch my face with my palms so the ash and dirt from St Teresa's can rest on me.

'You're meant to be able to go back home,' I say.

'This will always be your home,' she responds.

'I walked around the village and … saw parts of me everywhere and it felt like maybe those spirits have more right to be here. But then I came back to this place, and it's a ghost as well.'

She brings out a handkerchief and wipes my face, then pulls me in for a hug. I collapse into her arms.

'Sister Alma…' I say into her chest.

'She woke up this morning. She's fine. She'll be glad you're here.'

'I spoke to her.' I pull out of the hug, disorientated.

'She's not up to phone calls yet, it must have been someone else.'

'What?'

'We feared carbon monoxide poisoning from the smoke inhalation. She's been in a coma for over a week. But, by God's grace, she woke up this morning.'

I press at my temples, trying to calm the buzz in my head. None of it makes sense.

'Stay and help us rebuild,' Mother says. 'Sister Alma would love that. You studied architecture ... Alma said when she was asked to fax your certificates through, the university in Ghana said you were applying to study architecture, that's right, isn't it?'

'It's all gone,' I say, numb.

'The redwoods are here and the rest we can rebuild ... Sometimes fire is what's needed.'

'Is that a confession?'

'It is no such thing,' she snaps. 'The redwoods remain, the foundations remain, that is something to build on.'

I'm only half-listening. My mind is still on Sister Alma.

'They're fireproof,' Reverend Mother says. 'The trees.' She moves closer to one of them as though seeking reassurance. 'Redwoods survive forest fires; they need them, in fact. When their cones fall, they lie on the ground dormant, waiting for the flames. Fire opens them up and they take root and grow. You see, sometimes fire is exactly what's needed.'

'Said like a true arsonist. And what about Sister Alma, will she take root and grow?'

'The fire was an accident, Imani. Alma woke up this morning and she was a little weak but in good spirits. The first thing she asked for was that silly cat,' she shakes her head. 'He's fine,' she says at the panicked look on my face. 'She's not allowed to have him in the hospital, but she'll have him back as soon as she gets out.'

'How did it happen?'

'They don't know – something in the kitchen, maybe.' She observes me. 'I hope you haven't returned with that modern sense of entitlement.'

'You call it entitlement that I want to know why our home was destroyed? Or is it "entitlement" that I left, that I wanted to know where I was from?'

'Maybe I was selfish, but my selfishness made me want to look after you. Hers made her give you away.'

'My mother came back, though, didn't she? She wanted me back?'

'I couldn't run the risk of giving you to her – what if she changed her mind again?'

'She was my mother.'

'We are all from God. That's what matters ultimately.'

'Bullshit!'

'I can see that you've lived a colourful life while you've been away from us.' She looks at my dreadlocks with disdain. 'But I won't have you tainting this soil with words like that. This is a holy place.'

Taint. The word hangs between us. 'It used to hurt me so much when you'd say that word to me.'

'What word? Don't be ridiculous!' she snaps.

'*Taint*. It made me feel dirty, like it wasn't a good thing to be Brown.'

'You knew I never meant it that way!'

'Did I?'

She looks hurt.

'Now there's nothing left to *taint*. It's all gone.' I look down at my shadow on the ground – what would she tell me now if I could speak to her as I once did?

'I received a vision from God,' Mother says. 'I knew how to deliver it, not too much change, not all at once. The Bishop and the church board said they were supportive, but they wouldn't grant me leave to do it. They started to say that our practices weren't that of a Carmelite order. So they felt perhaps we shouldn't be using St Teresa's name; they threatened to take it away from us. This for a site that once housed a holy relic and has had sacred visitations.

'They started to question the integrity of everything. That doubt, the constant undermining, it infected everyone. Magdalene was the first to go; it was too much, it made her doubt herself. The younger sisters left the year after her, and the past two years have been an exodus. Alma was the only one who stayed. I prayed ... and then there was the fire. It was unfortunate, yes, but also, maybe, a blessing. Did I do it? No. Do I regret it? Absolutely not. Now it's too much work for them and they're no longer interested in our little convent ... we can call ourselves what we want ... and now you're back.'

She did this. I know that she did this. Fury rises within me. '*Imani, promise me something? Don't blame her. You mustn't blame her, ok?*' Sister Alma had said when she appeared to me. I reach into my bag and take out the jewelled relic, the Incorruptible Finger of St Teresa. I throw it on the ground at her feet. She looks down at it. At first she doesn't know what it is, then she grimaces and her face loses colour as she recognises it.

'Magdalene saw...' she stutters, '...an angel.'

'She saw *Amarie*.'

Mother kneels beside the finger but doesn't touch it.

'When you saw Amarie with me, you called her a demon. But when she was away from me, standing with this *thing*, you called her an angel.'

'It was Magdalene. She said...'

'It was all of you.' I gaze down at her kneeling in the dirt beside the jewelled reliquary that holds the missing limb of St Teresa of Avila. 'All of you, in a million tiny ways, too many times to mention.'

'You were loved. You were loved,' she says again, challenging me to deny it. 'You were loved and you were raised to be believe that you were destined for great things. We did the best for you.'

'You told me I had a great destiny, but you kept me ... caged. You taught me to fear myself ... kept me ignorant of what I came from, but still, somehow, managed to fill me with shame about it.

And I held all of that inside … along with this fear and hatred of something I thought was in me, but that *thing* was never mine – it was yours.' I look down at the finger; its jewels blink in the winter light. 'It's yours.'

Mother stands, brushes her knees and walks into the distance, disappearing behind the trees. Clouds clot the sky and the wind picks up. Alone, I start to shiver, realising what I've just said – hearing it myself for the first time.

Reverend Mother reappears from beyond the trees holding a shovel. I ask where she got it from and she says the hermitage and storehouse at the back of the grounds are undamaged. She starts to dig at the base of one of the redwood trees. She digs with an energy I haven't seen in her before; in that moment she appears less than half her age. She pulls the soil from the earth and throws it aside, digging and digging until the roots of the tree are revealed. She smashes the tip of the shovel against the relic; it cracks open, lying on the concrete foundations of what was once St Teresa's Convent. I pick it up. The two halves of the gold case come apart in my hands and a green jewel falls loose. Inside is dust, greyish-black fibres and three small fragments that must be bone. She signals for me to drop the remains at the root of the redwood.

Are you sure? I nearly ask. But then I tip it in without saying a word and throw the soil on top of it, burying it as quickly as I can. She stands back, surprised by the suddenness of my movements. Kneeling on the ground, I throw soil and leaves and everything within my reach on top of it, pushing it all further into the earth. I wipe away tears with muddy hands and keep burying. When I'm finished, it feels as though I'm waking from a trance. Mother has her hands on my shoulders, trying to pull me away, and it is starting to rain.

We relocate to the hermitage to wait for a break in the weather. It is simple, tiny and just as I remembered it: one bed that is shorter and thinner than a single bed should be, two small windows up high to let in the light, but no views that might distract you, and one small desk chair but no desk. It still has the heavy scent of incense, wax and mould. Mother offers me the bed to sit on and takes the chair for herself. She wraps the blanket around my shoulders, saying she doesn't want me to catch a cold after my long journey. We sit there for the longest time in silence, listening to the rain against the windows and roof tiles of the hermitage.

'Why was keeping the name of St Teresa so important to you?' I ask. 'If they let you continue under a new name, wasn't it worth the compromise?'

'St Teresa is our spiritual mother, our heritage. And names have meaning.'

'Why did you call me Imani?' I ask, her response reminding me of a conversation I'd had with Aunt Esi years ago.

She looks surprised by the question.

'If names are important, why did you give me a random one?'

'It's not random,' she says softly. 'It means Faith.'

Did my mother have a Christian name? / Yes, Faith. / What's the difference between faith and reality?

'I named you after your mother.'

'You knew my mother's name!' I lean forward, shocked. 'You knew her?'

'Not exactly. I named you after your mother because I thought it's what Yaa would want.'

'Yaa?' My mind circles as I try to make sense of what she's saying.

'By now they would be calling her Nana Yaa. She's about my age... Did you visit Dosu?'

'Maame Yaa?'

'They still call her Maame?' she laughs; the sound is playful and giddy. I've never heard anything like it from her before.

Maame Yaa and Reverend Mother knew each other. I try to take in this new information. Maame Yaa and Reverend Mother knew each other. I grab my rucksack from the floor and search for the dictionary. Maame Yaa and Reverend Mother knew each other. I put the cloth-covered book in her hands. Her face lights up and her cheeks flush when she sees it.

'You're the white woman who taught her to read...?'

'That's an unfriendly description,' Mother says, her lips tightening into a small cramped line. 'She told you about me?' she asks, tentatively.

'Nothing. She never mentioned you.' It comes out sharper than I intended.

Mother's face falls.

'Maybe giving me this was her way of telling me,' I offer gently.

'I was there volunteering with a mission. I was a child really, not yet eighteen. We were great friends ... we were very dear to each other ... how is she?'

'Well. Sprightly. Full of thunder,' I say. 'She never married. But she raised everyone's kids, she's been a mother many times over.'

Reverend Mother strokes the pages of the book. 'I made this for her so we could share our languages. She taught me words in their language, too.'

'Twi,' I correct.

'Yes, Twi. You know, she was the only female who got involved in building. And she was young, so it was quite a taboo. I was very impressed; she was there with all the men. I imagine you'll have seen it, how they build with the earth around them. I also taught her to make cob – it's an ancient British building method; you add straw to the mix and it sticks better, it goes much further as well. Are they still doing that?'

'Ghanaians have been using grass to build for generations.'

'Is that right?'

'Yes.'

'So, are they still doing it?'

I want to explode at her – at her presumption and arrogance. But suddenly she seems frail – old, bent and vulnerable – and I feel sorry for her.

'If you stay, you can go back as often as you want on mission; we'd cover all of the costs,' she says.

'Why don't *you* go back – visit her?'

She remains silent.

We sit quietly, listening to the strum of the rain.

'I always wondered if it was Yaa who sent your mother to me. Faith was at a university in London and she chose to bring you here – she could have taken you anywhere. I wondered if Yaa sent her ... sent you to me... We were very dear to each other ... very dear... She really didn't ask about me?'

'Really,' I say, as softly as I can.

When the rain stops, we venture outside. Mother suggests we go to the post office and ask them to call us a taxi to the mainland. The teenage boy at the counter says that at this time, it would be easier for us to walk across the causeway and get a car from the other side.

'In this weather?' Mother asks, indignant.

'That's the last of the rain. You might get some mud on your shoes, but that'll be the worst of it. It'll be a canny wait if you call one to come out here, I'm just telling you.'

Mother is about to disagree with him, but I take her elbow, steer her out and thank him over my shoulder as we leave.

'I'd like to walk through the causeway.'

She looks disgruntled.

'It's just a bit of mud.'

Reverend Mother takes my arm. At the edge of the island, we go down into the path that will lead us to the mainland.

'Did you ever think that maybe this was your purpose?' Mother says. 'Maybe you were meant to come back and use what remains to build something new for us all?'

I haven't said I'll stay, and I don't respond to the question.

'The baby in the snow … she didn't just leave me like that, did she?'

'She left a note at the convent the day before, telling me where to find you and when.'

'You never met?'

'Not on that day, no.' Mother shakes her head.

'Was it really snowing? She didn't leave me naked, did she? That was just you … storytelling?'

'I'm sure Yaa will have told you that to explain every element of a story is like unpicking a tapestry to see the colours of the individual threads.'

'That's a no then, she didn't leave me naked.'

Mother smiles and we walk on. When we reach the middle, something makes me look back. The island rises behind us. In the distance, Beblowe Hill looms above the village with its castle-fort on top. A brown woman stands on the incline and places a wrapped bundle carefully on the ground. She runs to the top of the hill and hides at the corner of the castle. Reverend Mother walks up; she finds the child, picks her up, hides her in her coat and shields the baby with her white-grey hair before walking away. The brown woman steps out from behind the shadow of the castle and watches the two of them leave. In the middle of the causeway, I turn and walk to the other side.

ACKNOWLEDGEMENTS

I'd like to thank my family, friends, and colleagues for supporting and championing my writing for so many years and in so many ways. I owe a particular debt of gratitude to:

Lisa Baker and Sara Hunt.

Will Mackie, Chitra Ramaswamy, Ellah Wakatama Allfrey, Ali Moore, and Aisling Holling.

Linda Anderson, Tina Gharavi, Jackie Kay, Margaret Wilkinson, and Sean O'Brien.

Newcastle Centre for the Literary Arts, York's Centre for Applied Human Rights, S. Y. Killingley Trust, New Writing North, Arvon Foundation, Helix Arts, Arts Council England, Saraband and Aitken Alexander Associates.

Peter and Sue Stark.

Ms Clayton.

Carinya Sharples and Geri Chapman.

Eve, Laura, Ali, Katrina, Naz, Choman, Giada, Alessia, Kalina, Sofia, Karen and Jill.

Giorgos, Thomais, Theodoris, Natalie, Kostas, Eirini and Ifigenia.

Gloria, Yaw, and Aunt Vida.

Eric, Duke, Doreen, Belinda, Precious and Nana Yaw.

Aunt Anne, Ken, and Helen.

Uncle James and Aunt Christel.

Mary, Martha, Leona and Mama Viv.

Nikos and Konstantina.

Mpampa Stelios and Mama Katerina.

Aunt Evelyn.

My dad and mum, Joe and Solome Mensah.

And my Panos.

THE AUTHOR

J. A. Mensah is a writer of prose and theatre. Her plays have focused on human rights narratives and the testimonies of survivors, and her short stories have appeared in several collections.